Easy in the Islands

Easy in the Islands

Stories by Bob Shacochis

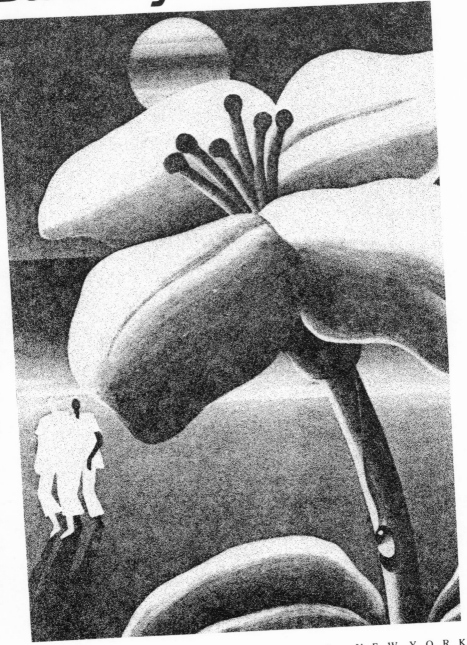

CROWN PUBLISHERS, INC. NEW YORK

All of the Author's stories in this book were initially published in magazines and periodicals as follows:

"Lord Short Shoe Wants the Monkey," "Mundo's Sign," and "Easy in the Islands," © 1982, © 1983 and © 1985 respectively, in *Playboy* magazine.

"Dead Reckoning" and "Redemption Songs" in 1983 and 1984 in *Esquire* magazine.

"The Heart's Advantage" in 1984 in *Tendril* magazine.

"Hunger," © 1980, in *The Missouri Review*.

"The Pelican" in 1984 in *The Iowa Review*.

"Hot Day on the Gold Coast" in 1984 in *Black Warrior Review*.

The author wishes to thank the National Endowment for the Arts and Yaddo Corporation for their generous support and the Copernicus Society for a James A. Michener Award.

Published by Crown Publishers, Inc.,
One Park Avenue
New York, New York 10016
and simultaneously in Canada
by General Publishing Company Limited

Printed in the United States of America

Library of Congress Cataloging in Publication Data

Shacochis, Bob.
Easy in the islands.

1. Caribbean area—Fiction.   I. Title.
PS3569.H284E27   1985   813'. 54   84–15570
ISBN 0-517-55549-2

Designed by Camilla Filancia

10 9 8 7 6 5 4 3 2 1

First Edition

These stories are for Miss Fish.
And for William Peden.

"Watching a coast as it slips by the ship is like thinking
about an enigma. There it is before you—smiling, frowning, inviting, grand, mean, insipid, or savage, and always
mute with an air of whispering, Come and find out."
—Joseph Conrad
Heart of Darkness

Contents

Easy in the Islands

Easy in the Islands

The days were small, pointless epics, long windups to punches that always drifted by cartoon-fashion, as if each simple task were meaningless unless immersed in more theater and threat than bad opera.

It was only Monday noon and already Tillman had been through the wringer. He had greased the trade commissioner to allow a pallet of Campbell's consommé to come ashore, fired one steel band for their hooliganism and hired another, found a carpenter he was willing to trust to repair the back veranda that was so spongy in spots Tillman knew it was only a matter of days before a guest's foot burst through the surface into whatever terrors lived below in the tepid darkness, restocked on vitamins from the pharmacy, argued with the crayfish regulatory bureau about quotas. And argued with the inscrutable cook, a fat countrywoman who wore a wool watch cap and smoked hand-rolled cigars, argued with both maids, muscle-bound Lemonille and the other one who wouldn't reveal her name, argued with the gardener who liked to chop everything up, argued with the customs house, argued with the bartender Jevanee. And although he had not forthrightly won any of these encounters, he had won them enough to forestall the doom that would one day descend on Rosehill Plantation.

But now the daily defeats and victories were overshadowed by a first-class doozy, a default too personal to implicate the local population. The problem was to decide what to do about his mother—Mother, who had thought life wonderful in the islands. Now she rested stiffly in the food locker, dead and coated with frost, blue as the shallow water on the reefs, protected from the fierceness of the sun she once loved without question or fear, a sun that was never really her enemy, no matter how it textured her skin, no matter what it revealed of her age.

In her room on Saturday, Mother had died mysteriously. As Lemonille had said when the two of them carried her out after the doctor had been there, *Mistah Till-mahn, it look so you muddah shake out she heart fah no good reason. Like she tricked by some false light, ya know.*

—His mother's body had been strong and brassy, her spirit itself unusually athletic for a woman only weeks away from sixty. In her quick laugh was as much vitality as a girl's, and yet she had died. In bed, early in the evening, disdainful of the bars and clubs, reading a book—Colette, rediscovered on her latest continental visit—her finger ready to turn the page. Tillman was astonished. Only after Dr. Bradley had told him that he suspected his mother was poisoned did Tillman begin to calm down, his imperturbable self returning by degrees. Such a conclusion made no sense. The terms of life in the islands were that nothing ever made sense, unless you were a mystic or a politician, or studied both with ambition. Then every stupidness seemed an act of inspiration, every cruelty part of a divine scheme. There was no dialectic here, only the obverting of all possibilities until caprice made its selection.

~ Dr. Bradley couldn't be sure though. Neither he nor any of the other three sanctioned doctors on the island knew how to perform an autopsy with sufficient accuracy to assure each other or anybody else of the exact nature of death when the cause was less than obvious. Still, Bradley earned moments of miraculous credibility, as when the former Minister of Trade was brought into the hospital dead of a gunshot wound in his chest. To the government's relief, Bradley determined the cause of death as "heart failure," an organic demise, and unembarrassing.

"I will take your permission, mahn, to cut de body open ahnd look in she stomach," Dr. B. had said to Tillman as they stood over his mother's corpse in the sunny hotel room on Sunday morning, a breeze off the ocean dancing the curtains open, billowing sunlight throughout the room and then sucking it back outside. A spray of creamy rosebuds tapped against the louvered window, an eerie beckoning in the air silenced by death.

"For God's sake, why?" Tillman had said. It sounded like an ultimate obscenity, to have this fool with his meatcutter's stubby hands groping in his mother's abdomen.

"To determine what she eat aht de time of succumption."

"I told you what she was eating," Tillman said, exasperated. "She was eating a can of peaches with a spoon. Look here, there are still some left in the can." He shook the can angrily and syrup slopped onto his wrist. In disgust, Tillman wiped the sticky wetness on his pants, half nauseated, associating the liquid with some oozy by-product of dissolution. "Take the peaches if you need something to cut into, but you're not taking Mother. This isn't one of your Bottom Town cadavers."

Bradley had reacted with a shrug, and a patronizing twist to his smile. "Dis racial complexity—what a pity, mahn."

How often Tillman had heard this lie, so facile, from the lips

EASY IN THE ISLANDS

of bad men. "One world," he said, biting down on the syllables as if they were a condemnation, or a final sorrow. "We all live in one world. What's so goddamn complex about that?"

Tillman refused to let him remove the body from Rosehill. He wrapped his mother in the mauve chenille bedspread she had been lying on, restacked several crates of frozen chicken parts, and arranged her in the walk-in freezer until he could figure out just what to do. It was easy to accept the fact that you couldn't trust a doctor in such circumstances. What was most unacceptable was that Bradley had told the police there was a possibility the old lady had been murdered. The police, of course, were excited by this news. They sent Inspector Cuffy over to Rosehill to inform Tillman that he was under suspicion.

"You're kidding," Tillman said.

He suggested the inspector should walk down to the beach bar the hotel maintained on the waterfront and have a drink courtesy of the house while he took care of two new guests who had just arrived in a taxi from the airport. "I don't believe it," the new man said in an aside to Tillman as he checked them in. "The skycaps at the airport whistled at my wife and called her a whore." His wife stood demurely by his side, looking a bit overwhelmed. He could see the dark coronas of nipples under her white muslin sundress.

"Hey, people here are more conservative than you might think," Tillman told the couple, and to the woman he added, "Unless you want little boys rubbing up against your leg, you shouldn't wear shorts or a bathing suit into town."

"But this is the tropics," the woman protested in an adolescent voice, looking at Tillman as if he were only being silly.

"Right," Tillman conceded, handing over the key. He escorted the couple to their room, helping with the luggage, and wished them well. Wished himself a dollar for every time their notion of paradise would be fouled by some rudeness, aggression, or irrelevant accusation.

He crossed back over the veranda out onto the cobbled drive, past the derelict stone tower of the windmill where every

4

other Saturday the hotel sponsored a goat roast that was well attended by civil servants, Peace Corps volunteers and whatever tourists were around, down the glorious green lawn crazy with blossom, down, hot and sweaty, to the palm grove, the bamboo beach bar on its fringe, the lagoon dipping into the land like a blue pasture, Tillman walking with his hands in the pockets of his loose cotton pants, reciting a calypso and feeling, despite his troubles, elected, an aristocrat of the sensual latitudes, anointed to all the earthly privileges ordinary people dreamed about on their commuter trains fifty weeks a year. No matter that in a second-class Eden nothing was as unprofitable as the housing of its guests. Even loss seemed less discouraging in the daily flood of sun.

Jevanee was glaring at him from behind the bar. And the inspector sat grandly on his stool, satisfied with being the bigshot, bearing a smile that welcomed Tillman as if they were to be partners in future prosperity, as if the venture they were to embark on could only end profitably. He gave a little wink before he tipped his green bottle of imported beer and sank the neck between his lips.

"Dis a sad affair, mahn," he said, wagging his round head. Jevanee uncapped a second bottle and set it before the inspector, paying no attention to Tillman's presence. Tillman drew a stool up beside Cuffy and perched on its edge, requesting Jevanee to bring another beer, and watched with practiced patience as the bartender kicked about and finally delivered the bottle as if it were his life's savings.

"What is it with you, Jevanee? What am I doing wrong?" The bartender had come with Rosehill when he had inherited the hotel eight months ago. Somebody had trained him to be a terror.

"Mistah Trick!" Jevanee whooped. He was often too selfconscious to confront his employer head-on. Nevertheless he would not accept even the mildest reproach without an extravagant line of defense or, worse, smoldering until his tongue ignited and his hands flew threateningly, shouting in a tantrum that would go on forever with or without an audience, a man who would never be employed to his satisfaction. He turned his back on Tillman and began muttering at the whiskey bottles arrayed on the work island in the center of the oval bar.

"Mistah Trick, he say what him doin wrong, de devil. He say daht he mean, Jevanee, why you is a chupid boy ahs black as me boot cahnt count change ahnd show yah teef nice aht de white lady? He say daht he mean, Jevanee, why you cahnt work fah free like you grahnpoppy? Why you cahnt bring you sistah here ta please me?" Without ceasing his analysis of what the white man had meant, he marched out from the bar and into the bushes to take a leak. Tillman forced himself not to react any further to Jevanee's rage, which appeared to be taking on a decidedly historical sweep.

The inspector, who had not shown any interest in Jevanee's complaints, began to tap the long nail of his index finger on the surface of the bar. He made a show of becoming serious without wanting to deprive Tillman of his informality, his compassion, his essential sympathy, etcetera—all the qualities he believed he possessed and controlled to his benefit.

"Who else, Tillmahn, but you?" Cuffy finally concluded as if it hurt him to say this. "Undah-stahnd, is only speculation."

"Who else but me?" Tillman sputtered. "Are you crazy?" The inspector frowned and Tillman immediately regretted his choice of words. Cuffy was as willfully unpredictable as most everybody else on the island, but in a madhouse, an outsider soon learned, truth was always a prelude to disaster, the match dropped thoughtlessly onto tinder. He should have said, Look, how can you think that? or Man, what will it take to end this unfortunate business? But too late. The inspector was pinching at his rubbery nose, no longer even considering Tillman, looking out across the harbor, the anchored sailboats bobbing like a display of various possibilities, playing the image of artful calculation for his suspect.

Tillman sighed. "Why do you think I would kill my own

mother? She was my *mother.* What son could harm the woman who carried him into the world?":

— The inspector pursed his lips and then relaxed them. "Well, Tillmahn, perhahps you do it to have title to dis property, true?"

The absurdity was too great even for Tillman, a connoisseur of island nonsense. "To inherit this property!" Now Tillman had to laugh, regardless of the inspector's feelings. "Cuffy, nobody wants this place. In his will my father was excessively sorry for burdening me with Rosehill Plantation and advised I sell it at the first opportunity. My mother had absolutely no claim to Rosehill. He divorced her long ago."

Tillman paused. As far as he could tell, he was the only one in the world, besides the government, who wanted Rosehill Plantation. It had been on the market for years, not once receiving an honest offer. Its profits were marginal, its overhead crushing. But the hotel was his, so why not be there. What he had found through it was unexpected—the inexplicable sense that life on the island had a certain fullness, that it was, far beyond what he had ever experienced back home, authentic in the most elemental ways.

Cuffy had become petulant, studying him as if he were spoiled, an unappreciative child. Tillman was not intimidated. "Why should I tell you this anyway? It has absolutely no relevance to my mother's death."

"Um hmm, um hmm, I see," the inspector said. "So perhahps you muddah take a lovah, a dark mahn, ahnd you become vexed wit she fah behavin so. You warn her to stop but she refuse. So ..." He threw out his hands as if the rest of the scene he conceived was there before him. "Is just speculation."

Tillman was tiring fast. Inspector Cuffy had no use for what was and what wasn't; his only concern was his own role in the exercise of authority. It killed boredom, boredom amid the splendor. It created heroes and villains, wealth and poverty. No other existence offered him so much.

He discovered that he was grinding his teeth and the muscles in his jaw ached. Jevanee had slipped back behind the bar, and every time Tillman glanced over there, Jevanee, now bold, tried to stare him down.

— "My mother was an old lady," he told the inspector. "She was beyond love. She liked books and beaches, fruit, seafood, and rare wines. Traveling. There was no man in her life. There never was. She was even a stranger to my father."

"You just a boy," Cuffy noted in a way that made Tillman think it was a line the inspector must use frequently. "Nobody beyond love, ya know."

"So?"

"So, nobody beyond pahssion, ahnd nobody beyond crime." Tillman blinked. Damn, he thought, Cuffy's starting to make sense.

"Even ahn old womahn need a good roll to keep she happy," the inspector concluded.

"Oh, for Christ's sake," Tillman said, standing up. "I have to get back."

He couldn't get away before Jevanee butted in. Ignore Jevanee and life might possibly go on. The bartender used his mouth like a gun, the words popping spitefully while he focused on whatever spirit he had summoned to witness his oppression.

"Daht ol boney-bag he call his muddah grabbin aht every blahck boy on de beach. I see it wit me own eyes."

"Jevanee, shut up."

"Oh, yes, massa, suh. Yes, massa." He feigned excessive servitude, wiping the bar counter, the cash box, the bamboo supports with his shirt sleeve. The time would come when Tillman would have to face up to Jevanee's vindictiveness. He had been steaming ever since Tillman had told him not to hand out free drinks to his friends from the village. Jevanee insisted no one but Rosehill's tourists, who were not regular, would ever patronize the beach bar if it weren't for him. Maybe he was right. Nobody was coming around anymore except on Friday nights when the band played. More and more, Jevanee wanted Tillman to understand that he was a dangerous man, his every move a challenge to his employer. Tillman was still trying to figure out how to fire the guy without a lot of unpleasantness.

"Don't listen to Jevanee," Tillman told the inspector. "He's pissed at me these days because of a disagreement we had over a charitable instinct of his."

"I give me bruddah a drink," Jevanee said in a self-deprecating way, as though he were the victim and Cuffy would understand. Jevanee's mood would only escalate if Tillman explained that the bartender's "bruddah" was consuming a case of Scotch on his drier visits, so he refused to debate Jevanee's claim. The inspector turned on his stool with the cold expression of a man whose duty it is to make it known that he must hurt you severely, that he may cripple you or make you weep, if you disobey him.

"Look now, you," he said, taking moral pleasure in this chastisement. "Doan you make trouble fah Mistah Tillmahn. You is lucky he give you work."

"Dis white bitch doan give me a damn ting," Jevanee snarled, shaking an empty beer bottle at Tillman. "I work in dis same spot a long time when he show up. Ahnd what you doin kissin he ahss?"

"Doan talk aht me daht way, boy, or I fuck you up. Hell goin have a new bahtendah soon if you cahnt behave."

Jevanee tried to smile, a taut earnestness that never quite made it to his mouth. Tillman arranged chairs around the warped café tables, backing away. "Okay then, Cuffy. I'm glad we had this opportunity to straighten everything out. Stay and have another beer if you want."

Cuffy looked at his gold wristwatch. "You will be around in de aftahnoon?"

"Why?"

"I wish to view de deceased."

"Uh, can't it wait till tomorrow?" Tillman asked. "I have

EASY IN THE ISLANDS

errands to run in town. A shipment of beef is coming in from Miami."

From his shirt pocket, Cuffy had taken a note pad and was scribbling in it. He talked without raising his head. "Okay, dere's no hurry. De old womahn takin she time goin nowheres."

Tillman nodded, now in stride with the process, the havoc of it. "Cuffy, you're a thorough man. If anybody's going to get to the bottom of this mess, it's you."

The inspector accepted this flattery as his due, too certain of its validity to bother about the subtle mocking edge to Tillman's voice. His eyes were relaxed, hooded and moist. Tillman started up the footpath through the palms, kicking a coconut ahead of him, a leaden soccer ball, turning once to check what fared in his absence: and yes Cuffy and Jevanee had their heads together, the bartender animated, swinging his hands, the inspector with his arms crossed on his wide chest. Jevanee had too much energy today. Maybe his attitude would defuse if he were somewhere other than the bar for a while. He seemed to live there. Tillman shouted back down to them. "Jevanee, after the inspector leaves, lock everything up and take the rest of the day off."

The bartender ignored him.

Tillman jogged up the perfect lawn along an avenue of floral celebration—tree-sized poinsettias, arrow ginger, bougainvillea, oleander—a perfumist's tray of fragrance. On the knoll, graced with a vista of the channel, was the old plantation house, a stubborn remnant of colonial elegance, its whitewashed brick flaking in a way that benefited the charm of its archaic construction, the faded red of the gabled tin roof a human comfort against the green monotonous sheets of the mountains that were its background. Farther south, the cone shell of the windmill stood like a guard tower or last refuge. Tillman had huddled there with his guests last summer during a hurricane, the lot of them drunk and playing roundhouse bridge, the cards fluttering from the storm outside.

When he was a teenager Tillman had flown down to the island during a summer off from Exeter to help his father build the two modern wings that flanked the manor, one-level box rooms side by side, as uninspired as any lodging on any Florida roadside. Tillman's father was a decent man, completely involved in his scheming though his interest invariably flagged once a puzzle was solved, a challenge dispatched. The old man had worked for J. D. Root, one of the big ad agencies in New York, handling the Detroit accounts. His final act was an irony unappreciated—he perished in one of the cars he promoted, losing control on the Northway one rainy evening. He had gone fishing up on the St. Lawrence, convinced this time he would hook a muskellunge. Rosehill Plantation was his most daring breakaway but he never really had time for the place. Throughout his ownership, Rosehill lost money and after his death the checks from the estate in New York flowed like aid from the mother country. When a lawyer's telegram reached Tillman, asking if he wanted to pursue more aggressively the sale of the plantation, he decided to dump the Lower East Side loft where he had been sweating out the draft for two years since graduate school and make his claim on Rosehill. Nixon had just been reelected. The States no longer seemed like the right place to be.

Awash in perspiration, Tillman turned the corner around the east wing, his blood pressure a little jumpy, the skin on his face at the point of combustion, wondering if all the friction of a fast life could suddenly cause a person to burst into flame. Sometimes he felt as if it were happening. It wasn't very easy to find peace on the island unless you hiked up into the mountains. Whereas it was very easy to catch hell.

In the exterior courtyard behind the estate house, the new arrivals, husband and wife from Wilmington, Delaware, were inspecting one of Tillman's few unequivocable successes, the gazebo that housed his parrot aviary, in it seven of the last rainbow parrots on earth. The project was really the veterinarian's at the Ministry of Agriculture, a man who hated goats and cows but spent all his spare time bird-watching or digging up pre-Columbian artifacts, storing them in his living room until the far-off day a museum would be built. Together he and Tillman waged a public campaign on the island, the parrots' sole habitat, to prevent their extinction. A law was passed for appearances, its advantage being that it clearly defined for the bird smugglers *who* needed to be paid off and *who* could be bypassed with impunity.

After the crusade, Tillman decided to contact some poachers himself. They were kids, tough miniature bandits, the nest robbers. One was nine, the other eleven. Basil and Jacob, tree climbers extraordinaire, both as skinny as vanilla beans. They lived in a mountain village, a clump of wattle huts, one of the outposts before the vast roadless center of the island, all sharp peaks, palisades and jungle. When the hatching season had ended, Tillman and the boys trekked into the lush interior, camping overnight, Tillman's neck strained from looking up into the canopy, his ears confused by the wraithish shrieks and skraws—*skra-aaa-aw!*—unable to pinpoint where the sound came from in the infinite cathedral of growth. But the kids knew their business. They were fearless, scaling to the top of the highest mahogany or madrone, indifferent to the slashing beaks of the females who refused to abandon the nest, shinnying down the trunks with the chicks held gently in their mouths, polycolored cotton balls, the fierce tiny heads lolling helplessly out from between the embrace of boyish lips.

Tillman thought he would tell his guests from Delaware the story. The woman was scrutinizing the birds rather sternly. She would cluck and whistle at them, tap the chicken wire wall of the cage, but she did so without affection. When he finished talking, she turned to look at him, her eyes obscured behind oversized sunglasses, her mouth in a pout. Tillman guessed she was a bank teller, something that had made her very sure of herself without placing any demand on her intelligence.

"It's cruel," she said.

"It is not cruel. It's heroic. These islands have a way of

forcing everything but the lowest common denominator into oblivion."

"Hero," she said sardonically. The husband looked skeptical. Light reflected off her glasses and sliced back at Tillman. He shrugged his shoulders. Perhaps he should bar Americans from Rosehill. Canadians made the better tourist. They allowed for a world outside themselves.

The Land Rover started painfully, a victim of mechanical arthritis. Soon it would take no more to the prosthetic miracle of wire, tin, and hardware junk. Spare parts appeared from across the ocean as often as Halley's comet.

Onto the narrow blacktop road that circumnavigated the island, Tillman drove with reckless courage and whipping flair, showing inner strength when he refused to give way to two flatbed lorries painted up like Easter eggs, one named *Sweetfish,* the other *Dr. Lick,* passengers clinging to everything but the wheel hubs, racing down the coastal hill side by side straight at him, *Dr. Lick* overtaking *Sweetfish* just as Tillman downshifted reluctantly to third and toed the brake pedal. Someday the lorries would spread carnage across this highway, Tillman thought. It would be a national event, the island equivalent of a 747 going down.

In the capital, a pastel city breathtaking from the heights above it but garbage-strewn and ramshackle once you were on its streets, Tillman honked his way through the crowds down along Front Street, inching his way to the docks. On the quay, three pallets of frozen steaks destined for Rosehill were sweating pink juice onto the dirty concrete. Beef from the island was as tough and stringy as rug; if a hotel wanted to serve food worthy of the name, it had to import almost everything but fish. He located the purser in one of the rum-and-cake sheds that filled every unclaimed inch of the wharves like derelict carnival booths. There was no use complaining about the shipment being off-loaded without anybody being there to receive it. That was Tillman's fault—he had been too preoccupied. He signed the shipping order and then scrambled to hire a driver and boys to break down the pallets and truck the cartons out to Rosehill's freezer before the meat thawed completely.

There were other errands, less urgent—to the marketing board in search of the rare tomato, to the post office, to the stationer for a ballpoint pen, to the pharmacist, who was disappointed when Tillman only bought aspirin. Most of his regular white customers spent small fortunes on amphetamines or Quaaludes. When Tillman had finished there, he drove over to the national hospital on the edge of town. Without a death certificate from Bradley, Mother was destined to be the morbid champion of cryogenics, the Queen of Ice in a land where water never froze in nature.

The old colonial hospital was a structure and a system bypassed by any notion of modernity. Someone yelled at him as he entered the shadowed foyer, but it wasn't apparent who or why. The rough wooden floorboards creaked under his feet. The maze of hallways seemed to be a repository for loiterers —attendants, nurses, nuns, clerks, superfluous guards, mangled patients, talking, weeping, spending the day in rigid silence. One naked little boy asleep on the floor, hugging the wall.

He found Dr. Bradley's office and went through the door without knocking. Bradley, chief surgeon, head physician of St. George's National People's Hospital, an agnostic operation if Tillman ever saw one, was reading a paperback romance, a man hovering over a fallen woman on its cover. The room smelled of sweet putrefaction and Lysol. The scent of jasmine wafted in through open screenless windows. Tillman sat down on a wooden bench against one bare wall. Flies buzzed along the ceiling. Bradley slowly broke off from his reading, dropping his feet one by one from where they were propped on the broad windowsill. His lab coat, smudged with yellow stains and laundered blood, sagged away from his middle. He recognized Tillman and smiled grudgingly.

"Mahn, I been callin you, ya know. I examine dem peaches

you muddah eat. Dey was no good. I think we solve dis big mystery."

Tillman knew this was his chance to end the affair but he could not forgive Bradley his smugness, his careless manner, the suffering he had sown.

"You're sure? What'd you do, feed them to a chicken and the chicken died?"

"Mahn, Tillman, you doan have enough troubles, you must come make some wit me? Why is daht?"

"You're telling me she died of botulism?"

"It seem so, seem so."

Tillman was incited to fury. "Botulism, Doctor, causes vomiting and extreme pain. How can you not know that? My mother died a peaceful death."

Bradley turned with eyes murderous. "If it's so, de autopsy prove so. I cahnt know oddahwise."

"You're not touching her. Somebody else can do it, but not you."

"Mahn, daht's irrational."

Tillman jumped up from the bench and stood in front of the doctor's cluttered desk. "You'd be the last person on earth to touch her."

"Get out, Tillmahn."

Tillman was in no hurry to leave. "Remember Freddy Allen?" he asked.

"Who?" Then Bradley remembered and his face lost its arrogance.

"He was a friend of mine, a good one. He helped me out at Rosehill whenever I needed it."

"Tillmahn, consider I am only human."

"Yes, you are. So was Freddy until he came to you. You gave him bromides for acute appendicitis. The damn vet can diagnose better than you."

Bradley stood so fast, his eyes full of menace, that Tillman tensed to defend himself. "Get out," he shouted, pointing his finger at Tillman. "You muddah now a permahnent guest aht

Rosehill till you come to you senses. Get out." The doctor came around from his desk to open the office door and then kicked it shut behind him.

Tillman, island hotelier, master of the business arts, student of impossibility, fond of weather that rarely oppressed, a man of contingencies and recently motherless—Tillman knew what to do. Whatever it took.

Whatever it took, Tillman told himself, back out on the streets, heedless in the late afternoon traffic. Sometimes that meant nothing at all, sometimes the gods spared you muckery, blessed you with style, and everything was easy.

At the airport he parked next to a single taxi out front, no one around to note this familiar island tune, the prolonged pitch of tires violently braked. Through the dark empty airport that always reminded him of an abandoned warehouse, Tillman searched for his friend Roland, the freelance bush pilot from Australia, a maverick and proven ace. Roland leapt around the warm world in his old Stearmann, spraying mountainsides of bananas with chemicals that prevented leaf spot and other blights. Tillman suspected the pilot was also part of the interisland ring sponsored by the most influential businessmen to smuggle drugs, whiskey, cigarettes, stereos—whatever contraband could be crammed surreptitiously into the fuselage of a small plane. He seemed to be able to come and go as he pleased.

Roland's plane wasn't on the tarmac, or in the hangar. Sunset wasn't far away. Wherever Roland was, waltzing his plane through green, radical valleys, he would have to return before dark if he was coming in tonight. Tillman left a message with a mechanic in the machine shed for Roland to come find him at Rosehill.

Twilight had begun to radiate through the vegetation as he arrived back at the hotel, lifting the mélange of colors to a higher level of brilliance, as if each plant, each surface, were responding to the passage of the sun with its own interior luminosity. Inspector Cuffy was on the veranda of the west wing, laughing with Lemonille, her eyes flirtatious. They clammed up when Tillman appeared beside them.

"You haven't been waiting for me, have you?"

"Well, doan trouble yourself, mahn. I been interviewin dis pretty young lady."

Tillman looked at Lemonille, who averted her eyes shyly. "Perhaps we cahn view de body of you muddah now." Cuffy said this without the slightest conviction. Tillman understood that, for the time being, the inspector was only interested in chasing Lemonille.

"I've had a hell of a day. Can I ask you to wait until tomorrow?"

"Daht strike me ahs reasonable," Cuffy said, allowing Tillman to experience his generosity.

"Besides, case solved, Cuffy," Tillman said, remembering the doctor, the hospital. "Bradley says something was wrong with the can of peaches my mother was eating when she died." If you want to believe such crap, Tillman added under his breath.

"I will study daht report," the inspector said. From the way he spoke, Tillman knew the investigation would drag on for days, weeks—especially if Lemonille played hard to get.

"Mistah Till-mahn?" Lemonille buried her chin, afraid to speak now that she had drawn attention to herself. More woe, thought Tillman. More hue and cry.

"What's wrong?"

"De cook say she fraid wit you dead muddah in de freezah. She say she not cookin wit a duppy so close by."

"All right, I'll go talk to her."

"She gone home."

"All right, I'll take care of it." He began to walk away.

"Mistah Till-mahn?" The big woman's soft and guarded voice made him stop and turn around.

"What, Lemonille?"

"De men come wit de meat, but dey won't stock it."

Tillman inhaled nervously. "My mother again, right?"

Lemonille nodded. "Damn!" Tillman said, and scuffed the dirt.

Lemonille had one last piece of news. "Jevanee in a fuss cause you fire him."

"I didn't fire him. I told him to take the day off."

"Oh."

"Cuffy was there. He heard me." Cuffy looked into the trees and would not support or deny this allegation.

"Oh. But Jevanee tellin every bug in de sky you fire him. Daht mahn be fulla dread you goin put him out since de day you poppy die."

"Well, it's not true. Tell him that when you see him."

Tillman took these developments in stride, closing the restaurant for the evening by posting a scrawled note of apology at the entrance to the modest dining hall in the manor. For an hour he shuffled the cartons of dripping steaks from the kitchen to the freezer, stacking them around the corpse of his mother as if these walls of spoiling meat were meant to be her tomb.

Event upon event—any day in the islands could keep accumulating such events until it was overrich, festering, or glorious, never to be reproduced so wonderfully. This day was really no different except that his mother had triggered some extraordinary complications that were taking him to the limit.

After showering in cold water, Tillman climbed the stairs in the main house to the sanctitude of his office, his heart feeling too dry for blood to run through it, another fire hazard. What's to be done with Mother? On a hotplate he heated water for tea, sat with the steaming mug before the phone on his desk. Ministry offices would be closed at this hour and besides, the Minister of Health was no friend of his so there was no use ringing him up.

Finally he decided to call Dr. Layland. If Layland still were running the island's medical services, the day would have been much simpler, but Layland, a surgeon who had earned international respect for his papers on brain dysfunction in the tropics, had lost his job and his license to practice last winter when he refused to allow politics to interfere with the delicate removal of a bullet from an opposition member's neck. Although the case was before the Federation there was little hope of reinstatement before next year's elections.

Frankly, Layland told him, his accent bearing the vestige of an Oxford education, your position is most unenviable, my friend. A burial certificate, likewise permission to transfer the corpse back to its native soil, must be issued by both the national police and the Chief Medical Officer. The police, pending their own investigation of the cause of death, will not act without clearance from the CMO. In cases where the cause is unclear, it is unlikely that the CMO will agree to such clearance, especially for an expatriate Caucasian, until an autopsy is performed.

"But Bradley said it was the peaches, a bad can of peaches." Tillman jerked his head away from the telephone. How absurd and false those words sounded.

"Unlikely, but I see what you're getting at. Any cause is better than none, in light of your problem. But you know what sort of humbug that foolish man is. And you shan't have him on your side since you refused to have him do the autopsy."

Layland further explained that there was no alternative to removing the corpse from the walk-in freezer unless he had another to put it in, or unless he committed it to the island's only morgue in the basement of the prison at Fort Albert— again, Bradley's domain. The final solution would be to bury her at Rosehill, but even this could not be accomplished without official permits. The police would come dig her up. Tillman asked if it was a mistake not to allow Bradley to cut open his mother.

"I'm afraid, Tillman, you must decide that for yourself," Layland answered. "But I think you must know that I am as disgusted by my erstwhile colleague as you are. Well, good luck."

Tillman pushed the phone away, rubbed his sore eyes, massaged the knots in his temples. He tilted back in his chair and almost went over backward, caught unaware by a flood of panic. Unclean paradise, he thought suddenly. What about Mother? Damn, she was dead and needed taking care of. Hard to believe. Lord, why did she come here anyway? She probably knew she was dying and figured the only dignified place to carry out the fact was under the roof of her only child. A mother's final strategy.

Outside on the grounds one of the stray dogs that were always about began a rabid barking. Tillman listened more closely, the sounds of squawking audible between the gaps in the dog's racket. The protest grew louder, unmistakable; Tillman was down the stairs and out on the dark lawn in no time at all, running toward the aviary.

There was some light from the few bulbs strung gaily through the branches of frangipani that overhung the parking area, enough to see what was going on, the wickedness being enacted in blue-satin shadows. In the gazebo, an angry silhouette swung a cutlass back and forth, lashing at the amorphous flutter of wings that seemed everywhere in the tall cage.

"Jevanee?" Tillman called, uncertain. The silhouette reeled violently, froze in its step and then burst through the door of the cage, yelling.

"Mahn, you cy-ahnt fire me, *I quit.*"

Tillman cringed at the vulgarity of such a dissembled non sequitur. All the bad television in the world, the stupid lyrics of false heroes, the latent rage of kung-fu and cowboy fantasies had entered into this man's head and here was the result, some new breed of imperial slave and his feeble, fatuous uprising.

"I didn't fire you. I said take the day off, cool down."

"Cy-ahnt fire *me,* you bitch."

The parrots were dead. Hatred exploded through Tillman. He wanted to kill the bartender. Fuck it. He wanted to shoot him down. He sprinted back across the lawn, up on the veranda toward the main house for the gun kept locked in the supply closet behind the check-in desk. Jevanee charged after him. A guest, the woman recently arrived from Wilmington, stepped out in front of Tillman from her room that fronted the veranda. Tillman shoulder-blocked her back through the door. She sprawled on her ass and for a second Tillman saw on her face an expression that welcomed violence as if it were an exotic game she had paid for.

"Stay in your goddamn room and bolt the door."

Tillman felt the bad TV engulfing them, the harried script writer unbalanced with drugs and spite. Jevanee's foot plunged through the rotten boards in the veranda and lodged there. An exodus of pestilence swarmed from the splintery hole into the dim light, palmetto bugs flying blindly up through a growing cloud of smaller winged insects.

At the same time, stepping out from the darkness of a hedge of bougainvillea that ran in bushy clumps along the veranda, was Inspector Cuffy, pistol in hand. Tillman gawked at him. What was he doing around Rosehill so late? Lemonille had been encouraging him or the investigation had broadened to round-the-clock foolishness. Or, Tillman surmised, knowing it was true, Cuffy apparently knew Jevanee was coming after him and had lurked on the premises until the pot boiled over. A shot whistled by Tillman's head. Jevanee had a gun, too. Tillman pitched back off the deck and flattened out in the shrubbery.

"Stop," Cuffy shouted.

What the hell, thought Tillman. Where's Jevanee going anyway? He was near enough to smell the heavily Scotched breath of the bartender, see his eyes as dumb and frightened as the eyes of a wild horse. Another shot was fired off. Then a flurry of them as the two men emptied their pistols at each other with no effect. Silence and awkwardness as Cuffy and Jevanee confronted one another, the action gone out of them, praying thanks for the lives they still owned. Tillman crawled away toward the main house. He couldn't care less how they finished the drama, whether they killed each other with their bare hands, or retired together to a rum shop, blaming Tillman for the sour fate of the island. There was no point in getting upset about it now, once the hate had subsided, outdone by the comics.

He sat in the kitchen on the cutting table, facing the vault-like aluminum door of the refrigerated walk-in where his mother lay, preserved in ice, her silence having achieved, finally, a supreme hardness.

He wanted to talk to her, but even in death she seemed only another guest at the hotel, one with special requirements, nevertheless expecting courtesy and service, the proper distance kept safely between their lives. She had never kissed him on the lips, not once, but only brushed his cheek when an occasion required some tangible sign of motherly devotion. He had never been closer to her heart than when they cried together the first year he was in prep school, explaining to him that she was leaving his father. She had appeared in his room late at night, having driven up from the city. She tuned the radio loud to a big band station and held him, the two of them shivering against each other on his bed. For her most recent visitation she had not written she was coming but showed up unannounced with only hand luggage—a leather grip of novels, a variety of modest bathing suits, caftans and creams. Behind her she had left Paris, where the weather had begun its decline toward winter. Whatever else she had left behind in her life was as obscure and sovereign as a foreign language. He wanted to talk to her but nothing translated.

The pilot found him there sometime in the middle of the night, Tillman forlorn, more tired than he could ever remember feeling. Roland looked worn out, too, as if he had been stuck in an engine for hours, his cutoff shorts and colorless T-shirt smudged with grease, his hiking boots unlaced, and yet despite this general dishevelment his self-confidence was as apparent as the gleam of his teeth. Tillman remembered him at the beach bar late one night, yelling into the face of a man dressed in a seersucker suit, "I get things done, damn you, not like *these* bloody fools," and the sweep of his arm seemed to include the entire planet.

Tillman smiled mournfully back at him. "Roland, I need your help."

The pilot removed the mirrored sunglasses he wore at all times. "You've had a full day of it, I hear. What's on your mind, mate?"

Like an unwieldy piece of lumber, his mother's corpse banged to and fro in the short bed of the Land Rover, her wrapped feet pointing up over the tailgate. With a little effort and jockeying, they fitted her into the tube-shaped chemical tank in the fuselage of the Stearmann after Roland, Tillman standing by with a flashlight, unbolted two plates of sheet metal from the underbelly of the craft that concealed bay doors. You can't smuggle bales of grass with only a nozzle and a funnel, Roland explained.

Tillman was worried that an unscheduled flight would foul up Roland's good grace with the authorities. Man, Roland said, I've got more connections than the friggin PM. And I mean of the UK, not this bloody cowpie. He thought for a second and was less flamboyant. I've been in trouble before, of course. Nobody, Tillman, can touch this boy from down under as long as I have me bird, you see. Let us now lift upward into the splendid atmosphere and its many bright stars.

The chemical tank smelled cloyingly of poison. With his head poked in it, Tillman gagged, maneuvering the still-rigid body of his mother, the limbs clunking dully against the shiny metal, until she was positioned. Roland geared the bay doors back in place. The sound of them clicking into their locks brought relief to Tillman. They tucked themselves into the tiny cockpit. Tillman sat behind the pilot's seat, his legs flat against the floorboard, straddled as if he were riding a bobsled.

The airport shut down at dusk, the funding for runway lights never more than deadpan rhetoric during the height of the political season. Roland rested his sunglasses on the crown of his blond head as they taxied to the landward end of the strip, the mountains a cracked ridge behind them, the sea ahead down the length of pale concrete. Out there somewhere in the water, an incompatibly situated cay stuck up like a catcher's mitt for small planes whose pilots were down on their agility and nerve.

Roland switched off the lights on the instrumentation to cut all reflection in the cockpit. Transparent blackness, the gray runway stretching into nearby infinity.

Roland shouted over the roar, "She's a dumpy old bird but with no real cargo we should have some spirited moments."

Even as Roland spoke they were already jostling down the airstrip like an old hot rod on a rutted road, Tillman anticipating lift-off long before it actually happened. The slow climb against gravity seemed almost futile, the opaque hand of the cay suddenly materializing directly in front of them. Roland dropped a wing and slammed the rudder pedal. The Stearmann veered sharply away from the hazard, then leveled off and continued mounting upward. Tillman could hear his mother thump in the fuselage.

"Bit of a thrill," Roland shouted. Tillman closed his eyes and endured the languid speed and the hard grinding vibrations of the plane.

Roland put on his headset and talked to any ghost he could rouse. When Tillman opened his eyes again, the clouds out the windscreen had a tender pink sheen to their tops. The atmosphere tingled with blueness. The ocean was black below them, and Barbados, ten degrees off starboard, was blacker still, a solid puddle sprinkled with electricity. Along the horizon the new day was a thin red thread unraveling westward. The beauty of it all made Tillman melancholy.

Roland floated the plane down to earth like a fat old goose who couldn't be hurried. The airport on Barbados was modern and received plenty of international traffic so they found it awake and active at this hour. Taxiing to the small plane tarmac, Tillman experienced a moment of claustrophobia, smelling only the acrid human sweat that cut through the mechanical fumes. He hadn't noticed it airborne but on the ground it was unbearable.

They parked and had the Stearmann serviced. In the wet, warm morning air Tillman's spirits revived. Roland walked through customs, headed for the bar to wait for him to do his business. Two hours later Tillman threw himself down in a chair next to the pilot and cradled his head on the sticky table, the surge of weariness through his back and neck almost making him pass out. He listened to Roland patiently suck his beer and commanded himself up to communicate the failure of the expedition.

"Bastards. They won't let me transfer her to a Stateside flight without the right paper."

"There was that chance," Roland admitted.

All along Tillman had believed that Barbados was the answer, people were reasonable there, that he had only to bring over the corpse of his mother, coffin her, place her on an Eastern flight to New York connecting with Boston, have a funeral home intercept her, bury her next to her ex-husband in the family plot on Beacon Hill. Send out death announcements to the few distant relatives scattered across the country, and then it would be over, back to normal. No mother, no obligations of blood. That was how she lived, anyway.

"Just how well connected are you, Roland?"

"Barbados is a bit iffy. The people are too damn sophisticated." He left to make some phone calls but returned with his hands out, the luckless palms upturned.

"Tillman, what next?"

Tillman exhaled and fought the urge to laugh, knowing it would mount to a hysterical outpouring of wretchedness. "I just don't know. Back to the island I guess. If you can see any other option, speak out. Please."

The pilot was unreadable behind the mirrors of his glasses. His young face had become loose and puffy since he had located Tillman at Rosehill. They settled their bar bill and left.

In the air again, the sound of the Stearmann rattled Tillman so thoroughly he felt as though the plane's engine were in his own skull. He tried to close his sleepless eyes against the killing brightness of the sun but could not stop the hypnotic flash that kept him staring below at the ocean. Halfway through the flight, Roland removed his headset and turned in his seat, letting the plane fly itself while he talked.

"Tillman," he shouted, "you realize I didn't bolt the plates back on the fuselage."

Tillman nodded absently and made no reply.

Roland jabbed his finger, pointing at the floor. "That handgear there by your foot opens the bay doors."

He resumed flying the plane, allowing Tillman his own thoughts. Tillman had none. He expected some inspiration or voice to break through his dizziness but it didn't happen. After several more minutes he tapped Roland on the shoulder. Roland turned again, lifting his glasses so Tillman could see his full face, his strained but resolute eyes, Tillman understanding this gesture as a stripping of fear, tacit confirmation that they were two men in the world capable of making such a decision without ruining themselves with ambiguity.

"Okay, Roland, the hell with it. She never liked being in one place too long anyway."

"Right you are, then," Roland said solemnly. "Any special spot?"

"No."

"Better this way," Roland yelled as he dropped the airspeed and sank the Stearmann to one thousand feet. "The thing that bothers me about burial, you see, is caseation. Your friggin body turns to cheese after a month in the dirt. How unspeakably nasty. I don't know if you've noticed, but I never eat cheese myself. Odd, isn't it?"

Tillman poked him on the shoulder again. "Knock it off."

"Sorry."

Tillman palmed the gear open. It was as easy as turning the faucet of a hose. When they felt her body dislodge and the tail bob inconsequentially, Roland banked the plane into a steep dive so they could view the interment. Tillman braced his hands against the windscreen and looked out, saw her cartwheeling for a moment and then stabilizing as the mauve chenille shroud came apart like a party streamer, a skydiver's Mae West. The Stearmann circled slowly around the invisible line of her descent through space.

"Too bad about your mother, mate," Roland called out finally. "My own, I don't remember much."

—"I'm still young," Tillman confessed, surprising himself, the words blurting forth from his mouth unsolicited. Tears of gratitude slipped down his face from this unexpected report of the heart.

He looked down at the endless water, waves struggling and receding, the small carnation of foam marking his mother's entrance into the sea, saw her, through the medium of refraction, unwrapped from her shroud, naked and washed, crawling with pure, unlabored motion down the shafts of light and beyond their farthest reach, thawed into suppleness, small glass bubbles, the cold air of her last breath, expelled past her white lips, nuzzled by unnamed fish. Now she was a perfect swimmer, free of the air and the boundaries of the living, darkness passing through darkness, down, down, to kiss the silt of the ocean floor, to touch the bottom of the world with dead fingers.

They had watched her plummet with a sense of awe and wonderment, as boys would who have thrown an object from off a high bridge. The pilot regained altitude and they continued westward. The realization came into Tillman, a palpable weight in his chest. I don't belong here, he said to himself, and immediately resisted the feeling, because that must have been the way she felt all her life.

Then, with the rich peaks of the island in sight, the heaviness dissipated. "It's beautiful here," he heard himself saying.

"What's that?" Roland shouted back.

"Beautiful," he repeated, and throughout Roland's clumsy landing, the jolt and thunder of the runway, "Mother be at peace."

Dead Reckoning

When I dropped out of Old Dominion, I took the first job I could find, flipping hamburgers in a fast-food place near one of the marinas in Ocean View. My education wasn't helping me one way or another, and it was time to do something that would enrich my life—as if anybody's life is like a loaf of bread you can press vitamins into. I was ambitious, I thought, but not strong. Working in a place like that seemed a fitting penance to endure until I figured myself out. Dumb, I know. Not the inspired thinking that really changes lives. I would come home greasy and exhausted, my hair unhealthy and smelling like onions. I felt like a floozy. Occasionally I would find enough energy to barhop and sleep with men I didn't know very well. You've heard stories like this, I'm sure. But it was the best time, the right place to lose hold of myself. If you don't do it when you're young, then I think you must get stuck forever being perfect and unreal.

The bleakness just kept increasing until they switched me to a morning shift. It was the end of March—the azaleas and dogwoods tried to make me appreciate that although I think spring is a phony season, hardly there at all before winter forgets what it's doing and summer bears down with its heat and humidity. I hated waking up early at first because I could never seem to spend the night decently. No matter how much I worked on myself in front of the bathroom mirror, my eyes still looked dulled, my mouth decadent, my skin subterranean, my pride—my thick blond hair—unmanageable, an expression of how untied I was. I'd bicycle down Oceanside to the hamburger joint and start heating up the grease. From the very first day this guy would come in every morning around eleven to get a cup of black coffee, a bag of french fries, which he'd soak in vinegar, and a piece of apple pie. Sometimes I'd take his order, sometimes Janine would. Janine obviously knew the guy. She'd ask, "How's it going?" He would look serious and say something like, "No turnbuckles. I can't find the right turnbuckles," or, "I'd like to know just how the hell anybody can afford teak?" Then he'd march off to one of the tables, unroll the big piece of graph paper he always had tucked under his arm, spread his order out on the diagrams and scratches, and study them while he ate, doodling atop the doodles he had made the day before. The plans were so coffee-stained and sticky I don't see how he got the boat built.

It was clear that he cared as much about food as I did about my job. His name was Davis and he was, whenever he came into the place, filthy. His jeans were caked with epoxy, his T-shirt looked like a painter's palette. He wore tennis shoes that could have been chewed on by a shark and he had the worst fingernails I've seen on anybody. They were smashed and black and jagged, with enough dirt beneath them to occupy a geologist. I liked his body, though. For all the junk he ate he was handsomely lean, and yet his arms were so muscular they seemed swollen. He never bothered to comb his rusty hair, but it was too short then to give him the wild Leif Ericsson look he has now. If I had created him I would have had more sympathy for his face. Davis had a face you expect to see scars on, like a tally of what's been paid, but he only had a little one, a thin white line that italicized his left eye. I don't know how he got it. His skin was much redder than his hair, his features so abrupt—he looked like a man whose element was fire, who could only be happy with the world ablaze, which was odd, because he loved the sea more than anything else. He was not a romantic figure; his appearance was too haggard—scary— for that. I was attracted to him nevertheless. I was intrigued, glance by glance.

He walked in one day after I had gone through a long, depressing evening in a bar with Janine, that old scene, not caring how much I drank, half wild from this great reservoir of ambivalent desire I felt was in me. By eleven I was a zombie; it took me a second to realize Davis was standing across the counter from me and talking.

"What?" I said wearily, pushing the hair out of my eyes, hating the oily touch of it. I just wanted to go home and sleep for a year.

"You look terrible," he said.

"Thanks. So do you," I told him. "You always do, you know that." He smiled, and the smile was more than I imagined it would be.

"So you built a boat?" I already knew he had but I asked him anyway.

"Yeah. Finishing up. She goes in the water in three or four days."

"Need a crew?" I blurted out. I had not really intended to speak that sentence, only to test out the feeling on myself.

"Oh?" he said suspiciously, the grayness of his eyes bearing down on me, critical, but not by the same standard as the guys in the bars. "Do you sail?"

"Sure," I answered. "Well, a little bit anyway." The only boat I had ever been in or on was a canoe. I was more of the horseback, hiking type—I'd grown up in the Blue Ridge Mountains outside of Charlottesville. Nothing strange or special about me; I was an ordinary girl.

"Well," said Davis slowly, as if he wasn't sure he was being smart. "If the sailmaker gets off his butt we'll go out on the bay some Saturday. Next week. Maybe."

It did not take three or four days for Davis to get his boat in the water—it took him more than a month. The entire time he acted mad or preoccupied so I stopped talking to him about it. Then one afternoon he showed up as I was getting off work and took me sailing, more or less.

Davis was a master craftsman, and a wry bastard of a perfectionist. It had taken him four and a half years to build *Impetuous*—a gaff-rigged sloop, thirty-two feet long, and double-ended, her black hull ferrocement. The design was seventy years old and somehow, even though the boat was brand new, Davis had succeeded in giving her an ambiance of graceful age, as if she had been day sailing the Chesapeake since before our parents were born. Everything aboard was not bright and polished and packaged, but quiet, comfortable, and loved. Under full sail *Impetuous* was breathtaking, something bigger in my life than had ever been there before.

A lot of time passed, though, before I learned these details about the boat, learned what gaff-rigging meant and that *Impetuous* had it. When I first went aboard I didn't know stem from stern, didn't have a nautical fact in my head. And I couldn't have guessed how stubborn a true perfectionist can be. I ran my hand along the beautiful woodwork in the cockpit. Davis frowned. "It's not right. Doesn't drain right." Every time I made a compliment, he would say something to undercut it. That's the way he is: it's one of his characteristics I strive to ignore.

That first day on *Impetuous* was like petitioning to join a club that you desperately want to belong to, even though the

3 1   DEAD RECKONING

club's only function is to confuse and harass people who fit your description.

"Let's do it," said Davis. I'm sure I must have looked like a silly belle, eyelids fluttery, clapping my hands, my heart so certain I was meant for this.

I asked him what he wanted me to do. He wanted me to sit in the cockpit and be prepared to take the tiller when he told me to. I felt a nice warmth in my blood that came from being with Davis, and absolutely no apprehension about what was going to take place. I sat down innocently on the edge of the cockpit, my legs crossed comfortably, my fingers resting on the shaft of the tiller, feeling as grand as if I had the best seat in the house at the most spectacular show ever to hit town. And it started out like that. Davis, magician and sorcerer, salty and seaworthy, huffed and grunted and raised the mainsail, dazzling me with its white immensity, its thunderous rustling. It shone like snow and swelled as big as a mountainside. It was wonderful.

He began to winch up the anchor and call instructions back to me. Then he started yelling, curses like knots tied into the weave of my fantasy. I began to feel unworthy, a moron, a bug. "Starboard, damn it, starboard." When he saw I didn't understand he yelled *Steer right, for Chrissakes!* so I swung the tiller right as far as I could, the boat began to circle the wrong way, and he screamed at me, "To the right, goddammit, what's wrong with you?" I felt terrible, but how was I to know that when you pushed the tiller right the boat went left? We ran aground there in the anchorage—serious taboo for a prideful sailor, an elemental failure, like a farmer who can't plow his rows straight. Somebody had to come pull us off because Davis had no money left over to put an engine in the boat. His yelling frightened me, but in the days ahead I got better. I don't know why he gave me the chance but he did, and I took it.

One Saturday in June we were out in the middle of the Chesapeake, a day of sluggish weather, no pressures. When the sun started to fade and drain into the haze of the far shore, we headed back in but the wind died before we were halfway there. We drifted in the humid evening light until the water shallowed enough to set an anchor out. Night closed us in gently and we lit the kerosene running lamps and hung them in the rigging. Out there in the middle of nowhere they looked cheerful and secure. I felt as if everything bad in my life had remained onshore and everything good was out on the water with me. We went below, shared a can of tuna fish with saltines and drank warm beer. On the quilt-covered bunk we lay in each other's arms until morning, whispering. Oh, he was so full of chivalry, this Davis; he could be tender and patient when he wanted to. I thought to myself I'd fall far in love with him someday. Maybe he'd fall in love with me, too, although I'm not certain what made me think that, unless it was that I was a woman willing to tolerate him, his quick shouting, the pick pick pick of his perfectionism, his demanding (and hypnotic) presence. I kept quiet and mostly tried to please him. It was just the right thing to do. I finally wanted something. I finally felt that something was worth the effort. I was that clear about Davis and the boat.

Davis was in the Navy, he had been for six years. His current tour was up in July and he wasn't going to reenlist this time. He served night duty as a radio technician. During the daytime he sweated over *Impetuous*. I don't know when he slept. He had joined the military because he was bored and because he was poor. That's how he came in, and that's how he was going out. The boat had taken all his money. Routine had neutralized his job. Now he planned to sail around the world, the hard way, through the Strait of Magellan, across the Pacific without a landfall to New Zealand, around the Cape of Good Hope—all of this without a motor to depend on. "So what?" he lectured me. "How long do you think engines have been on boats?" The first leg of the voyage would take him to the Grenadine Islands in the Caribbean, where he had already arranged to charter the boat out for the winter season. Enough money would come in this way to pay for food and whatever else was needed.

"Can I go with you?" I asked. He glared at the hesitation in

DEAD RECKONING

my voice and I wondered if I were crazy. Then I said, "Take me with you, Davis."

"I don't think you can handle it," he said. "It can get pretty rough."

"Yes, I can," I insisted. I hadn't the slightest idea of what he meant by rough. "You just can't go off and leave me," I said. "I want to be with you."

He didn't have an answer right away, but he did say yes. I withdrew what savings I had from my bank and bought a small diesel engine for the boat. He never really was a purist about it. He just didn't have enough money himself. It took about three weeks to get it in and running properly. *Impetuous* felt more like home to me after that. (But oh, the back talk I was to endure from that engine, the diesel muttering, and Davis muttering—a woman muttered against.)

Davis got his walking papers from the Navy, I moved out of my apartment, and we lived together on board. The Coast Guard offered courses in navigation and Davis wanted me to sign up even though we weren't going to be around long enough for me to be certified. The books weren't easy to comprehend and the instructor cared very little for women, but I enjoyed working with the equations and learned what I could. Now on our day sails we steered the boat out of the bay into the ocean. It was more rigorous but didn't seem impossible. The perpetual heaving made me sick but Davis said that was normal and I would get used to it. In the meantime without Dramamine I had no more equilibrium than a sedated duck.

Davis decided that Cape Hatteras, the graveyard of the Atlantic, might be too drastic an initiation for me, so we were going to follow the Intracoastal Waterway to the top of the Florida Keys, then do the long haul to Puerto Rico, replenish our supplies there, leave the Atlantic for the Caribbean Sea, island-hopping our way to the cluster of Grenadines. We had to be in Bequia by November 15 for our first charter group, three medics whom Davis played softball with on the base. On the map it all looked charmingly simple, islands like stepping-stones from one continent to another. I quit my job and phoned my parents. They said no and I said good-bye. We left Norfolk the first week in August.

The Intracoastal Waterway, I discovered, is a party circuit for weekend warriors. The three weeks we spent on it lulled me into the notion that traveling by sailboat was like driving a sleek but clumsy bus from one good time to the next. The developed stretches along the canals reeked of money and Southern idleness; in some marinas I felt the yachtsmen's disdainful eyes on *Impetuous,* as if she were an old Chevy wagon in a parking lot full of Mercedes and Porsches. We sneaked through Miami in the middle of the night into the free anchorage at Dinner Key. Our generator malfunctioned, costing us six days waiting for the new part to be hunted down. Davis stayed angry minute by minute; all he wanted was to get out on the sea where he didn't have to depend on other people. When the generator was fixed and we thought we could leave, Betty, a hurricane prowling Barbados, made us think again. We sat under sunny skies for another week until Betty blew herself out on the thumb of the Yucatan. On a Friday morning in September we motored out Government Cut, raised our sails, and surged into the Gulf Stream.

There is much to say about the voyage but only one thing that really matters: by the third day out from land I thought Davis had it in his mind to kill us. I honestly did. "You're navigating, you know," he'd told me days before in Miami. I'd said okay, accepting the task casually because I knew perfectly well he was a better navigator than I was and would catch any of my mistakes. At Monty's Raw Bar, I drank beer and munched conch fritters, leisurely charting out our course, an agent who had never actually left the travel office and therefore had no idea what the tickets, the reservations, the itinerary, represented.

We headed south-southeast through the Straits of Florida. My unsteady stomach was pacified by Dramamine; I felt brave and twice as alive as I ever had been. The Gulf Stream was calm, the wind well mannered but *there,* always there. After four hours on watch, Davis turned the boat over to me for two. Everywhere I looked the world was blue. I was alone with my man and that was it, that was all that was left of the planet.

When the sun went down I started worrying like an old lady. I had the sensation of being blind, moving too fast, out of control. We were in the shipping lanes and I imagined one of the big tankers crunching right through us. They have so many lights that at night on the sea they show up like cities rocking in a void. You can't see where you're going; you have to have faith, and faith was something I was beginning to lose. I stood watch from ten till midnight and from four to six. My grip on the tiller seemed to be my only hold on life. I stared at the compass as if it were a crystal ball. Everything I needed to know was spinning around under the faintly lit dome, and yet I felt I hadn't the power to read it correctly. I felt this grave loneliness—more than anything else I wanted Davis to wake up and be next to me, wanted to touch him, have him reassure me. Davis and the sun both came up at the same time. I was cold and afraid, crying inside from the responsibility that cut into me like the blade of an ax. Davis looked relaxed—strong and liberated. He brought me a cup of hot coffee, said he was proud of me. Everything's going to be okay, I thought then. Everything's all right.

The second day we were becalmed. The ocean never appears more endless than when the wind stops and the surface slows like gelatin. I studied the charts. How much were we losing to the current? How much drift did I have to compensate for? At noon I raised the sextant in my sore hands and shot a fix on the sun. I computed and drew lines and checked the books, eventually marking a little x on the edge of the Grand Bahama Bank.

"I think we're right here," I told Davis, spreading the chart out on the hot deck in front of him.

"What do you mean, you think?" he answered me. "Don't think, just know."

"It's hard to know for sure, Davis," I said. "Don't get upset."

"I'm not upset," he said. "But your well-being depends on knowing, not thinking you know. Aren't I right?"

I went back down to the cabin and tried to work out the position again. I was doing the best I could. By sundown the radio was broadcasting storm warnings. Davis seemed to look forward to the bad weather gathering out there in front of us, invisible only to our sense of sight. He was hungry so I cooked him spaghetti for his supper, throwing up into a bucket after five minutes of smelling the sauce heating on the stove.

On my first watch of the night the clouds absorbed the range of stars above us. Davis came up at midnight to take the helm. Nothing had changed, but I was so keyed up I thought I could hear the forces gathering out there in the darkness ahead, like armies beyond the next rise. Exhausted, I went below and collapsed on the bunk, pulling the quilt over my head. I don't know how long I slept but I was awakened violently, thrown out of bed across the beam of the boat, shanghaied and suddenly at war. From very far away Davis was shouting at me to come on deck. *Impetuous* was experiencing a bucking and pitching that didn't make sense to my body. I had to crawl to where Davis was. The boat had heeled severely in the wind; the oceanic floodwaters churned over half the deck. The rain and blackness were impossible to see through, the noise horrendous, a ripping apart of the soft world that floated us. I had to take the tiller while Davis reefed the mainsail and dropped the jib. I remember this—the terror blooming in my throat, making me a blind animal; the pain as the storm raced through the sky and ocean, transferred to the boat and centered, like electricity, into the tiller as I fought against it; and the extreme loneliness again, as if the universe could offer no truer moment than this, ever.

Davis screamed at me hysterically: "You stupid-ass bitch, get her into the wind, goddammit, put her up into it. Dumb fucking cunt." It was no time to be sensitive, I suppose.

We lost the jib. It blew out, its clean geometrical precision

DEAD RECKONING

exploding into tatters before I could command the boat to come about. He seemed to blame me for that. "We almost lost the boat," he said. "No boat—no more me, no more you. You have to react quicker, you have to be on top of it, you have to be ten times stronger than you think you are. When you think you've reached your limit, that's when you really have to start pushing ahead."

I didn't want to hear it. "You bastard, Davis," I told him. "I'm not tough. I know you want me to be. I'm trying, I honestly am, but I'm not tough. I'm just afraid."

The rest of the night I refused to leave his side. The seas were huge, invisible until they crashed down onto us. The boat shuddered continuously with their impact, lurching as the water swept across the deck. The cement hull made an eerie humming sound. Even with Dramamine I kept puking. To comfort me, Davis tied a rope between us, from waist to waist. I could not tolerate the thought of being separated from him, being alone in the sea, struggling for however long it took me to give in. Davis ate amphetamines and battled against the weather. Eyes blazing, he seemed well suited for the horror of it. By morning the wind was not as renegade. The waves still held their size though, each one a rushing continent about to bury *Impetuous*.

"Davis, let's head into port somewhere and wait until this passes," I pleaded. "I can't take it."

"There's nothing nearby but Cuba and we can't go there and there's no need to run away," he said. "This isn't something we can walk away from. Boats teach you to stick with your trouble until it's over."

"Please don't lecture me," I said quietly, my one courageous moment. Mostly I was so fundamentally shocked—by the power of the water, by Davis, by the taste I had of my life's end—that I just closed up completely.

"We're beating it," Davis said, surveying the slab of purple clouds overhead. "The worst has passed."

He was right about the weather—we would not have to go

through a night like that again. But the worst was not over for me. The cloud cover remained for six days; a front had stalled on top of us. There would be occasional rents of blue sky, progressively bigger and longer as the days went by, but for six days I could not get a satisfactory noontime fix on the sun.

"Davis," I said hopelessly, "I don't know where we are. You've got to help me navigate."

"That's your responsibility, isn't it?"

"But I don't know where we are," I said. I couldn't keep my tears back anymore.

"Find out," he said without emotion.

"Why, Davis, why won't you help me?"

"Learn to depend on yourself." I couldn't stand the holy, self-satisfied look on his face when he said that. "If something happens to me you should be able to take over. Otherwise you shouldn't be here."

"Maybe I shouldn't be here."

He didn't reply and I hated him. I had to rely on dead reckoning, which is a system of estimating where you're going based on where you've just been. It's primarily guesswork, especially if as the days go by you're less and less certain where you've been. I studied and studied the chart, worked it all out over and over again, but kept arriving at different answers. By the seventh day I couldn't think straight.

"Davis," I begged, "I still don't know where we are. Please, let's just head due south. We should be able to sight the coast of Haiti by nightfall. I think so, anyway. If not, we're in a lot of trouble."

None of this made the impression I expected. "No," he said. "Get us to Puerto Rico."

I became paralyzed with my own inability to change things, hardly speaking to Davis over the next two days. On the tenth day I told him I wanted to get off the boat. He laughed at me. "Where you gonna go?" he said.

"I can't stand it anymore. I'm out of Dramamine and sick all the time. I'm fed up with everything always moving, moving,

moving. Every inch of my body is black and blue. I can't even brush my teeth."

"I told you not to leave anything lying around on deck. This isn't the Chesapeake Bay. There's no margin of error here. Stop acting like it's my fault we can't brush our teeth."

At breakfast on the eleventh day I said, "Davis, let's just stop for a day or two. We've got to be pretty close to the eastern tip of the Dominican Republic. I need a rest from all this. Then we can go on."

"Find Puerto Rico," he said, again pointing to the scope of the horizon. "Find the Mona Passage. Get us into the Caribbean."

I was too battered to implore or argue any longer. The following day, at midafternoon, I commanded with very little confidence, "Steer due east. We'll mark the west coast of the island and take it down and around to Ponce." As the sun set behind us we still sailed forward into an empty seascape.

"It's not there," I told Davis sadly. "We should have crashed into it by now. I knew it wouldn't be there. You're letting me kill the two of us, Davis. And I don't understand why."

I could not go on watch that night, I felt so utterly defeated. I resigned myself to hell and Davis knew that but didn't do a damn thing to comfort me. At sunrise I came up on deck and stared blankly at him. His face seemed raw and worn out. He had eaten a bagful of amphetamines during the past four days to keep going—the Navy's secret weapon, he called them.

"I'm sorry I can't do anything," I said. "I'm sorry for everything."

"You can," he answered. "Take the tiller while I wash up."

He disappeared for five minutes and then was back up, letting the boom swing out over the starboard gunwale.

"What are you doing?" I asked him. My shorts were damp and itchy. All of a sudden I couldn't sit still.

"What does it look like? Change your course to one-sixty."
"Why?"
"Don't ask me why, just do it. Stop feeling so sorry for yourself and take a look around."

Sargasso weed was scattered everywhere in gold lines along the surface. The blueness had become subtly richer, less opaque, less threatening. It appeared to be, despite my gloom, a gorgeous day. I could see other boats, a fishing fleet, trawlers stiffly waving their tall arms, on the horizon in front of us. After a minute all this information sank in.

"My God, are we near land?"

"Can't you smell it?" Once he said it I could. It smelled like newly broken soil, fresh and safe.

"Where's Puerto Rico?"

"Stand up and look."

I popped up but had to turn around before I could find what it was I needed to see—a hazy gray smudge, and below it green hills, the white and red lines of rooftops. I didn't understand.

"Davis, how can that be it?"

"That's it all right. We passed it during the night."

I started to shriek—not at Davis, but at myself. How could that be? The island was on the wrong side of the boat; it should have been off our port stern. I looked back at Davis, a crazy woman, my voice shaky.

"We're supposed to stop. Why aren't we stopping?"

"It's too late. We missed our turn."

"Don't joke with me, Davis. I'm too upset. Just tell me what's going on."

"What's going on, lady, is that your navigation has been wrong for the last six days. Ever since Cuba your course has been too slow and too high and too easterly. What's going on is that you have passed the Antilles and are on your way to fucking Africa."

That is our history. That is where we have been. Why couldn't Davis have told me, why couldn't he have spared me the extent of my suffering? He knew all along, had been keeping our course secretly on a second chart, verifying it with a radio direction finder I didn't even know was aboard. What did I learn, except to despise his coldheartedness and hate my own acquiescence? Hardship builds character, he was always re-

4 1

minding me. Well, not when the odds are bad and nobody's lifting a finger to help. So that's where we've been, and yet, knowing our tracks, I could not accurately predict where we were going. Davis had hurt me and I wanted to leave him. We reached St. Croix that night and docked at Frederiksted. He wished only to order a new jib and proceed immediately to Nevis to wait for it to be flown down. St. Croix was too American, he felt, and he didn't want to hang around until the sail was ready. He didn't bother to ask me what I wanted. When we got off *Impetuous* for the first time in twelve days I thought I had made up my mind.

"I'm going home," I said.

"That's your decision," he answered calmly, meeting my eye without the customary arrogance the sail had given him. "But I wish you'd stay."

"How can you expect me to believe that! After what you did to me out there."

He took hold of my arm as we walked to a café. "It won't happen again. It won't happen because now you know how bad it can get. You have no illusions."

"You're such a shit."

"That's right."

"Why can't you lighten up on me, Davis?"

"Stay with me until Nevis. Nevis will give you what you want."

"What do I want?"

"You want everything to be beautiful and perfect and easy."

"What do you think I am, damn it? That's not true. I'm just trying to survive. Can't you see that?" Davis rolled his eyes when I said "survive" as if it were the biggest cliché. His attention was already someplace else on the busy street. But something in me couldn't stop, was compelled to go on. I was back at sea with him the next day.

Nevis was indeed beautiful—a perfect island, a perfect paradise, if you could relieve it of its history and its bittersweet poverty. Alexander Hamilton was born there, the son of a Scottish aristocrat. America's saint of the well-to-do, he lost his blue blood defending the manliest of virtues, his honor, or *Honor,* I guess he would have said, the imprudent fellow. I can't think of the island without seeing him lounging around as a young blade, a pretty boy who wore a sherbet-colored velvet coat and silk stockings and shoes with red wooden heels, a sword always knocking against his leg. He must have loved it. I know Davis would have. Davis, the picaroon.

The sail over from St. Croix took thirty hours, thirty hours under flawless conditions, but I could not release myself from my paranoia to enjoy it the way I should have. I fell for the island, though. It was my reward, my redemption song. After going through what I had, I felt I deserved a place like this; I felt as if I owned Nevis. We dove in clear turquoise water, poked around the reefs like two lazy turtles, bathed naked, bathed on beaches as empty as the moon. Soaking in mineral springs, I stopped focusing on what was wrong with Davis and again saw what was good. We hiked into lush mountains to a waterfall too cold to swim in. Clouds encircled us on our way down. For a while I felt once more that dread sensation of being lost, but we were on land, sweet land, and it passed without effect. In Charlestown we sat in palm-thatched bars and yakked with the locals, drank moonshine rum, ate curried goat stew. We walked and we walked and we walked, hand in hand, sailors ashore on legs still wobbly from the sea.

Each morning we would row our dinghy in from the anchorage to the public dock, busy in a slow way with stevedores and children, the dirty concrete piled with lumber and cases of glistening bottled beer, lumpy sacks of vegetables, hands of bananas, slaughtered animals, all steaming in the tropic sun. We wandered through the quayside markets and stalls, buying fruit from the hucksters and hot loaves of bread from an old woman who cooked them in a Dutch oven over an open fire. The bread was delicious, the days exalted, unlike any I had ever known. And yet Nevis questioned me, burdened my heart with its children—preschool beggars with big eyes, kids growing up on the hot streets. Most of the population was poor, but not pathetically so. Some people lived in scrap shacks, but most owned small two-room wooden houses with rusted tin roofs and no plumbing. In these latitudes that's not as stricken as it sounds. The worst of it was they couldn't get ahead no matter how hard they tried. In Nevis people had enough to carry on, sometimes a little more. Other than that they were stuck. Everybody but the merchants seemed terminally unemployed, although it was common for families to have a little garden or a piece of land in the hills where they could pick mangoes and grow sweet potatoes or tether a cow. Only the shop owners and civil servants could afford to dress the way they wanted; otherwise people wore clothes that were ill-fitting or torn, the zippers always busted, but rarely dirty. That's how it was in Nevis, my first true touch of paradise. I've been to better places since, but mostly I've been to worse.

The little kids in the countryside were shy and withdrawn, very formal when you did get them talking. They would say yes, sir, yes, missus, good day to you. In Charlestown, though, the kids begged whenever a white person appeared. Davis hated them.

"That's what tourism does," he said.

The first morning we bought bread from the old woman, a black boy—he was probably ten or eleven years old—was there. His feet were bare, as ours were, and he wore a pair of shorts cut off from shiny black pants and a white T-shirt with one of the shoulders ripped out. He watched us buy bread and then approached with his hand held out in front of him. I looked down because I thought he wanted to show us something.

"Mistah," he said to Davis, "please fah a dime. Me muddah dead ahnd me faddah blind."

Davis ignored him.

"Can't we give him something?" I asked.

"No way," Davis said. "All these people think every white

person in the world is a Rockefeller. I work for my money and I don't have enough of it, either. I'm not giving it away."

I dug into my pocket to find a coin for the boy. Davis grabbed my wrist. "Don't," he said. "If you give to him you're going to have to give something to every kid on the road watching you right now. How can you justify giving to him and not to the others?"

Since I didn't have an answer for that I gave in to Davis. "Is this your son?" I asked the bread lady. She grimaced and ground her loose jaw, shook her head, scolding me. "I doan raise no rude pickahninny."

Each morning after that the boy was there, and each time he'd wait until after we had purchased our bread and then he would say to Davis, "Mistah, please fah a dime. Me muddah dead ahnd me faddah blind." I tried to close my eyes to it. He was such a handsome little boy though, long-lashed eyes, an elegantly boned face, brilliant teeth, sticklike arms and legs that he was striving to grow into. I wish that my perspective on him wasn't distorted by what Davis saw. The boy was not sullen; there was a gay spirit about him that I couldn't dismiss.

I didn't want to leave Nevis but I understood that *Impetuous* would have to leave soon if she were going to make her deadline in the Grenadines. As our time on the island shortened I felt the tension between Davis and me rekindle. I still wasn't positive that I wanted to continue on with him. He wasn't pressing me for an answer, at least not verbally, but the pressure was there anyway.

On what turned out to be our final morning in Nevis we went to the bread lady to buy our breakfast. The beggar kid was there, too, but this time he had a pack of his brethren behind him. For moral support, I supposed. They were all in raggy clothes, all pretty and smooth like beach pebbles, the way black children are. Some of them just looked curious, some attempted to look very tough or serious. Davis paid for the bread. The black kid stuck out his hand. It was the longest-running show on Nevis.

"Mistah, please fah a dime. Me muddah dead ahnd me faddah blind."

Maybe it was because of the audience, the knowledge that his message would be heard by many ears, or maybe it was because he already knew this would be our last day here, since the new jib had arrived, and therefore he could say good-bye to the island by bringing to a conclusion his ritual with the kid, but Davis finally conceded to talk to him.

"What's your name?"

"Willessly," the boy readily answered, pleased for the opportunity. He had a languid, musical voice that sounded like the middle range of notes on a clarinet.

"Your mother's dead, right?"

"Yes, mahn."

"Your father's blind?"

"Yes."

"Look here, Willessly. If I were you I wouldn't smile when I say that."

Giggling erupted among Willessly's comrades. His bright smile only increased. Davis glared down at them all. Willessly wouldn't withdraw his hand.

"Me hungry, mahn. Please fah a piece ah bread."

"Jesus, he's so good-natured about it," I whispered to Davis. "Why don't you give him some? There's plenty."

"You don't get it, do you?" he said, turning on me. His look was empty of everything I thought it should be full of—the intimacy we had established in Norfolk, cultivated in the garden of Nevis. "It would be a sign of weakness. When you give to people like this, they're not grateful, they don't respect you. What happens is they hate you. They think you're a fool for giving in to them."

"But, Davis, he's just a little boy."

"Me hungry, mahn."

"Let's go," Davis said, stuffing the loaves into his haversack. "Go eat a coconut," he said to Willessly. The audience of kids thought this statement was extremely funny. They laughed, not at us but at Willessly, teasing and taunting him. A game was being played here but I couldn't tell what it was. There we stood in the tiny square of the marketplace, the stalls abundant with a rainbow of fruits and vegetables, the air luscious with the smells of spices, of frying coconut oil and garlic and cumin, the scents of frangipani and lime. Palm trees sprouted up everywhere against the cloudless sky like exaggerated flowers. Calypso music screeched from several radios in the nearby buildings.

"Me hungry, mahn." Willessly bent down, scraped up a handful of dirt and put it in his mouth. The black kids responded as if this act were inspired.

"Look de boy dere goin ahll out."

"He mahd. Him dizzy."

"Oh, sweet Lahd, him eat de dirt now."

And a shrill little-girl's voice sang, "Momma goin beat you, Willessly. Momma goin strike."

"Let's go," Davis said. He spun me around and we started walking away down a grassy alley that led to the water. I looked over my shoulder. Willessly was spitting out the dirt. He wiped his mouth with the bottom of his T-shirt, leaving muddy streaks on the overbleached whiteness, and followed us.

We walked along the beach away from town. I could hear the kids behind us having a grand time.

The ocean on this side of Nevis was like a mountain lake, serene and glassy, bluer than the sky. As you walked along the shore, the water was so transparent you could easily spot fish. Long skinny fish like Willessly, fat clown fish, fish dressed for carnival, sleek hot-rod fish. The bay was crescent-shaped and we stopped in the middle of it to eat our food, a shadowy grove of sea grape and palms behind us, the cool sea in front. We sat in the sand and stripped down to our bathing suits. Willessly advanced on us. Somewhere he had gotten hold of a baby. Maybe the infant had been with the kids all along and I just hadn't seen her. He toted her haphazardly, his arms wrapped under her arms and around her chest, the rest of her dangling loose, facing us, her cheeks like bowls of chocolate pudding.

"You want to buy dis baby?" he asked Davis.

Davis squinted at him. "How much?"

"Twenty dollahs U.Ess."

"Get lost," Davis said, chewing his bread.

"She too dahk fah you? I cahn get you a clear-skin one, ya know."

Davis didn't bother to answer. The kid handed the baby over to one of the girls backing him up. Willessly spoke directly to me for the first time. "You husbahnd doan like blahck peoples." It was no accusation; there was no bitterness.

"No," I said nervously. "No, I don't think that's true. You shouldn't say that."

"Yes, it's true." He insisted upon it in such a friendly, straightforward way, his dark eyes playful but firm, that I smiled. "He doan care fah de color ah shit."

"What?"

"God made blahck peoples from his own shit," he said, holding out his thin arm as if the evidence were there.

That's the most terrible sentence I ever heard anyone speak, let alone a child. I think my heart shrank and burrowed into my stomach when he said it.

"Who told you that?" Davis snapped.

"Me muddah."

"Your mother's dead."

"Yes."

"You *are* full of shit, you little bastard."

"Davis, don't say that."

"Where's your pride, boy?" he demanded.

Willessly had a quizzical look on his face, a veteran player determining his opponent's newest strategy. He rubbed his snotty nose, went over to his group of friends and came right back to us.

"You want to buy dis?" He held out an old swim fin, its rubber cracked and faded.

"No," Davis said. "I want you to get out of here right now."

"You want to buy dis?" Willessly now had in his small hands a conch shell that looked as though it had been lying in the sun for years, all but a trace of its inner pinkness burned away.

"Go away. I told you I don't want to buy anything."

"Lady, you want dis?" I shook my head no.

"I give it to you. Fah free." He thrust the shell into my lap. I thanked him and he retreated back to the group.

I stretched out in the sand, letting the sunshine cook me. If you'd taken a picture of us it would have made a nice postcard, I guess, another enticing image for a travel brochure. The kids were in the water, splashing and laughing with no thought for keeping their clothes dry. The baby was left by herself propped in the bone-colored sand. A schooner under full sail edged by close offshore. The jungle soared behind us, climbing the volcano to a height that could no longer support it. And here was this rugged fellow beside me, my man, ready to kick the world's ass.

After an hour or so we started back to Charlestown, the kids still tagging behind us. We planned to catch the morning bus—not a bus, really, but an old flatbed truck with benches nailed down to it—to the windward side of the island. Davis was going to skin-dive for lobster on the barrier reef; I had heard about some women in one of the villages over there who still made pottery the same way the Arawak Indians used to, and I wanted to watch them.

We stopped in a rum shop near the corner where we were supposed to pick up the transportation. It was dark inside and smelled like rancid butter. An old phonograph played reggae music, intolerably scratchy and loud. We had not entered into this shop before. It was full of black men who stood along the counter or sat balefully against the wall. The atmosphere was oppressive. For the first time I felt we were unwanted here, that we were resented. All our immunities were canceled: We were not tourists spending money. We were just there sharing the island.

Willessly followed us in, the other kids crowded around the doorway. Davis bought a can of Tennant's ale and some Aristocrisp peanuts that came packaged in old Heineken bottles. The peanuts were grown and roasted in St. Vincent, the mother island of the Grenadines. Davis loved them, said they were better than any you could get in the States. He shook some out of the green bottle into his mouth, crunched on them, took a gulp of his ale.

"You want anything?"

"No," I said. "Just to leave."

"Mistah, buy me a Coke," Willessly said. He had not retired his smile. I decided I liked him a lot. He didn't care that Davis was deaf.

"I'm real tired of you annoying me," Davis said. I thought he was going to challenge the boy to a fight from the way he spoke.

"Please fah a groundnut," Willessly persisted.

"Piss off."

"I'm going," I said. "We'll miss our ride."

I started toward the door. Faces creased with malice loomed up at me, thick, gagging smells, unhealthy air. The shop seemed more crowded than when we first came in. I had to push through people, all men, their muscles tight, their eyes reddened with an appetite foreign to me. Someone began to hiss, *pssst.* The sound was ominous but it only made me feel hard. The younger men scowled at me and called out, "Busy, busy." In the islands, a "busy" woman is a whore. I wasn't going to let it penetrate me; my determination to handle it all coolly just kept building. I should have been afraid but if I was I can't remember. I was being bumped around. I looked back for Davis and felt a hand grab and pinch one of my tits. That did it for me. I felt walled off by sharks on one side, this righteous lion on the other, me and the kid in the middle trying to stay alive. There was this teenager in front of me, cocky and leering. He winked at me and snarled with laughter. His teeth were dirty and he wore a red beret that was puffed up with the wool of his hair. I knew he was the one who'd grabbed me. I reacted without even considering the consequence. I punched him in the ear.

"Wha I do?" he protested, his high voice wounded, a charade of injustice received, waving his hands in front of him. "Wha I do? I doan do a dahmn ting. Dis bitch womahn cra-zee."

"Don't tell me that, man," I screamed at him. "Get out of my way."

He stepped aside and I passed out the door through a chorus of snickers, Davis and Willessly in my wake. I felt as if I had blood all over me and that that entitled me to anything I wanted. I kept on screaming.

"Davis, goddammit, give the kid a peanut."

I waited with my hands on my hips. Davis didn't do anything. Actually, he finished off his ale and chucked the can into the gutter.

"If you don't give the kid some peanuts, I swear to God I'm going to go back to the boat right now, unlock the shotgun and write you a good-bye letter on the sails in buckshot."

"Okay, okay," Davis said reluctantly, although I believe he had a private desire to see me play out my rage. He called Willessly over. "Here," he said. He gave him a peanut—one lousy peanut. I would have smashed the bottle out of Davis's hand if it hadn't been for the way Willessly responded.

He held the peanut up in the air like a trophy. He jumped up in the dirt street, displaying the tiny gold nut to his friends. They each examined it enviously. He went from one to the other until they had all seen it.

"What I tell you," he called out to them. "What I tell you, Mahcus? You owe me, mahn. I tellin you now, I ahm de best."

They weren't concerned with us anymore. I watched as they tramped back toward the marketplace, Willessly in front of them, walking backward, full of bravura, ten feet tall, the peanut still raised triumphantly between his thumb and index finger.

"You see that," Davis said. "All he wanted to do was make a fool out of me."

"All you wanted to do," I told him, matching his awful smirk, "was teach him a lesson he didn't need to be taught."

That evening, under a waxing moon and sharp northeasterly breeze, we took up anchor and sailed away. I knew that going out to sea would not be an act of war this time, and I saw, like Eve, that paradise had become just another place to leave behind. I felt good about that, because I could tell myself that across the waters, with the winds and sometimes against them, somewhere there would be another. I could move ahead without even thinking about it. And to hell with Davis.

There's a jazz club in Barbados that you end up in after hours. You come in hot from the streets, fight your way to the bar for an ice-cold Banks beer, and take it easy taking it all in. Tonight there's a big deal going down. Lord Short Shoe wants the monkey. He says he's willing to pay.

The tropical night is kinetic and full of potential. In a place like Bridgetown, there's something going on somewhere, and it won't be right—you'd be stealing from yourself—unless you're there, too. So you come in from the streets, a damp ocean breeze coaxing you through the wrought-iron gate that leads up the stairs to the second story of this run-down Victorian relic, its pink gingerbread crumbling with termites. You are already sort of perfectly oriented—the fact is, you feel great.

On the streets the people were good-looking, carefully dressed, friendly. There's no rampant poverty here to close you up or make you defensive. You have witnessed the subliminal movement of moon from sea, the silhouettes of palm trees and sailboats framed in its orange hoop. Dinner at the Frangipani was excellent, the superlative cuisine of this island: flying fish, baked christophene, an arsenal of curries, blood pudding. You drank a rum punch that turned out to be a solvent for every piece of trouble and bad luck you ever experienced. The conversation at the table was full of adventure and brotherhood and, between the men and women, love was ripe and sticky and abundant—enough for all. You felt so much a part of it, and to be a part of it all is what you've always wanted.

So you push through the crowd at the door, into an atmosphere of latent sex and laughing words and jazz, past the drunks and the heroes, past the world-class drifters and lean sailors, the silent dealers, the civil servants, and the deadly men with politics in their heads, the sunburned tourists and the beautiful Bajan women who flare their dark eyes at you as you rub past them and say, *"Here now, watch yourself, boy. You think you cahn handle a brown skin gy-url?"*

At the bar you wait several minutes for your bottle of Banks to be snapped down in front of you by a lanky bartender who's got on Ray-Bans and an undersized T-shirt with the logo *Survival Tour '79*. It's not like the rum shops on the side streets and alleys; there's paint on the walls, no one pays attention to you, and the clientele seems safely cosmopolitan.

The jazz is sweet enough to keep a dying man alive until the set is over. Sitting in at a table next to the musicians, there's a stunning black woman singing a soft scat that explores the melody just below the acoustical level of the instruments. You think you recognize her and you're right, you do. The lady is Melandra Goodnight, backup vocal for the calypsonian from Antigua, Lord Short Shoe. The group performed earlier tonight at the cricket stadium. Melandra's still dressed in the white sequined gown she wears onstage, a piece of sartorial luminescence in front of the spotlights, string straps supporting coconut breasts that spark like the flashbulbs of paparazzi, the skirt slit on both sides to the top of her hipbones. What a sight Melandra is onstage when she spreads out her glowing black legs and the front and back flaps of her gown swing down between them like a long, elegant loincloth, her hips marking the beat while she grips the microphone with both hands and sings, sings with every muscle of her body. If you're a woman you respond to her with awe and envy. If you're a man, the sight of Melandra cripples you with lust.

Eyes closed in concentration, her head bobbing, she's floating in the music and you stare at her freely, wondering if you should move closer, be bold enough to sit at her table, buy her another Coca-Cola, which she seems to be drinking. At least she has one hand wrapped around a half-empty bottle of it, the long, red-tipped fingers encircling the glass. The inevitable image rises in your brain and you can't get rid of it, can't stop imagining that hand on you, so you turn away to watch the musicians. There are seven of them, seven old black men, five parked on wooden chairs arranged in a semicircle in the shadowy corner, the sixth on one side caressing the keys of an ancient upright, the seventh dusting the traps on the opposite side, behind Melandra, all of them unmindful of the audience, unmindful of the years by the dozens on the road spreading the gospel of jazz to houses that loved the message but not always the messengers. They have come here, like you, to take it easy, to do what they want. Luckie Percentie, the octogenarian on the alto sax, a New Orleans man with a lot of wind left. Shake Keane, the man who conquered Europe with his trumpet. After twenty-odd years he's come home to the islands. The Professor on clarinet. Few people in the States know he's still alive. Little Dalmar Gibson on the big baritone sax. It was Mezz Mezzrow who showed him how to blow the beast, in Harlem back in the thirties. Dulceman Collins hasn't been back to East St. Louis since he was a teenager, but they still call him Poison Ivory there and talk about him like he never left. Rubin Hopper,

LORD SHORT SHOE WANTS THE MONKEY

the dark-skinned Krupa, and Les Harvey, the guitarist, both Chicago-born and bred on the blues. There's no way you can put your finger on what they're doing. One ear hears a tangle of roots, the other a hedge of flowering hibiscus, and Melandra's voice dipping from bloom to bloom like a hummingbird.

You stand there taking it all in, drinking two or three fresh Banks, brewed down the street. More and more your attention returns to Melandra. You begin to throb; it starts in your heart and works its way down. Your hand shakes somewhat as you light a cigarette. She's moaning now, following the saxophone up into the hills, into the bush. The air is suddenly wet and dripping and all you smell is her sex. A monkey screams nearby. Something somewhere is howling. People turn to look at you. *My God!* You reel down the length of the bar to get outside on the balcony.

On the narrow balcony that hangs over Front Street, Harter and Short Shoe are squeezed around a tiny café table. Several bottles of Guinness between them, the white man passive and serious, the black man passive and serious, trying to come to terms. The monkey is there, too, behaving itself, eating coco plums and a wedge of papaya. Both men look up briefly at the guy who comes staggering out from inside the club, knocking into chairs, his eyes glassy, his crisp chinos stretched by a terrific hard-on. A coke head, thinks Harter. He looks back at Short Shoe, who nods with insincere pity.

"Dere's anuddah white mahn come too close to Melandra," Short Shoe says. Harter, irritated by the calypso singer's sly, mocking tone, sighs and flicks his cigarette down into the empty street.

"What's wrong, bruddah?" Short Shoe says. "You cahnt take a joke?"

Harter insists he doesn't want to sell the monkey, says he loves it, but talks like he has a price even though his one proposition so far was said in jest, at least that's what Short Shoe figured, and Short Shoe wants the monkey, wants it to put in his act to promote his recent hit, "Dis Country Need a Monkey":

> *We need a monkey*
> *To govern dis country*
> *Take any monkey*
> *From any monkey tree*
> *Give him a big car*
> *Ahnd a pretty secretaree*
> *Den dis little monkey*
> *Make a big monkey*
> *Outta we.*

There are four more verses, each progressively broadening the insult against the island's prime minister.

When the record aired on Radio Antilles last month, the fellows at Government House in Antigua sat down to discuss the pros and cons of grabbing Short Shoe and giving him a lesson in lyric writing. He got the word that the bigshots were visibly unhappy with him, knew it was only temporary but decided it was time to take the band out to the islands, work down the chain to Trinidad, and then maybe a couple of dates in Georgetown before taking the show north to Brooklyn and Toronto. He was airborne in a yellow Liat Avro before the bookings were confirmed. The performances they did were sellouts, sneak-ins, crowd crazy. The record shops in each place couldn't keep the forty-five stocked.

But Short Shoe knows that something is missing in the repertoire. He has a fondness for props and gimmicks and drama, anything that will make him stand out and contribute to his growing legend. Wearing shoes with the toes cut out of them was a decision of this nature. They symbolize, he says, his boyhood and his humble background, his ties with the people. When his momma couldn't afford anything but trouble, her son inherited charity shoes from the Bosom of Love First Baptist Church. No size seemed to fit his awkward feet, so he chopped off the toes of the pair that appealed to him—dusty black wingtips—with his machete. He wore them for eight years. Now he wears Adidas with his meaty toes poking out the front. He will not tolerate any humor about big feet. The shoes, he says repeatedly, are a symbol, not a joke.

Melandra first joined the group with the debut of "Coffee Grinder." During the chorus Short Shoe would leap up against her and grind away from behind. With the song "Leggo Tourist Lady," he became more ambitious. On the beach, he found a plump white girl down vacationing from the States. Prepared to pay, in one way or another, for her services, he was still not at all surprised when she immediately agreed to accommodate him in any way she could. He waited for carnival and the ca-lypso-king competition. He waited until the end of the set to do the song. As he began the second verse, she pranced out onstage from the wings and took his arm, put her pink cheek against his chest. "Leggo lady," he sang and shook her off. She persisted, hugging him around the waist. "Leggo tourist lady," he sang breathlessly, and danced away from her. She fell to her knees and crawled after him, wrapping her arms around his shins, trying to pull him down. "Leggo tourist leggo." The crowd on the parade grounds took up the chant. The percussionists banged down into it with brake drums and congas, unleashing total bacchanal, a frenzied, drunken spree. Short Shoe sank lower and lower onto the white girl until almost on top of her. Then the horns drilled back into the beat and Melandra, undaunted Melandra, pulled Short Shoe up by his ear and kicked him in the ass. He finished the song in triumph.

The King.

He realizes that he has a reputation to uphold, that he must give the people all he can, and in return they will love him and allow him the wealth they themselves will never have. There's a vision he's had since he first picked out the notes of the monkey tune on the old Buck Owens guitar, red-white-and-blue paneled, he keeps next to his bed. He sees himself as he knows his fans must see him under the lights: clean and big and randy, his beard the right stroke of revolution, a savior in extrasnug white bell-bottoms, or at least a prophet, the voice of his people, a bull, a rogue angel, a star.

He sees himself onstage. The shrill brass salutes Melandra's entrance with the monkey. They dress the little fucker in an executive blue shirt jac and schoolboy shorts. The word *Boss* is screened on the back of the monkey's shirt in red letters. Melandra straps a toy holster and pistol around the primate's waist. The monkey dances around in a circle, does back flips, pretends to shoot at the crowd with the gun. At the end of the song the monkey hops onto Short Shoe, climbs him like a tree and balancing on top of Short Shoe's ropey head, pulls down its tiny shorts and moons the audience. Glorious. This is what Short Shoe pictures in his mind, but so far he hasn't been able to re-create it for the world.

The first time they tried to use a monkey was in St. Kitts. The monkey bolted offstage as soon as Melandra let go of it, never to be seen again. In Montserrat, Short Shoe made his next attempt, asking around if anybody had a domesticated monkey for sale. Nobody had one on hand, but as soon as the news spread that Short Shoe wanted a monkey, every ragged kid on the island went up into the mountains to find him one. Out of the many brought down from the bush, he chose the one that seemed the calmest. He purchased a light chain at the hardware store; some ganja-soothed Rastafarian in a leather shop took an entire day making the monkey a little collar. The calypsonian introduced the monkey into the act three nights later. Short Shoe clipped his end of the leash around his wrist so his hands would be unencumbered while he danced and sang. When Melandra tried to put the clothes on the monkey, the monkey sprang onto Short Shoe's thigh, viciously biting him over and over. The music stopped, the band members rushed to help. The monkey drew blood from all of them before they could unfasten the leash from Short Shoe's wrist. But the dream still lives for Short Shoe. It is a good idea, and good ideas make money. He knows he can make it work if he only

LORD SHORT SHOE WANTS THE MONKEY

finds the right monkey. As always, the knowledge that he must give the people what they want drives him onward.

Indeed, before he even reached Barbados two days ago the word had been passed through the grapevine that Short Shoe was looking for a monkey. Anybody who gave any thought to the problem arrived at the same solution: *Hahtah got himself a good monkey.* And that's what they told Short Shoe when he landed.

"So what about it," Harter says. "You like this jazz stuff?"

"Yeah, nice," Short Shoe answers quickly, peering around like his attention should be elsewhere. He's tired of bullshitting, which is a very new feeling for him, but all he can think about is getting the monkey. They've gone through five rounds of Guinness and gotten nowhere. Harter has been tonelessly monologuing diesel engines and Hollywood. The monkey looks bored, rolling a papaya seed under his hairy forefinger around the wet tabletop. Short Shoe decides it's good strategy to call for a bottle of Mount Gay.

Nobody knows much about Harter, but everybody claims to know him, and everybody has a different version of who the slim, aloof, sandy-haired Californian living in quiet luxury out on Bathsheba Beach is, and what he's doing on the island. He's going to build a hotel, he's filming feature-length pornography, he runs a safe house for Bolivian smugglers, he's a retired pirate, he's involved in some baroque deal with the government, a casino or banking scam, he's a Hollywood star who decided to dump it all, he's CIA investigating that Cuban plane somebody blew out of the air awhile ago. Nobody knows, but everybody's sure it's something big, because in his quietness, in his stylish solitude, in his tense but confident movements, Harter appears to be a man of importance.

The waiter brings the bottle of gold rum, two clean glasses, a small bucket of melting ice. Short Shoe pours a full load for both of them. As politely as a Boy Scout, the monkey reaches into the bucket, fishes around, and takes one small piece of ice to suck. He watches Harter expectantly, letting out little chirps every once in a while, birdlike and questioning.

"My monkey here has a lot of talent," Harter says assertively. "You couldn't ask for a better monkey."

For lack of much else to do, Harter has been training the monkey for the last six months. Somebody out at Bathsheba shot its mother for a stew, found the terrified baby clinging to a dead teat underneath her protective arms. Harter heard about it and on impulse went to see the hunter. The mother's skin, pink and fly-covered, was stretched and nailed to dry on the door of the man's shanty. Not knowing exactly what to do with the baby, the hunter placed it inside one of the many empty oil drums in his dirt yard for safekeeping until the proper time came for him to study the situation. Harter stared down into the darkness and saw the honey-sheened, cat-sized ball of baby monkey hiding its face, trembling in the absurd immensity of the drum. He paid fifty cents for the three-month-old vervet. He named him Frank. They had had some good times together.

"Dese monkey too much like politician," Short Shoe says, now readily suspicious of both breeds. "How I know dis monkey trustable?"

"Because I said he is, pal." Harter is trying to work himself up to the deal.

"Take it easy, mahn." Short Shoe explains what it is he wants the monkey to do in the act. Harter, another State Express stuck in his mouth, stands up and slaps the surface of the table.

"Come here, Frank," he says. The monkey scurries out of his chair onto the table, stops erect in the center of it at the point Harter has indicated. Like a gymnastics coach, Harter works through a dry run of a black flip with the monkey, picking him up and turning him in the air and setting him back down. He does it three times, finally rewarding Frank with a coco plum from a canvas bag next to his chair.

"Okay, Frank," Harter says, taking a step back from the table. He snaps his fingers and the monkey executes a precise back flip, landing in a half-crouch right in place, the bottle and glasses undisturbed. "Again," Harter commands, snapping his fingers. Frank does it again. Harter takes another step away from the table. "To me, Frank, to me," Harter says. The monkey back flips off the table, onto Harter's shoulder, and is given a coco plum. Frank squeezes the fruit as if it were a lump of clay.

"Hey," yells Short Shoe, jumping up from the table. "Hey," he yells to nobody in particular. "You see daht? My God, mahn, dis a smaht monkey. I must have dis fella."

"Sit down and let's talk about it," Harter says. All three of them, black, white, and monkey, take their former seats. Harter doesn't want to sell the monkey, but he does have something else in mind, something that lodged there like a wild bullet the first night Short Shoe brought the band to the island and Harter went to catch the show. There's an urge gnawing away at him, growing out of control. He makes his proposition, the same one he joked about before.

"Holy Christ," Short Shoe says, withdrawing, but he's already puzzling over the diplomacy he will have to use to make it happen.

The success of their negotiation can be measured by the bottle. Two-thirds full and they're both still insisting the other wants too much. At the halfway mark, Harter is assuring himself that Short Shoe will come across, and the calypsonian realizes he will, after all, leave the place with the monkey. The details just have to be fleshed out. With only a shot left for each of them in the bottle, the deal is struck, and they toast each other. Short Shoe will take the monkey on tour for six weeks and then return him to Barbados. Harter will take Melandra for a night. The monkey has fallen asleep, curled up on the seat of his chair.

Was there coke, too, a little snow to clear the muggy air? You can't remember. Nor can you remember the woman you were with earlier in the evening, nor why you left her and came here to the jazz club. Lately life has seemed so fragmented, a blurred series of wonderful postcards, of clever vignettes. There are so many excuses available: the dizzying tropic sun, the high-octane rum, the lethargy of many days at sea, the casual violence of West Indian streets, the wrenching juxtaposition of an expensive sports car racing through the ghetto. Yet you have resisted the slow disintegration of moral certitude that is a part of it all, right? The unexpected blow to your senses that plunged your brain down between your legs was nothing more than a normal reaction to an exotic woman, and what you imagine is not lurid, sweaty sexual acrobatics but a seaside cottage, Melandra singing for you alone, toffee-colored babies playing in the sand, a milk goat in the yard, a parrot in the lemon tree. Sounds nice.

Leaning on the balcony for the last half-hour, trying to calm yourself, to regain the cool you walked in with, you have eavesdropped on their conversation. And now, you think, it is your responsibility to speak. Possessively, protectively, you approach the table where the imposing black man and the humorless expatriate face each other. With obvious satisfaction, they are polishing off the last of their bottle of Mount Gay. You stand there unsteadily but with righteous fortitude until they glance up. Maybe Harter figures you want to pet the monkey. Short Shoe guesses you are a fan of his, that you will congratulate him, ask for an autograph. You clear your throat, which wakes the monkey.

"Gentlemen, forgive me," you say. "You cannot trade a woman for a monkey." It sounds so right, so absolute. You are pleased with yourself.

"Where dis fella come from?" Short Shoe cries. You recoil from the threat in his voice. "People buttin around like dey own de fuckin world. Mind you own business, Jimbo."

"Get lost," Harter adds, scowling at you.

You suddenly feel fatuous, and a little hurt. You escape to the bar.

Short Shoe wanders back in, the monkey clinging to his side, and sits down next to Melandra. Her hair has become less sculptured in the humid air, the silver eyeshadow blotchy and creased, her lip gloss flat. She is dying to get back to her room at the Holiday Inn, slip off her dress and high heels, take a shower and collapse into bed.

"Let's go, Shorty," she says. "I am tired."

"Rushin, rushin, ahlways rushin," Short Shoe says. "Gy-url, I believe you mus be commu*nist.*" Instead of laughing, she cuts her eyes at him. "Look here," he continues, "I get de monkey."

"I see it."

His mood changes abruptly. Melandra's enthusiasm, he thinks, should match his own. Leaning over the table, he strokes the monkey and looks straight at the woman with what he hopes is the right amount of regret.

"Darlin, I get meself in a terrible jam wit dis white fella," he says with great seriousness. "Be nice to him ahnd he say he forget de whole thing."

Melandra's eyes narrow as if she's taking aim on Short Shoe. She feels on the edge of a temper but pushes it back. Her voice is her pride and her living: to let anger race through it would be like dropping a cooking pepper into hibiscus honey.

"How you mean, Shorty," she asks, her silky voice just the slightest bit strained, " 'be nice'?"

The monkey fidgets in his big hands as he pets it harder. Short Shoe knows he was lucky to find such an exceptional monkey, luckier still not to pay cash. The woman is not going to ice such a sweet deal, even if Short Shoe has to hold her down himself.

"Doan play de fool wit me, womahn," he says, shaking a finger in her face. She looks at it, a mongoose watching a snake. Then she sighs wearily and turns away.

"Do ahs I say."

"No."

"He want more dahn just a night, ya know. I tell him no. I thinkin in your best in-*trest.*"

"No."

Short Shoe's voice rises an octave. "How you mean, 'no'?" he shouts, and smacks the table loudly with his palm. "I tellin

you *yes.* You forgettin a lot ah things, darlin. How many womahn in de world want to sing with Short Shoe? Ahnswer me
daht." Short Shoe is proud of the fact that he always takes an
international view of his affairs.

"Shorty, doan do dis to me."

There is such a look of disappointment on her face that
Short Shoe is momentarily confused—actually on the brink of
catastrophe, because he is *never* unsure of himself. But the
people in the bar begin to applaud the jazz musicians, who
have just finished their set. Short Shoe multiplies the applause
thousands and thousands of times and throws it all down on
himself, letting it swell his chest with glorification. His is the
voice of the people, he must give them what they want.

"Go now, I tellin you," he orders her. "Go!"

She smooths her hair back over her ears and then fans
herself with a paper napkin. Melandra realizes that whatever
magic Short Shoe performs onstage, however great he truly is
in front of an audience, he can still be a clod at the dinner
table, a half-literate fisherman. She likes him enough so that
working with him isn't a hardship, she is grateful that it was
her he chose to sing with him, because that changed her life in
a way she never believed could really happen, but Short Shoe
is like most men she has ever met—selfish and single-minded.
Men were all just schoolboys in uniforms diddling with their
little peckers.

She pictures herself out in the countryside at her momma's
house back in Antigua. She and Momma are in the kitchen,
talking about all the troubles and woe *men does give dem.*
Melandra opens the cupboard and takes out the tin can
Momma keeps full with hibiscus honey. She takes it out to the
garden, to the pepper bush, covered with the small green cooking peppers that must be taken out of the stew before they
burst and make the food too hot to eat. *One cookin peppah,
two cookin peppah, tree cookin peppah*—into the honey. She
takes the can back inside and puts it on the kerosene stove.
Momma, I goin to boil dis up ahnd give it to de next mahn try

to make a fool of me. Momma looks at her and shakes her head sadly. *Gy-url, you does de boilin ahll you life den.*

"Ahlright, Shorty," she says in a deadly voice. "But dis monkey goin come bahck to haunt you, ya know." She sneers, sucks her teeth in disgust, and walks away. On the way out to the balcony she brushes up against Shake Keane, the trumpet player, and whispers in his ear, "Bruddah mahn, check me out in a while, hmm? I goin outside fah some action."

"Yeah, baby," Shake says. "What's up?"

"Showtime," Melandra answers wickedly.

There's been too much rum. Harter really doesn't know what he's doing but he knows there's more than just a rum spell on him, that he has a powerful yearning for a black woman, that he heard their skin is always, permanently, as hot as the Tunisian desert, and it sends a fever running right through you, that some white men can't stand the heat, their blood pressure or something can't take it, but for those that can, heaven is a step closer. And he knows that Melandra is one of the most majestic women he has ever seen, and that these moments with her might knock him out of the drift he's been in for the past year.

Harter watches Melandra approach his table. She stays in focus and everything else gets blurred. His head hangs loosely but his eyes are geared up and he watches her, watches her perfect hips dance through the mostly empty chairs and tables, the long graceful dark arms shining, her huge chestnut eyes, her thin nose that suggests some East Indian blood, lips as full as pillows, straight shoulder-length hair that he recalls puffed up in a big Afro on Short Shoe's last album cover. She has taken a pink hibiscus flower from one of the tables and placed it behind her left ear. Harter can feel his pulse struggling up through the alcohol.

"Please sit down," he says in what he thinks of as his Hollywood voice. Charming and jaded. "You are beautiful. Absolutely."

"You such a polite mahn," Melandra answers coyly. Harter

hears the staged quality in her voice but he's too far gone to infer anything from it. "Shorty say you lookin fah me. True?" She pulls a chair next to his and sits down, crossing her legs so that the skirt of her dress falls away, exposing one leg fully up to her hip, the other almost so, and the elastic fringe of a black G-string. Harter tries to keep his attention from this area, knowing that he must produce some facsimile of romance and sensitivity if this is all going to work right.

Melandra's surprised that he's as handsome as he is, and as drunk. She expected some pasty bastard, dressed like an off-duty cop, a good decade older than Harter, sober enough still to enjoy the nasty little routines that men buy women for. She thinks maybe she might be interested in Harter under different circumstances. His eyes aren't totally cold like she imagined, but green and cautious and lonely. Maybe she can talk him out of this foolishness, let him buy her dinner tomorrow night; Short Shoe can keep his monkey, and she can go home to bed.

Harter unfreezes, reaches over and grabs her arm, not painfully, but hard enough to annoy her. Her first instinct is to slap him. She stops herself—it's too easy, it might well do more damage to her than put anybody in their place. Harter and Short Shoe would shrug it off, absolved, and she did not want that, she did not want to defer to stalemate or forgiveness. Not this time. Not against a monkey. It's clear that the only way out of it is her way.

"I—love—you," Harter says, as though he has searched long and hard for each word.

"Is daht right?"

"Uh-huh."

"Well, love mus have its way," she says, throwing her arms around his neck, tugging him forward, smothering his mouth with hers, her tongue driving, she hopes, far enough down his throat to choke him. Harter's bewildered resistance lasts about two seconds. He never knew he had it in him, that *any* man had it in him, but he feels as if he's about to swoon. Melandra is running her fingers through his hair, raking his scalp mercilessly with her sharp fingernails. His lips are being pulped by her forceful kisses. His eyes are closed and feel like they are never going to open up again, as though there's some electrical glue being pumped into him. It all feels so natural, so deep, so meant to be. He's lost in what he believes is the sudden inevitably of their passion, lost to the world, sailing on some mythological ghost ship with the Queen of Africa. He slips a hand under the top of her dress and clutches one of her breasts. It *is* hot. Her nipple feels like a pencil eraser.

Melandra's hand glides from Harter's shoulder to the top of his shirt. She pops all of the buttons in one aggressive rip, peeling his shirt back so she can rub and knead his bare chest. A groan hums in the back of Harter's throat. There's some thought, some urgent information, trying to form in his head but he can't make it clear. *Baby,* he gasps, but then his mouth is locked up again by Melandra's. Her hand crabs its way down his tan stomach. Before it registers with him, his belt is unbuckled, his fly unzipped. Her hand snakes into his linen pants and grabs him. The vague feeling he's been trying to define spears through the darkness like a spotlight. *Not here,* he shrieks to himself. The light dims, the power fails. This is Harter's last coherent thought of the evening.

Melandra cocks her head slightly, steals a look out of the corner of her eye at the faces gathering around her. They affect her the same as any audience does: A part of her performs for them, a part of her sits back and observes it all ambivalently. She's as good an actress as she is a singer, lets her imagination accept whatever role is required of her—Shorty's stupid on-stage games have at least given her that. Her hand works deftly, conscientiously; she hopes the rings on her fingers aren't bruising the man too terribly. She imagines she's rubbing ointment on a baby's arm, or milking Momma's cow, which is easier because of the noise Harter is making. She suppresses the desire to fall out of her chair laughing; Short Shoe's foul covenant has the right-of-way here. Harter begins to arch his hips off the chair. Melandra stops, but too late, for the spasm has begun. She wonders if she should feel sorry for him for what she's about to do. It's a curious thought, and maybe some other time she'll allow herself to explore it. But right now she imagines the cooking peppers bursting one by one.

You are sulking, having one last Banks before you call it a night and head back to where you're staying. Most of the jazz musicians have sidled up to the bar around you. Short Shoe's there with them, showing off the monkey. You'd like to talk to them but you can't think of anything appropriate to say, something to let them know you're not just another drunk tourist hanging on the bar. The trumpet player strolls in from outside, a generous grin on his face, and announces loudly, "Look here, check this scene out on the balcony."

Everybody moves out from the bar and you follow them. Before you can even get outside, Short Shoe is already pushing his way back in, a grim, uninvolved expression on his face, muttering *Dread, dread.* He hurries for the exit, wearing the skinny string-bean monkey like a necktie.

There's hardly room for you on the small balcony. Beyond the weak illumination provided by a single, bug-swarmed light bulb above the doorway, the night is at its darkest point. You squeeze through the crowd, excusing yourself, begging the pardon of those you perhaps shove more than you should. You break into the front line. The sight of Melandra fondling Harter before your astonished eyes turns your heart upside down.

"Mmm hmm, lookit that gal bone the chicken," one of the gray-haired musicians next to you drawls. "Gawd*damn,* that looks good."

Harter might as well be knocked out. His head lolls over the back of his chair, his arms and legs sprawl out to the sides. Melandra has moved away from him just enough so the audience can witness this most flagrant of hand jobs, delivered under the auspices of Melandra's professional devastating smile. As Harter begins to ejaculate, the spectators clap and hoot. Harter reacts to the noise as if it were cold water. His

LORD SHORT SHOE WANTS THE MONKEY

head snaps straight, his eyes click open wide with horror. You watch the stain on his pants spreading and think, oh yes, this is a fine specimen of sin and shame in front of you. Harter stares dumbly down at his lap, at the dark relentless hand that still grips him. He tries to wriggle backward, to get the hell out of there, but Melandra has him tight.

"Fellas," she calls out triumphantly, "look aht dis little vahnilla bean." She waves Harter's prick at them, which can't seem to lose its erection. "Looks like it might be ready fah busy-*ness,* if de boy evah grow up."

She wags him stiffly at one or two faces. "Somebody got a nice disease dey cahn give dis mahn? Something to help him remembah dis ro-*mahnce?*" Harter struggles up. Melandra plants her free hand on his chest and shoves him back down.

"Monkey," she hisses, pointing at Harter. "Womahn," she says, jerking a thumb at herself. She repeats the distinction: *Monkey. Womahn.* "Lissen to me, fella. Monkey ahnd womahn doan mix. It seem you make a big mistake. Now get you ahss away." She releases him and steps back, her arms folded over her breasts, glaring at Harter, threatening him with every last ounce of trouble she can.

You shudder, regaining your senses, tasting the bitter-sweetness of such severe and utter humiliation. But you have to hand it to Harter. He doesn't panic. He composes himself quickly and with, you must admit, a certain amount of dignity. Slowly he puts himself back together, beginning with sun-glasses which he takes from his shirt pocket. He lights a ciga-rette. Only then does he straighten out his torn shirt, and only after his shirt is right does he return himself to the sanctuary of his linens and zip up. When he is finished, he stands sol-emnly in front of the gathering, exhaling the smoke from his State Express. You suspect he is going to speak, but he only shrugs, offering a half-smile that concedes the evening to Me-landra. Then, with athletic sureness, he vaults over the railing of the balcony to the street below and is gone.

Months later, in a bar in Mustique or Negril or maybe St. Lucia, you hear the end of the story. Someone who knows will tell you that in Port of Spain, at Short Shoe's first performance at the Boomba Club, the Calypsonian was attacked by a man in a gorilla suit who proceeded to beat him with a stick. And Melandra, the fellow at the bar will say, has signed a solo contract with Mango Records. They even gave her her own backup band to tour with. She has a new single that's just been released.

"Maybe you've heard it already on the Voice of the Antilles," the guy says. "It's called 'Troff de Monkey.'" Sure, you tell the guy, waiting for the foam to settle in your beer. You've heard it. Throw off the monkey.

The Heart's Advantage

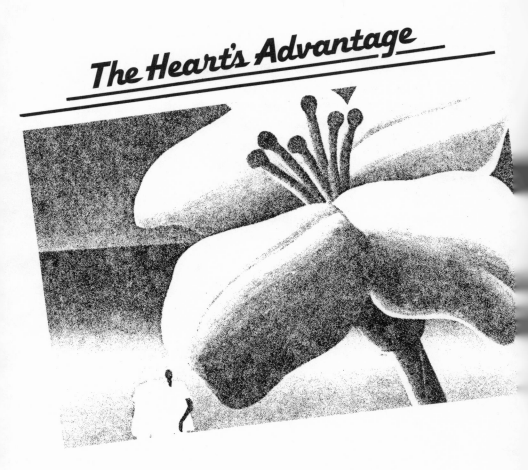

Lindy, I said, are you even there? Get up and let me in the door. It was a Saturday morning, not so early. I'd been away in Africa for a month, a hired hand for the government charged with spreading money across the Sahel, the only green they've seen there in generations. The ticket was *appropriate technology*, the words that make clouds of cash wing across oceans to rain change down upon the lives of other men.

I pounded on the door and shouted but it was a full five minutes before I heard her on the other side clawing at the deadbolt. I had been in the air for eight hours. My shirt was like wet celluloid layered to my back, and my intestines gurgled, invaded by microbes. There was a clear joy in me to be back home.

"Lindy?"

"Just a minute. I don't have my contacts in."

"What are you doing in there? Were you still asleep?"

Yes, she was. Lindy, a determined early riser, had to be roused. The curtains were still drawn, the house itself in a soporific state. When the door cracked open, I felt an alien proliferation spreading out of the cool dimness beyond. Then she stepped forward and I saw her hair.

For months she had been fussing about a perm, tearing through women's magazines, pricing some of the shops in Coral Gables, pausing in front of mirrors to study herself. I chastised her for being indecisive and said quit whining and just go do it. I don't know, she said. There's no going back once they squirt the gunk on. What if I don't like it? What if *you* don't like it? Take a chance, I advised. You're adventurous. Only stop throwing yourself around and sighing.

"You don't like it, do you?"

She looked like a juju queen. Wrapped in the bars of her yellow, blue and green terry robe, she appeared untended, underslept, last night's makeup rendering her face experimental, ghoulish, asymmetrical. Her myopia gave her an intensely dazed stare, and one smudged eye looked a centimeter or so off from its set. She needed a good wipe.

"Dear God, what have you done?"

I could not speak in a calm voice about her once precious hair. Why is the head of a treasonous woman shaved? Why else butcher and abominate those delicate threads if they are not emblematic of her soul? Women used to bundle, braid and bind their tresses, let them tumble down at night for their husbands, the first gift of bedtime. They washed their hair lovingly with exotic soaps and rare milks, spiced it with mint extracts and herbs, stroked it over and over into glorious waves, scintillating spills, their proud crop, heavenly curtains parted over the cold fact of the face so that even the ugly could take advantage and be redeemed by exquisite curls. So it is that we soon become estranged from women who allow their hair to depreciate.

Lindy had hair the color of an Irish setter's, a singular color

THE HEART'S ADVANTAGE

to be envied, no matter that it is the color of a dog. It was as rich in sight as a brogue in sound, a visual lilt. It crowned her in thick and luscious loops that swayed on small shoulders. You can imagine the pleasure of having it fed to your lips, or seeing it glide strand by strand across the taut cone of a nipple and gather between breasts, watch it open and close the rapture of her face. I smelled long life there in Lindy's hair, good-heartedness and babies. And I felt, as she approached permhood day by day, she will honor her sex.

She did not. To my horror she did not. What I now observed through a dulling shock was a pumpkin-headed debutante of naughtiness, her tresses lopped off inches from her skull and spiked like a guard-dog's collar. The spikes were needle-tipped and apparently simonized so they would hold their shape, and there was a hatching grid of distasteful white scalp around the base of the roots.

"You don't like it."

I said That's right. I said You bet I don't. By her tone it was obvious that she knew I didn't—*had known* I wouldn't—and had prepared herself not to be affected by my reaction. She arched her eyebrows defiantly and stepped back to let me in. Her arms were crossed on her chest, but when she moved, her hands dropped unconsciously and the robe fell open.

"You've slept in your clothes, I see."

She glanced down at herself and frowned.

I am a happy witness to the caprice of fashion but I believe each generation identifies itself and marches on, true to its code. Lindy wore one of those crotch-high synthetic knit ba-bydoll dresses—low-waisted to a flounced skirt, a loose bodice shaped like a sack, spaghetti-strapped, the style popular among tough high school girls who gag at the idea of cute. The fabric was the color of spotted banana peel with broad stripes of tinsel running through it. She had gone beyond vogue, gone a step past the glamour of the magazines.

"You look eighteen and dirty."

She folded her robe closed stoically and tied herself in, the cinch of the belt making the outline of her hips appear. The terry knot bulged with the foretelling of permanence. "Come in," she said. "The air conditioner's on."

There are moments, even days—longer still, phases— when we're not ourselves, when we inhabit foreign moods and obscure desires. We're somebody else for the duration. Blame a planet or odd chemicals in the breakfast cereal. I'm not refer- ring here to such temporary phenomena. I'm talking about a genuine change of character, like a color television transmut- ing to black and white without hope of repair, or a nation falling from the grace of its past. What is Persia today, what is Egypt? That's what I mean. Something, from all evidence, irre- versible. A cheating, a betrayal.

Lindy's reluctance to let me back in—no hungry kiss, no hug of relief—made me suspect, together with her wretchedly flamboyant hairdo, that she had been unfaithful, not sexually, but to the life we had fabricated as a couple. Decisions with impact had been made that I knew nothing about. Suddenly I was an occupying force, she *le résistance.* It was a flat way to come home from abroad, dragging my absence like a bum who had attached to me.

She whirled toward the bedroom and I tramped straight for the bath, where I showered petulantly. Not to be found in its dish was my brand of soap. I scrubbed myself with something similar to a hunk of potter's clay, the lather no more than oily flecks of foam. Searching through the medicine cabinet for a Q-Tip I discovered a sinister rainbow of nail polish, the shades of Lindy's current fascination—Avocado Whip, Midnight Scream, Angel's Throat, Chocolate Bunny. A bright undented tube of spermicide mystified me. Lindy had been on the pill when I departed in June. In place of her round hairbrush was a rattail comb and a squat jar of gel treatment labeled *Spic n Spike.* Whoa, stop, I said, sliding the mirror back carefully, my breathing shallow.

I emerged fresh, clad in navy running shorts, resolved to

THE HEART'S ADVANTAGE

adjust to Lindy's remarkable appearance now that the shock had withdrawn, diluted by clean pearls of North American public water, the common blessing of comfort. In the Sahel you go unwashed for as long as you can or people object. Lindy was in the kitchen seated at the table, her eyeballs lacquered into focus, her legs crossed once at the knees and again at the ankles, everything otherwise the same. She blew steam off a cup of coffee. A second cup sat waiting for me. I wrapped my grateful fingers around it, thinking nothing had really changed after all. I lowered my head, waiting for the resolution and the nerve to look at her once again, this time honestly, prepared for kindness. She tapped one foot and sniffed.

"So how'd it go?" she asked.

"I now have seven native wives." I diverted a cruel thought —each less garish than you.

"I bet you do."

"Actually, it went okay. Nobody believed in the windmills. We drilled deeper and I designed a prop that generated more rpms. They now have a few drops of water to fight over, and we have more money for the boat. So goes the division of wealth in the world."

She sipped her coffee, her expression unchanged. I kept staring at her, the familiar core. Somewhere there beneath the trendy masquerade was my personal historian and book-keeper, my partner in escape from various numbing realities, the only person in the globe whose ear I dared whisper into, my night-stilled companion, my arm crooked on the future. Nostalgia took its gummy bite. But then I thought, *thrill to this, thrill to this, man,* she's a strange presence that bears your mark.

"So how was it for you? Did you miss me?"

"A month's a long time," she answered cryptically.

"I missed you. I did. Really." The emotion stalled in my voice and the words blanched. I regretted opening my mouth —no songbird had flown out, only the processed warbling of mealy notes. I wanted to hear an appetite in her voice. I wanted the distance reconciled, the love more splendid for all the anticipation absence had forged. I want it, I thought, battling resentment, like the last time I came home from who knows where.

She cocked her head. The spikes rotated like a satellite positioning itself to fire laser beams. She grimaced, her eyes showing a small impatience for what I had said or how I had said it. I had been standing, hesitant, but now I sat down next to her at the table.

"I meant what I said."

"I know."

"We can do better than this," I clucked.

"It takes awhile to get used to you again. I haven't even brushed my teeth."

Her lips looked like a brittle red lariat slipping off the rim of the coffee cup. The gold chain around her neck I hadn't seen before. It encircled the tendons that arched from her collarbone, an aristocratic sweep of lines that had become more pronounced since we first met, she an auditor sent over to our department to punch holes in our budgetary exuberance. A bead of amber dangled from the center of the chain, what looked like a baby cockroach embedded within, an ancient pest that proved the high alchemic value of whatever is stolen from time.

"So," I said, fishing for anything wonderfully nice to say. "So."

She watched me expectantly, her headdress bobbing with each of my Sos. I had nothing more to say about her hair. That was to be treated in the same manner as if she had wrecked the car—don't worry about it, it's only the fender, we can have it knocked out. But I wanted somehow to reach into her month alone, to extract the thorns she had accumulated deprived of the shield togetherness provides. So I said with all the earnestness of a half-wit priest, "Lindy, I'm sorry I had to be gone so long. I know it must have been terrible for you."

I leaned forward on my elbows, pushing aside my mug, ready for her sad account of life without me.

"Of course it wasn't." She laughed in girlish eighth-notes,

like a piccolo, a silvery confident melody that made me first ashamed, then defensive. "Oh, Lord, don't be mad, Sims. It's nice to have you back, but I have fun, too, when you're gone. I don't dry up, you know."

"Oh." I swallowed my coffee like a frog. The cries of the *hajis* echoed in my ears. *What?* windmills in the desert. Water sucked forth from barrenness? No, *monsieur.* No no.

"Well, don't be so surprised," she said.

"Actually I'm not," I sputtered. "This is in fact good news. I worry about you being lonely."

We had struggled through elaborate discussions before I chose to quit the department and join the press of part-time consultants feeding off the huge carcass of foreign policy. It was for the best, we concurred, if we were ever going to get the boat in shape and one day sail off to what we dreamed could happen in our lives. The gaps that would separate us would be no more than the slight blips, the blind spots, encountered on a dial between one level of intensity and the next, like a furnace building heat, a light increasing wattage. I would fly off, a return ticket in my pocket, and then I would retract like the wandering leg of John Donne's compass to the center of the circle, the geometric conceit of love well architected.

"No need to worry about me," she insisted, giving a cheery toss to the ghost of her hair, a pang of loss sent into my blood.

She had picked up three new accounts in her freelancing work, read a dozen books, started an aerobics class at Miami-Dade. We were edging back into our rhythm as we talked. I felt better all the time. Her hair impressed me as less angry and ominous than when I first saw it, a loud game that would soon stop. Yet I felt on the verge of unwanted discovery. She saw my look and forced it. Her mouth puckered, her eyebrows plumed. She nailed a finger into my arm.

"Well, go ahead," she snapped. "Don't hedge, it's not like you. You're dying to say something."

"It's just that I didn't expect to find you quite like this."

"Quite like what?"

"Asleep, for one thing. In your clothes, *those* clothes. Was it wrong of me to expect something else? Now come on, be honest."

She was. "I forgot you were coming today," Lindy said.

I pretended unsuccessfully that this failure was of no importance.

"Don't lock up," she said, tugging my arm, taking my hand in hers. "I was out too late. I was drunk."

I pulled my hand away. "What do you mean you were drunk?" I said stupidly. She crossed her eyes to reinforce my stupidness.

"I had too much to drink. I was dancing and worked up a sweat. The drinks felt like they ran right through me."

"You never sweat," I reminded her.

"I do when I dance."

I was astounded by the implication of this report. "You don't sweat when you dance with me."

"You haven't asked me in ages. Besides, the dances are different today."

I slammed my coffee mug on the table. I seemed to have been invalidated. "Today?" I said loudly. "Today?"

"Look, we've talked enough for now," she proclaimed. "You're just getting mad. I'm going to go shower."

I retrieved my luggage and trudged into the bedroom, disoriented from the moment I set foot in there. Our platform bed had completed a 180-degree turn and now faced south, underneath the double windows, instead of north, underneath the full security of a heartpine wall. The batik had disappeared from the wall, replaced by a chrome-faced abstraction, pink paint splashed and dribbled on a beige background, the impression that of a muffled scream. The curtains had turned white as had the comforter on the bed. My antique oak bookcase was gone. Glass shelves climbed the walls. White gladioli thrust from large raku vases with pinched necks, one in each corner. I flopped down on the mattress and lit a cigarette. Lindy returned from the shower, a black towel wrapped like a sari around her, a black plastic bathcap pulled over her scalp. Her face is pretty, I thought, no matter what she does to herself. She stopped abruptly, scrinching her nose.

"Please don't smoke in the bedroom, okay?"

"Why not?" I said, becoming annoyed again. She knew I liked to lie in bed and smoke, think.

"No stinking up the bedroom. Smoke somewhere else."

"Christ." I reared up from the bed and stamped out, looking for an ashtray. When I came back she was stretched out naked on the sheets, her legs raised and bent, the knees splayed, pelvis tilted. The image I got was of a baby about to have her diaper changed. In a second I realized she was inserting her diaphragm. I regarded her position, her exposure, her assumption. Her hands dipped downward between her thighs, one wrist flipped under, pushing up. She rolled her head and looked over at me.

"I think you should keep your mouth closed and come here, boy."

She had never stooped to such strategy and blatant intent before.

"It's different in here. Why have you done this?" I demanded.

"I was bored with the way things were."

"That new canvas on the wall, I hate it. Where's the batik?"

"In the garage. Why don't you climb over here?"

"Whose rain slicker is that on the couch in the living room? It's not mine."

"It must be Champ's. He left it in the car."

"Who?"

"Champ Ransome, this guy."

"That's a preposterous, awful, ridiculous name."

"I think his name is perfect," she said, propping herself on her elbows to stare guilelessly at me.

"For what?" I bitched. A gigolo, a failed actor, a racehorse. "I suppose now you're going to tell me that you slept with him." I ripped out of my shorts and pitched them toward the closet where the wicker hamper had been relocated and waited, the scorned man, hands on my hips, unadorned before my fate.

"My dear Sims," she said, her eyes inspecting the ceiling, bored with my accusation, "I haven't slept with anybody but you, believe it or not."

I slouched into bed on all fours and hovered above her, sniffing like a bear for the scent of a stranger on the body beneath me, eying the sheets for the stains of carnal labor. She held out her arms for me to collapse into and then, thank God, she smiled, cracking the hard red candy of her lips.

"What'd you bring me from Africa?"

"Disease," I answered, colliding with her bones.

Our life. The plural possessive pronoun, the singular noun. What a pair they can be. Lindy slowly accepted me back into it, yet it seemed more hers than mine or ours. I felt I wasn't all the way home, I felt I had missed it by a house or two. There was something going on, as if the woman now worshiped strange idols. Meals were more planned and formal. She wanted us to eat at the table instead of the back porch or cross-legged in front of the news on television. Where before there was serendipity, now there were cookbooks. Vegetables became suddenly exciting, artichokes prepared as feasts, vinaigrette splashed on anything. Pasta in drab colors filled the freezer. Coffee beans arrived UPS from New Orleans. Wine was ordered by the case from a store in Pompano. She subscribed to magazines that glorified people whose only talent appeared to be hanging out, the street elite. Jewelry achieved some vague level of meaning. Besides the gold and amber, she took to wearing an elephant's-hair ring, a baroque pearl, a pop-top from a beer can, and a tiny emerald cluster, all on her left hand, a band of studded leather above on her wrist. A ladder of holes was pierced into each ear, small gems descended to plastic or enamel hardware, household objects, pen caps, and on one occasion, teaspoons. Jogging was also important and she braved the roads at dawn and dusk in wine-colored briefs and a lemon Danskin, a Walkman delivering ska to her brain. In the bathroom you could browse the *New York Review of Books* or *Vanity Fair*. For the first time since I knew her she had a girlfriend, a Cuban woman of carbonated personality. The woman would pick her up in a black Firebird to go shopping over at South Beach.

Here is what I thought I understood, that Lindy was having one last fling with the dazzling, addictive fraud of American culture. She was revving up speed to hurl herself off the edge of the continent, to land with twenty-four dollars' worth of trinkets on an unknown shore, a parody of the urban frontier, a treat for savages she imagined out there.

I met up with Lindy's Champ Ransome down at the boatyard where our ketch had been sitting for two years, riding the dirt while Lindy and I prepared our life. The old ketch was a piece of sea trash I had saved from worms and disaffection. I could see in her lines the boat once had a passion for speed and enterprise. She was almost ready again to flout the crushing wallop of seas, the mammoth torque of full sail, Lindy at the wheel as I tuned the ropes until they hummed freedom.

Since I had left for the Sahel, the yard, a noisy cluttered city of boats, had dragged up a more unpromising pile of junk onto the rails down the way from the ketch, a stubby tramp freighter, ninety feet of negligence, a broad gray-hulled pig bleeding rust, a pilothouse on its stern like a whitewashed shanty. The craft resembled, remarkably, a giant high-topped basketball sneaker, the victim of brutal play. This filthy creation was Champ Ransome's ship. I took one look and said There's a vessel that advertises an association with crime, a dire picaroon. Lindy said no, Champ Ransome was certified clean, a purveyor of innocent cargoes, a man who believed in the benefit of trade. You never know, I said. Any Bowery bum might be a master captain, any saint a sinner. The ocean's chased by the best and the worst and sometimes you can't tell the difference.

"There, that's him."

Lindy raised her weird sunglasses and pointed with her

chin. The frames of her sunglasses were lavender and shaped like two obese blowfish kissing on the bridge of her nose. I followed the direction of her Celtic jaw. Up on scaffolding, a man attended a swarm of white sparks, welding a steel plate at the waterline of the freighter. I've always admired the concentration of men at work, the ability to calmly direct a tool whether the heavens sink or the doors of hell blow off. I see it as profound intent, the mojo to pull civilization back from the brink. I knew then and there that Champ Ransome was no flea, nor the punk darling I had envisioned, and if he posed a true threat there was no fast remedy for it. If he had cast this change on Lindy, she would stay changed.

Lindy tucked her fingers into the shallow pockets of her polka-dot bloomers. Rearing back as if she would spit the distance, she whistled like a longshoreman, a trick of hers I wish I had. When the man on the scaffolding didn't respond, she started to whistle again but I stopped her.

"Let him finish the bead or it's no good. The weld will be weak."

In another minute he cut the flame on his torch and monkeyed to the ground, the welder's mask still hanging from his face, his eyes a blur behind the scratched window.

"Champ Ransome," Lindy said. I suspected her tone would reveal intimacy but it didn't. She stepped forward, hooked a finger under the mask and tilted it up on its hinge, his face revealed. "Meet Sims. Of whom I have spoken."

"Endlessly," Ransome agreed. He nodded in my direction. Just nodded. No handshake, no smile, no wink, no Hey, nothing. He gestured with his head, the mask shoveling air. "She steers like a horse tank," he said, his accent bred in the glades and keys of southern Florida. "We creased her hip docking on the river." His mustache drooped off the corners of his mouth like Spanish moss, his chin captured underneath, as blunt as the toe of a cowboy boot, and his eyes, clear as they were with anglo blue, seemed perpetually half-lidded, reaching the unseen and far away.

"We'll let you be," Lindy said. She reached up and pulled

THE HEART'S ADVANTAGE

the black shield over his face again. It shut like a car hood, closing off the expression that was the beginning and the end of Champ Ransome's social grace.

We rambled back to the ketch. Lindy slipped her hand down into the waist of my cutoffs, her fingertips pressed smoothly against my rear. I believed she had shown me what I wanted to know, that Champ Ransome was a new friend and nothing more, no cause for furtiveness, no source of strain. So Champ became more of a mystery to me than ever. Champ was a crow out on the clothesline that wouldn't fly away, a bird that kept watching the house day after day.

I raised a wooden ladder against the sailboat's deck and climbed aboard. Lindy watched from below, sheltering her eyes against the sun.

"You coming up?"

"Only if you need me," she said. From my new perspective her head was a cocklebur.

"No, not really. Unless you feel like getting dirty."

"I don't. Not today."

She had done enough anyway, two years at my side in the industry of the yard. The payback wasn't so far off. The diesel would get an overhaul and the mainmast, stepped before the Sahel, would be rigged and fitted. The lease on the house expired in seven weeks. Our forwarding address would be as thick as an atlas.

She unfolded a beach chair in the shady lee of the hull and kicked off her pumps, a magazine in her lap, instantly remote. The breeze snuck in off Biscayne Bay and licked the propellor of my wind generator into a lazy spin. I went below, flicking on the cabin lights, inhaling the powerful aromas of canvas, turpentine, machine oil and mold. I crawled into the engine space and dug for gaskets, breaking for the surface after a couple of hours, greased like a cold-water diver. Lindy had abandoned her chair. I saw her down at the freighter, she and Ransome leaning on their elbows into the steel, face to face, their palms against their ears as if they were chatting on the telephone.

She in her clownish polka dots and electric jersey, he in black T-shirt, black jeans blushed with rust smears and dark burns. When she wandered back I was on the ground, scrubbing my forearms with a rag soaked in gasoline.

"He doesn't eat well," she said. "Cocoa Puffs and Coca-Cola and hot dogs, crap like that. I invited him for dinner."

Champ moved through the house as if it were a fragile affair and he couldn't quite trust himself under its roof. We drank rum together, spectating from the table while Lindy chucked things into a wok. He had a long brown neck, hands that weren't easily cleaned. I knew he didn't want to be my friend. He was taken by Lindy, a boyish infatuation, eager for her words, wary of mine. I only blamed him for the atmosphere of competition he sent through the room, the soft drumming of a have-not. Yet I don't deny he was a good enough man for me and the evening passed without great event under the dome of Lindy's fantasy—she would feed us and entertain us, we would love her, perhaps a community would be built upon such rocks. She would be modern, we would be rugged, so that the three of us together might balance the world on our toes like a circus ball.

Frankly, I don't know what Lindy thought.

Champ Ransome knew. Neither conspirator nor sneak but another restless man who sweated toward dreams like me, he was around when Lindy needed to unload and he carried the weight of the knowledge on his tongue until two days before he left for good, puttering out the Miami River bound for Haiti, his cargo three thousand cases of German beer. The hull repaired, auxiliary fuel tanks installed in the bow, Champ was itching to go. He took us aboard for an inaugural cruise, a cocktail chug out to the continental shelf to determine how the welds behaved before he stacked the hold with pallets, a bon voyage party for all of us, Lindy and I due to set sail ourselves within the month.

We drove down to the yard late on a Friday morning, the

THE HEART'S ADVANTAGE

top up on the Volkswagen at Lindy's request. She had been avoiding sunlight, I noticed, her fair skin fairer by the day. She wore pegged jeans, plastic sandals, a camouflage spandex tube top that squeezed her breasts back to prepubescent nubs, those same fish-kissing sunglasses and a Yankees baseball cap, the bill tugged so far down her face that she had to lift her head to see in front of her. I was better dressed for the squalor of Ransome's ship—Topsiders, khaki work pants and work shirt with epaulets, the young lieutenant look. We brought along a cooler of ice-cold beer, a jug of red wine, steak sandwiches from the deli. And I would not go without my fishing rod and tackle, for I was a man anxious to rob the sea of all its many pleasures.

Overnight the yard had eased the freighter back into the water, Champ's ship, the *Southern Wind,* which he had rechristened, inscrutably, *Sea-Bop-A-Baby,* I can't guess why. There she wallowed, lashed to the capstans on the dock, looking less malignant with most of her bulk submerged, the Stars and Stripes topping a white triangle imprinted with a martini glass, olive included, stirred by cool zephyrs on the flagpole off the stern. The hatchcovers were piled one on top of the other, revealing the grim cavern of the hold. Champ stepped from the wheelhouse, his skull bound in a red bandanna, his stringy pirate's body bare except for cutoff jeans and oversized workboots.

"Permission to come aboard," I called out, a good fellow.

Champ clomped up to midships, brandishing a wrench which he pointed at my stomach. We were several feet above him on the dock. "You like to fish?" he said, examining my pole with an unconcealed lack of esteem.

"You like to breathe?" I answered back.

"I don't give a damn about breathing," Champ said, squaring his shoulders. "I like to fish."

We gathered in the wheelhouse and stowed the gear and provisions. The short-wave radio buzzed nonstop, spoke to us in tongues. Champ rammed a tape, an untalented imitation of fifties rock and roll, into a cassette player mounted above the chart table. The music was so loud I couldn't see. Lindy plopped down on the bare blue-striped mattress in the lower bunk, her feet bouncing to the concussive rhythm. We were a party that had not yet found its mood though anticipation waxed second by second toward the exhilarated moment of leave-taking. A speedboat passed in the channel beyond our berth, transmitting a pattern of waves toward us that nudged and tickled *Sea-Bop-A-Baby.* My blood paced quickly in a happier heart, heated by rum Champ had harvested from an unpainted plywood cupboard in the narrow galley. I turned the music down so I could speak.

"I hear this is a seagoing vessel," I said to Champ.

"Those who say she is are not wrong."

"Well," I piped, "let's plow the dreadful deeps. Toot out around the yonder."

"Aye," he answered. "Prepare to blow port."

Lindy heard the two of us jawing this way and seemed pleased, I suppose, though I make no claim to reading her right. For all her transformations, she didn't act the way she looked, at least in my presence, and didn't look the way I thought of her.

Champ opened the single door inside the pilothouse and descended the stairs to the engine room. Out on deck Lindy helped me replace the heavy hatchcovers which we then tarped to keep any maverick sea from bathing the hold. Below deck the big diesel cranked like a helicopter. A black cloud puffed out of the stack that impaled the wheelhouse, followed at intervals by a steady emission of round balls of smoke. The steel deck vibrated under our feet. Champ's head appeared out the port window, ordering me to cast off the lines. We fell away from the dock in slow motion, opalescent mud churned in the blue space widening between us and land. Then we were in deeper water, clear of pilings and other craft, tracing the channel with vigilance out through the calm flats.

Lindy and I took position in the bow, shoulder to shoulder,

THE HEART'S ADVANTAGE

our arms resting on the flaked surface of the bulwarks, the water below us divided with a gliding hiss. Off starboard we passed the port of Miami, the wharves crammed with big tankers and cruise liners like captured factories. Behind us the skyline of the city radiated in the sun, a fantast's vision, a hummock where bears once pawed the sand for turtle eggs. We entered Government Cut. On the north side of the breakwater spray exploded skyward, its white fingers suspended and then crashing down, setting pelicans to flight. I saw the last channel marker ahead of us, the clang of its bell intensifying as we approached—*bong bong* do you know what you're doing? *Bong Bong* you're on your own *BONG BONG* have faith have faith. The water was darker but no less translucent, the mouth of the cut bleached with whitecaps. We passed from shelter into the fluid gleaming hill country of the seas, the bow where we stood a bastion above the almighty sweep of the Atlantic, rising and falling as the ship cantered onward, an old sow lunging again and again for the trough.

"Wonderful," I shouted. I turned to Lindy with a wide grin. "Do you have a better word? I want a better word."

"Yes," she said. "Reckless." She watched me for a time behind her sunglasses before she drew them down an inch and allowed her eyes to linger with mine. "What do we do now?"

I didn't like her attitude, I didn't like the slate-green reproach on her face. "We jig atop the pilothouse," I said with an exasperated flourish of my hand, "while your Champ Ransome chauffeurs us to New Guinea. We get drunk and fall overboard, never to be seen again. What do you mean, *what do we do?* Isn't this enough?"

As I finished my lecture *Sea-Bop-A-Baby* dipped with a force that bent our knees. A fan of water spread at eye level, held utterly still for a second, close enough to touch, broken glass in unreal suspension. Then it swashed down onto our heads, draining through Lindy's baseball cap.

"Oh, ugh! God," Lindy complained, flapping her arms uselessly. "I'm all wet. I'm going back and sit with Champ out of the glare."

She walked the lifeline aft to the wheelhouse. Straight on, its construction resembled an old-fashioned gunner's turret, the corners beveled off octagonally, ringed with windows tinted green like Coke bottles. Champ Ransome was a half shadow behind the glass, mastering the wheel, a beer in one hand. Strung between the staff and boom of the cargo crane was a hammock. I stretched open its edges and climbed into it, elementally secure in its hug, a friend to the world. I dozed off and awoke with Lindy standing watch over me, a sad and tender smile on her lips. I smiled back, in love. The wave had washed out her spikes. She was Peter Pan. A jungle version in a one-piece, one strap, leopardskin bathing suit.

"You look pretty," I said, swaying with the roll of the ship.

"That's the first nice thing you've said to me in ages."

"Is that right. I'm sorry."

"That's right," she sulked. "And you ought to be."

I dragged her down into the hammock and kissed her. "Why aren't you having fun?" I asked.

Her teeth nipped into the flesh of my shoulder. The shell earrings she wore scratched my neck. "Oh, I am," she said quietly. "Really."

"It will be better on our own boat," I assured her. "Much much better. *Sea-Bop-A-Baby* is like taking a gymnasium out on the ocean."

She pushed herself up off my chest. "Hey," she said. "Champ wants you back there. I think something's wrong."

We lurched and yawed, skating over a sequence of hard knolls that were in opposition to the easy cadence the ship had settled into, renegade thoughts bombarding the flow of meditation. Champ was spread-eagled at the helm, throwing the wheel left and right like a test driver. His bandanna was soaked in perspiration but he seemed well placed to the task. He had a brave start on a collection of empty beer cans along the window ledges.

"What's wrong?" I said, stepping through the doorway.

"Nothing." He grunted as he adjusted the wheel to the buck of a wave. I went to the cooler and opened a beer. On the

THE HEART'S ADVANTAGE

radar screen the fading shore was an outline of foxfire. "I'm going below to have a look-see," he reported. "Take the wheel."

Had I taken some long beast by the horns and tried to push it backward through an imaginary gate, the job would have been no different. The bow overswung to the north, overswung to the south, overswung to the north again as I steered twenty degrees past our heading in each direction until I got used to the slack in the linkage. This was Champ's idea of funny.

"Told you," he laughed hoarsely. "She's a straying bitch."

I steered for an hour while Champ played below and, let me tell you, it's a fine feeling to captain a ship, a liberation to power it over the depths, surely a magic, like flight. The horizon writhes. You go on and on. The horizon writhes, now brassed with daybreak, now colorless and baleful with the coming of night, and the distance irons out in your wake.

I followed the compass due east. Lindy, a slender pod, hung in the hammock in possession of a magazine. There was a change in the water ahead, a friction, like the line where a meadow ends and the scrub takes over. This was the Gulf Stream pouring northward through the Florida Straits, a wilder current than the one we hitched. Out there beyond the stream, unseen, were the islands, some as fragrant as cardamom, some with histories hidden like fat beneath a girdle, some as crummy as headaches, some with treasure so abundant it had no value, some only phantasms, some with the power to close on you like Ahab's whale. I wanted to discover each of them, to drive Lindy there on the wind. I never imagined such places, she'd say.

For its greeting the Gulf Stream echoed thunder into us. The old sow dug her snout into the ocean and shook, tossing blue water over the deck that flooded under Lindy and out the scuppers. Champ emerged from the belly of the ship, a man at home with grime and knuckle-busting. He clomped on deck and perched over the rail, his nose inches away from the highest rising swells. He clomped back in.

"Stay out of the stream," he said in passing. The machinery roared when he reopened the engine room door.

"What's up?" I yelled out.

"Not much," he said before disappearing again. "Bilge pump." He pointed toward Cuba. "Fall off to the south. Take it easy."

I jacked the wheel just as Lindy timed her dash back to the cabin. The change of direction threw her across the room in a stagger.

"What is going on?" she inquired breathlessly, grabbing my waist for support. "I'm getting sick."

"We're leveling off for the cocktail hour," I explained. "Eat one of those sandwiches. It'll settle your stomach."

She chewed a few bites and threw up out the lowered port window.

"Feel better now?"

"No."

"You will," I promised. I dropped the throttle one-third.

She crawled into the bottom bunk and lay on her stomach, moaning piteously, her arms draped over her head. Champ came up wiping his hands on a dirty rag, every crease in his skin penciled black.

"What's wrong with her?" he said.

"She feels bad."

"Hunh. Can't have that." But Champ did not come to Lindy's aid. He forgot about her immediately and opened another beer, wolfed down one of the sandwiches.

"How's that bilge pump?"

"What?" he said, distracted. He peered out the windows in each direction. "Where are we? You know?"

I tapped the chart in front of me. "About three miles northeast of Eliot Key."

"Yeah?" he said, not willing to commit himself to this information. He squinted at the water, tipped his beer can out toward the port bow. "Nice weed line out there."

"I've been looking at it," I said. "Why don't you take the helm back?"

THE HEART'S ADVANTAGE

"All right," he said, instinctively stepping forward, wiping mayonnaise on his shorts.

I took a direct path to my tackle box and pole. "I'm going to fish," I said.

Champ's eyes bulged. *"Fish?"* he grumbled as if I had tricked him. "Why, damn you."

"Take me right to them, pal," I said, and walked back to the stern. Our wake was a tail of smoky suds, the water we had passed over subdued, as if a gloved hand had smoothed it out. Champ must have fixed the bilge because I could hear it over the side, a mushed, sputtery *th-th-th* ending in a gurgle each time the ship dug in her heel. The waterline was about four feet down, adding or subtracting two feet with each change in gravity. I tied on a five-inch spoon with a yellow feather and sent it arcing into the air, the line dragging out fifty yards until it dropped the lure under golden patches of sargasso weed shrugged off by the stream, a gleaming irresistible whisk through the shade where dolphin schooled.

The line wasn't out five minutes before it jerked taut, a false strike that left a faint resistance. I reeled in twenty feet and a clump of grass levitated up, scooning across the surface. I brought it in so I could pick the spoon clean again. Our wake had taken on the aspect of doodling. This was Ransome's spite, I assumed, a maneuvering that would compel me frequently to adjust the tension on the line. Champ came running back to disprove this theory, swiping the air with his own pole. He saw me reeling in and glared.

"Whatcha got there?" he demanded to know.

"Nothing," I said. "Weed."

My poor luck cheered him. "Now we'll see what's what. You step back when I start hauling them in."

"We'll see about that," I said. Even square-fingered he could tie a leader with dexterity. He scoffed at my spoon and chose for himself a black and white jitterbug plug that was out in the water before I realized it.

"You won't catch anything with that," I said, but I didn't care to improve on his judgment.

"You ever fished before?" he said. "In the ocean, I mean." He feigned a rabid concentration as if that would make a difference.

If I took one step backward I could send Champ Ransome overboard with my foot. These impulses are better ignored, the sting of hormones suffered, or you throw yourself into nothing less than war. "Who's at the helm?" I asked, although I already had the picture.

"Why, who do you think?"

"She's sick," I said.

"No, she ain't. I gave her a pill."

Champ scouted the vista of sea, rubbing his unshaven cheeks, an angry, underfed osprey. Good-bye, crow. He whipped his pole impetuously on the spur of wishful thinking. He whipped his pole again and spit at his lack of success, looking over at me, his eyes squeezed in an outlaw version of a smile. "She wanted that wheel. I told her she could turn the tub around and head for port."

"It's early," I said.

"It won't be." Champ nodded at our crazy wake. "She wants land but she's running a slalom to get there."

We both knew that wheel was a lot of trouble. I suppose if I had another minute to think about it I would have reeled in my line and gone to help her. Maybe it was cruel of us to leave her up there by herself. Maybe it wasn't, since self-sufficiency is a virtue that must be tested. But as soon as Champ shut his mouth, my rod bent double, the drag whirring like a hand-cranked siren. I was occupied thereafter.

"Goddammit," Champ howled, wounded by my good fortune.

"Slow her down," I shouted back. The drag continued to burn out and the core of the spool began to appear through the wrap. "I'm out of line. Slow her down."

"Aw, goddamn," Champ muttered, gravely disappointed.

"All right. Hold on." He took in his line with great reluctance. I battled the fish against its dive. Champ moseyed forward and I reeled frantically when the engine cut to a purr and the line slackened. Champ jogged right back.

"What is it?" he asked suspiciously. I tugged and reeled, tugged and reeled. Champ answered himself. "I'll bet it's a damn barracuda."

The water broke about a hundred feet out, a metallic flash as sudden as lightning and gone. The energy discharged, the fish spent itself momentarily in a last plunge that brought it straight under the stern. Champ mounted the bulwarks, watching the water like a tomcat. He had outfitted himself on his visit to the wheelhouse, a leather glove on his left hand, an oak billy club clutched in his right. I brought the fish alongside the hull and let it exhaust its fight with a final thrashing.

"That's a big blue," Champ announced. His body twitched. "A big chopper blue. Damn." He tottered over the side and caught the wire leader in his leather paw. "I've got her," he said. "I've got her. Look out now." He yanked the fish with such force that it sailed above our heads and smacked down on the decking behind us. "Look out now," Champ said with high excitement and fell on the fish, beating it repeatedly on its fat nose with the club. The tailfin quivered violently and then relaxed.

"That's enough, Champ," I said. "Let's get the hook out." He had battered an eye from its socket and exposed the brain with his hard strokes.

"Jesus," he said, inhaling deeply. "That's a nice one."

"One good rap between the eyes will do it," I said. Big fish are dangerous once you haul them aboard and must be subdued in short order. The common style though is not to pulverize or mutilate beyond recognition.

"Let's get moving," Champ said, "I want mine."

I hoisted the blue under the beautiful span of its tail and trotted to the wheelhouse door. Lindy was crucified to the wheel, in loose control. I held the fish out for her approval.

"We're going back," she said between clenched teeth, an overzealous fire in her eyes.

"Look," I said beaming. "I caught the first fish."

"Get it out of here, man. It's dripping blood all over."

In the galley I exchanged the fish for the bottle of rum. I was shamelessly pleased with myself. "Push her back up to trolling speed, honey," I said. Immediately the engine rumbled and throbbed. "Ho ho," I said. "Old Champ's pissed."

"Hey, can you give me a hand here, Sims?" Lindy said, trying to wrestle the wheel. "My arms are going to break off."

"Yeah, in a minute," I said, and took off for the stern, leaving her alone again. Champ's line threaded out into the water. I noticed the black and white plug resting on top of his tackle box. "What are you using now?" I asked him, nudging the lure with my toe.

"You'll see before you want to," he said, "when you remove it from the jaw of a big yellowfin tuna." No sooner had he said that than he obliged himself with a Rebel yell. I didn't even bother to pick up my pole.

"Oh yes," he proclaimed with lust. "Oh yes oh yes." When his rod went U-shaped he reclined away from it, employing muscle and weight against the strike. I was sure the line would snap but it held. No one had to tell me what to do next. I sprinted to the wheelhouse and stuck my face in the doorway.

"Slow her down, honey."

Lindy turned at me and snarled. "No."

Champ and I were aroused now and such talk was mutinous. "What do you mean, *no?*" I said, charging forward. I cuffed the throttle back. *"Slow her down."*

I quickly retreated to the stern. Champ collected his line inch by inch, grinding it in. In our wake I spotted a gray torpedo in tow.

"It's a barracuda," I said.

"The hell it is," Champ insisted. "It's a big king mackerel."

I sighted it again. "Naw," I said. "Only a barra plays dead like that."

"You can go farm in Nebraska," Champ said. "It's a big king mackerel." I donned the leather glove and stood ready. "If it's a barracuda I'll shove it up my ass."

"Pull down your pants," I told him, leaning over the rail. I grabbed the leader and raised the fish. It was big but a barracuda nevertheless. "This is how you do it," I said, holding the wire with my left hand and slipping the thumb, second and third fingers of my other hand into the gill opening, then wrenching the hook from the wicked grin of the jaws.

"You fool," Champ observed. "You'll lose a finger doing that." The fish shook against my grip, the twist and squirm of a thick snake. I laid it on deck, placed my foot behind its head and clobbered it once with the billy club. Champ threw his pole down and stomped away. *Sea-Bop-A-Baby* came back to speed.

One more fish to go and it was my catch more or less. Our two lines out dragging their temptations, both of us not disinclined to knife the other in the back, Champ and I sat watch on the froth, the bottle of rum passed between us and emptied before the strike. It occurs to me now that Lindy must have thrown up her hands in disgust and frustration when Champ hustled into the wheelhouse for the third time to choke the throttle. At the time I was acutely aware that *Sea-Bop-A-Baby,* apparently unpiloted, had begun a lazy clockwise circle, batted by the waves, that threatened to cross my line and slice the dolphin free.

There was a split second when neither of us, or both of us, could claim the fish. The dolphin struck on a head-on run, hitting the lure at top velocity and springing into the air upright, an iridescence. Dolphins are bull-nosed, elite warriors, potent and brawny, their vivid colors, a greenish-blue and yellow, unpresent in the same living hues in the world above the surface. When you land one you feel you have ripped the sea's own muscle from the water.

At the strike neither pole reacted. We watched the fish dance and fall, each one of us declaring ownership. But I understood what was happening. I could sense the spirit of the fish like a heating coil in the butt of my rod, confirmed in a violent instant as my line erupted from its spool and I set my strength against the pure unyielding weight of the dolphin. Champ cursed until his tongue turned white.

The fish pierced the atmosphere once again, nearer the ship, its great size more evident, its resistance a ferocity. Bringing the beauty back up took a long time. Each attempt to haul it closer than twenty feet from the stern was denied with fresh power. I had to slack off or lose. The dolphin stayed out there just below the surface sweeping back and forth, a hot electric current, a blue curling form, flashing between the arc circumscribed by the limit of the line I allowed. My will and the will of the fish—this is a tired thought but true, the forces so precisely opposite and therefore exquisite, no chance for sentimentality, for hapless negotiation. Nothing was given. It could go either way—all rare joys are as simple as that.

To land the fish I knew would take good work and patience. It paced the water handsomely, back and forth, back and forth, and I took advantage of each turn to ease the fish alongside the hull. When it thought to duck under the ship I jerked its jaws skyward. They gaped at me through the spangled water and then the fish rolled so its huge yellow-ringed eye, a cold defiance, could form its last judgment on me. Each time I brought its blunt head out of the sea, the body still in its own world spasmed, and I would slack off in fear that the line would break.

"You're gonna lose it," Champ said.

"Stand back out of the way," I ordered. "We need a gaff."

"Well, of course we do," Champ said derisively, "but we don't have one. You're gonna lose it."

I glanced across my shoulder at him in an unfriendly way. "Now what would you know about it?"

"A fish that big won't take the test of the line."

"You just stand back."

Champ removed himself from my line of vision and I listened to him scuff away. My plan was to wait it out, to let the

THE HEART'S ADVANTAGE

fish defeat itself, and then try to fling it over the bulwark. The fish would exert its strength again once I committed myself. The line would snap when the fish was in the air, yet if I timed the move right and the momentum was good I had a chance.

I inched the head up through the sea and prepared myself.

"Hold her steady," Champ commanded from behind me. He stepped forward, a shotgun raised to his shoulder. I could not protest before he acted. My ears boomed with the report. The tall forehead of the fish vaporized, disintegrating into crimson molecules, a residue of pinkish foam. The body slip-slided back down into the depths like a fluorescent leaf until it eventually disappeared.

Champ said, "Well, damn, that was a little high."

"Son of a bitch," I shouted. "A little high? *You shot my fish.*"

"You moved it just as I pulled the trigger."

"You shot my fish."

Champ tried a pout but it didn't suit his nature. "It would have been all right if you hadn't moved it."

"You skunk, you shot my fish."

"You were gonna lose it."

I flung down my pole in a rage. "You're nothing but a damn thief," I said and stalked away. What I wanted more than anything was to have my own boat launched to the wind, out of sight to cities, banks and fools, blowing down to Barbados with Lindy. I couldn't endure Champ Ransome a minute more. I stormed into the wheelhouse determined to get us back on shore with all possible speed. Lindy had been waiting for me to show myself, boiling her words before she threw them in my face.

"You!" The intensity of her shriek popped the gold studs from her earlobes. I stood dismayed before her wrath. *"You with your toys and games.* What do I have to do to get you to see *me?"*

My mood wasn't right for taking rebuke or faultfinding. "Calm down," I said. "Let's concentrate on getting out of here." I punched the throttle forward. Lindy wasn't finished with me.

"I've told you every way I can," she cried.

"Told me what? What's this all about?" Innocence has always been a fine target and effective as provocation.

"Have you been blinded! My life has changed."

"Well, don't think I haven't noticed a difference," I said.

"You're always flying off and leaving me alone. Whenever you go, I learn about myself. Things I didn't know before."

"So what's wrong with that?" Champ had come to stand in the doorway and witness the knowledge arrow into me.

"The boat," Lindy said, seething, her hands trembling in front of her. I didn't know what she meant. *"The ketch."*

"What about it?"

"Sell it," she begged. "If you love me and I know you do, sell the boat and stay with me."

Did I bellow and kick the wall? Maybe I did. What I remember is saying, *Not-on-your-life,* each word measured hateful and numbing. The engine gagged and shut down. My voice resonated in silence, the smell of raw fuel and scorched circuitry. We were dead in the water, as if together we had murdered *Sea-Bop-A-Baby* with the splitting of our faith.

Throughout the night we drifted forlornly, Ishmaels on the water, Lindy in the cold solitude of her bunk, Champ banging below decks, correcting a variety of failures I won't go into. To prevent the ship from running aground, we let the anchor dangle over the side but it wasn't necessary. Our electricity had been lost, too. It was my responsibility to sit on top of the wheelhouse through those loneliest of hours with a flashlight and beam it out into the shimmering darkness whenever I sighted another vessel. Here we are, I'd signal. Down on our luck, a tub of infants in the night. Stay clear. Steer away. For most of the time I had only the void to examine—me, my nose, and zero. I lay back often, my hands pillowing my head, made despondent by the stars. There were too many of them, a cruel fact. Except for the most practical communications, Lindy avoided me until near dawn when the weakest light transmuted space and caused the black atmosphere to ripple and quake as if it were coming apart. Then she joined me up top and we talked.

"It *is* beautiful," she said, stretching out beside me.

"Tell me," I said, selecting my simplest fear, "who's Champ Ransome?"

"Nobody," she said ruefully. She paused and then modified her answer. "A nice guy, a pretty fair listener. A wanderer, like you."

"Tell me this," I said. "Why'd you ever do that to your hair?"

"Oh." She laughed, a quiet song on the ocean. "I thought you understood." She lifted herself up on an elbow and gazed down on me. "If you could understand that you'd understand a lot."

"Try me," I said. "Give it a go."

"It was a first step," she said haltingly. "I dared myself. It seemed the most bloodless way to begin to tell you I wanted other things. I guess it was the least, um, what—?" She searched for a word that she never found.

The sun came up, painting a distant shoreline to the west. "Look," I said, placing my hand on the warm nape of her neck and turning her head. "There are the beaches of Mauritius. Behind the low cloud is Mount Pelée in Martinique, the coast of the Seychelles. Sri Lanka, with elephants in the sand. Bali. The Azores."

"Stop," she said, shrugging off my hand. "It's only Miami. We live there, Sims. It's our home."

She signed a new lease on the house and enrolled in a graphics design program at the university. I have sworn to send her postcards whenever I'm in port. The ketch has been out in the anchorage for a week while I settled last-minute business, all the paperwork that appears on the eve of leave-taking. Two days ago I visited the animal shelter and conscripted an over-weight, cross-eyed cat as a shipmate.

I pulled anchor this morning. She had to go to class so I

said good-bye at the house and took a cab to the bay. Every-thing I have is hers for as long as I'm gone.

Through Government Cut and I'm out at sea. Where Champ Ransome's freighter rolled with the first swell, I nixed the engine and hoisted the sails, celebrating their silent powering ahead out to the ancient routes and mains, the currents that ushered men to new worlds. And now I've been talking to myself like an old salt, my voice returned to my mouth by the headwind I'm beating into. The cat dashes after imaginary mice, content as far as I can tell. Lindy, I said, honey, you should see this. You would be seeing this, had you shunned the lesser patriotisms, chose instead the outward passage, the heart's adventure. I suppose I'm still rather stunned, I can't get over it, I still can't believe she's not coming with me.

Redemption Songs

"These songs of freedom, are all I ever had."
Bob Marley

Glasford had been on the edge now for days.

"De whole friggin world on top of us, boy."

"Daht is so."

Glasford and Fish were in the Crabhole, a two-seat rum shop owned by Momma Smallhorne. In these two chairs they sat, an oil drum between them for a table, each man facing the open side of the shop, wisely studying the lights of Georgetown in the distance. A kerosene lamp glowed beside their bottle on the drum, buttering their faces with its light.

"Ahnd de whole world friggin us too, ya know."

"Yes, daht's so." Fish's nature was to be aggreable.

Glasford did not speak with undue anger or bitterness. His words were confident, as if he had finally discovered the exact methodology he would use to overcome his oppression. Fish, as always a composed soul, a man hard at work on understanding the world, provided an ear blessed with patience.

"We is like rocks on de bottom of de sea," Glasford continued. Each word was carefully enunciated in a low, scratching voice. "Cahnt move, cahnt go nowheres. Lissen, like rocks we is, ahnd everyting else swimmin by."

"Yes, daht is so, too," Fish replied matter-of-factly. "Look, gimme a smoke."

Glasford made a show of searching his pockets. "I have none," he said, and then called to Momma Smallhorne, "Momma, bring two cigarettes."

Momma rose up slowly from her cot behind the counter, troubled by her arthritis. From a single carton of Marlboros on the empty shelves of her shop, she took a pack and spent some time removing the cellophane with her crippled fingers.

"Save me a step, child."

Fish got up from his seat and gave her ten cents for the two cigarettes. When the fuss was over, Glasford spoke again. He spoke forcefully, although the only sounds to compete with him were the creaks of their overrepaired chairs, Momma's hard breathing in rhythm with the soft notes of the sea along the beach, an occasional car racing to Georgetown along the surfaced road behind the shop.

"We must do someting," said Glasford. Then he was silent, waiting for Fish to agree. Fish smoked his cigarette, puff after puff, enjoying it.

Finally Fish looked around. "Momma, bring de dominoes," he said.

"No, Fish. I tellin you, mahn, no dominoes tonight. We must do someting."

"What cahn fellahs like us do?" Fish asked. Glasford frowned into the night, his face beyond the cast of the lamp.

The man's insistence had teased out Fish's curiosity. There had been similar conversations between them ever since Glasford had returned from the States a few weeks ago. But now, somehow, tonight, Glasford was creating a sense of movement, a line of potential. "What cahn we do?" Fish repeated.

"Pray, now ahnd always," Momma Smallhorne croaked. She had started out on the journey to bring them the box of dominoes.

"Momma, be quiet," Glasford snapped at her. "Is mahn's talk we makin."

Fish looked at his companion again. They had been friends all their lives. There were no secrets, no mysteries between them, until Glasford had gone to the States. Glasford had his face set the way he set it when he wanted people to know that he was a warrior and bad news to anybody who bothered with him. That made no sense to Fish. There was no one to scare but Momma Smallhorne, and even the devil had given up on her.

"How you lookin so dangerous, Glahs boy?" The veins in Glasford's neck reflected the thick light as they swelled. Fish watched the glow race up them with each powerful throb.

"Dis mornin I wake up ahnd see a mahn burnin weed on his piece of land so he cahn plant some cassava. I tell myself, Glahsford, you been waitin ahnd waitin, ahnd now de time come."

"How you mean, bruddah?"

"I see in dis weed burnin how God trew down Babylon. Fah de great day of His wrath has come."

"Amen." Momma Smallhorne kept herself ready to punctuate the word of God wherever she encountered it.

"Come out of Babylon, my peoples, lest you share in her sins, lest you receive of her plague."

"Amen."

"Glahs," Fish said. "Doan get Momma excited."

"De Queen of Whores will be uttahly burned wit fire. Great riches have come to nought."

"Daht's true. Amen."

"Ah. Ah, I see," said Fish, nodding his head in understanding. "I didn't know you could scripturize so. You must get a callin, Glahsford?"

"We comin to a time of prophecy realization. Salvation reality."

"Upon dis rock you shall build a church," Fish said. He was enthusiastic about the idea of a theatrical Glasford, sowing fine language from a pulpit.

"Hallelujah," cried Momma Smallhorne.

"Mahn, doan play de arse. Is revolution I talkin now."

"Oh ho," said Fish. The tone in Glasford's voice had been condescending and Fish was offended. "Is Natty Dread I sittin wit. Johnny Too Bad. Mistah Castro."

Glasford stood up. "Momma, we leavin," he announced. Fish watched him disappear up the path that led to the main road. He finished the rum in his glass, and then the rum Glasford had left behind in his. He recapped the bottle and stood up also. Momma was just returning the box of dominoes to its customary spot beneath an unframed cardboard picture of Queen Elizabeth. He didn't want to trouble her further so instead of placing the bottle on the short counter for her to retrieve, he leaned over and put it away himself.

"Momma, you want company wit de light?"

She shook her head no and lay back on her cot.

"Good evenin, Momma," Fish said. He blew out the kerosene lamp and followed after Glasford on the path.

Glasford was in the bushes a few steps off the path, shielded from the nearby road. Fish saw the flare of a match and let it guide him to his friend. On his heels, Glasford crouched forward, sucking a cigar-sized splif he had just rolled.

"We is bruddahs, true?" Glasford asked, not bothering to look up.

"True."

"We is de same, you ahnd I."

Fish did not believe this was quite true but he said it was so anyway, not to humor Glasford but to avoid obstructing his point. There was a change taking place in Glasford. In island life, any change in anybody, the motivations, the possible consequences, was worthy of a lot of talk. Glasford inhaled, and inhaled still more, until a coal like a fat red bullet burned between them. Then he blew out so much smoke that he was lost behind it.

"Mahn, come to town wit me tonight," Glasford urged Fish.

Fish did not have to answer immediately because Glasford had passed him the ganja. Going into Georgetown with Glasford meant having to buy Glasford his beer and having to pay cash for it. At least Momma Smallhorne allowed him credit. And it meant giving up the bed of Althea, a woman he had been recently courting. Fish was not eager to make such a sacrifice.

"I cahnt do so, bruddah. My seed pointin me in de next direction."

Fish had discovered certain truths about his life that made him feel solid and steady. The most significant, the easiest to understand, was this: Women made him happy. He didn't even consider this much of a discovery until he noticed that for so many other fellows, the opposite was true: Women made them unhappy, women transformed their spirits, confused them, gave them their first breath of hatred.

The caresses, the smells, the closeness, the slick warm wetness, the words and thoughts he could only share with a female, these ran like a nectar through Fish's life. Some women were spiteful toward him because he had so many lovers, but he told himself simply that love had made him a free and honest man. When he made a baby with one of them, he did not run away as if he had committed a crime, but divided his spare time as best he could among the households. When he could not give them a few dollars, he gave them fish or conch, turtle meat, mangoes from a tree on his small property, and sometimes pretty shells or a long feather for the children to play with.

"Fish, come wit me tonight."

"Mahn, why you so in-trested in town? Daht's a bad spot, a place daht just eat de money right from a fellah's pocket."

"Come wit me," Glasford repeated, "come wit me," as if he were under a spell.

"Look here, why you need me?"

"Fah bruddah-hood."

"Bruddah-hood? Mahn, daht cahn wait till mornin."

"Fah witness."

"Witness! What, boy, you puttin youself on trial?"

"Bear witness to de lion."

"Glahsford, I feel you strivin, mahn. You lookin close at someting I cahnt see."

"You cahnt hear me now, Fish. I speakin de language of Jah Rastafari."

"How you cahnt speak a level daht make some sense to a guy like me? You might as well be monkey ahnd me jahckass. Daht's no bruddah-hood."

"Tell me, what dese words mean—guerrilla ahction, Babylon ahfire, ahnd Jah's people in liberation?"

"Mahn, who you? You a Jamaicahn fellah now?"

"As yet I find no boundary to corruption, ya know. Dis place deviled up too, same as Jamaica."

Fish scratched his head, thinking the matter over. Althea offered him sugar, Glasford wanted him to take salt.

"One mahn wit vision is ahll it must need to make a bettah world," Glasford added.

Fish sucked his teeth. "Daht's a simple line. You makin a joke."

"I jokin? *Me?* You come see, see how I joke."

Fish smiled without discretion. "Mmm," he said. "Mmm," as if he were savoring the dialogue, the smoke, the temptations now upon him. Glasford was blowing a big wind, talking a lot of movie house shit. But Fish would kick himself tomorrow if there was a show and he had missed it.

"Dere's a womahn callin my name," Fish said.

"Womahn must wait."

Fish stood up with a grunt and an exaggerated sigh so that Glasford would know of the sacrifice he was making for brotherhood.

It took a long time for Glasford to flag them a ride into town. Fish kept his distance from him on the side of the road, turned away as if he were just about to walk on, the visor on his cap pulled down toward the bridge of his flat nose. He was uncomfortable begging anything from a fellow he didn't know. Now if a friend drove past, he would wave his hand as hard as Glasford, but who could tell in the dark who was friend and who was not? This attitude had much to do with the second piece of knowledge Fish had learned during what he called his *self-studies*—the hours he spent alone fishing on the sea. It used to be, a few years ago, that he worked as a crew member on one of the sport fishing boats that were charted out to tourists. He didn't mind the work, but it wasn't worth the extra dollar a day to endure a boss. In fact, given the type of boss he had, and kept having as he moved from job to job, it made more sense to sleep in the rain and starve. To suffer under the hand of God, that was one thing. It was the hand of his fellow man that Fish could not abide.

This thinking led to a third truth that completed for Fish the extent of his destiny. A man's life was not to be perfect, but that was not to be worried over until other people pressed you with responsibility for that fact—a wife, a boss, or the salesmen, the politicians and preachers.

It didn't matter whose life was better, as long as his was the way he wanted it. Two years past, with no particular ambition in mind, he had signed a piece of paper that put him in the middle of the cane fields of Hendry County, working like a mule, swallowing enough dust to bury himself in, his forearms scarred from the sharp leaves of the cane.

He thought vaguely that in America he would see how the white people lived, live that way for a while, and then decide which life was better—island or Stateside, black or white. But in Florida, in the labor camps and fields, he never got close enough to a white person to talk. The rest of the fellows there were all Antiguans or Virgin Islanders, or dark, dark fellows who didn't know English. The women who came along with the laborers enjoyed the spectacle of men fighting over them. Fish, for the first time, felt lonely, bottled up. At night on his bunk, he relaxed only with thoughts of the warm Caribbean Sea, the spectrum of blues that colored it, the mood of reefs, of sand flats, of deep holes. He needed the sea as much now as when he was a boy spending idle days on the piers of Georgetown, studying the water for hours at the spot where his fishing line cut the surface and connected him to another world, one as familiar as a dream. When he had earned enough money to build a catboat of his own, he left Florida with no regrets.

Glasford had been to the States, too.

De States, Glasford said when he returned, *was baptism, was education.*

You ahsk how it was in New York, mahn? What, you doan know, nobody tell you so? No jobs, everybody have a blind eye to sufferin. You come today ahnd de fellah daht come yesterday tell you to go away, ain't have no place left fah you. Ahll de West Indian people dere does be up to tricks. You cahnt trust you muddah. Ahll de womahn too *busy.* White people afraid to look by you. Cahnt even have a piss witout trouble. Mahn, dis de sulfurous heart of Babylon.

"So how you not get rich in de States like my bruddah Granville?" asked another guy taking his refreshment in Momma Smallhorne's a few weeks ago when Glasford had first returned.

Glasford rolled his eyes. "Mahn, what you say, you ignorant? I beg everywheres fah a job. I weep ahnd pull up me shirt. Look aht dis, I say. My belly cavin in. I has nuttin to eat fah six days. I will work ahll day fah a piece ah bread, please. Dey point a big gun aht me ahnd chase me away. Den de cops see

REDEMPTION SONGS

you in Mahnhattan where ahll de white people does live ahnd make work in dese big prick buildins, ahnd dey beat you wit sticks, ya know. So how a mahn sposed to get by? You tell me. Den dis white bitch tycoonness find me. I will give you a tousand dollahs to please me, she say. I take de money ahnd poke she, but den I run away because she disgust me so."

Fish had laughed trying to picture Glasford fleeing a white woman with money.

"Mahn, you realize a tousand dollahs doan pay one month's rent in New York?"

"Yes, daht's so," said Fish to the other guy. He had heard some mention of that same information.

"See, what I tell you," Glasford had said, glaring at the other fellow. "Den it get so cold ice covah me face. I tell myself I dyin now, good-bye. I fall to de street. I look up at de sky—I cahnt see it. I see only dese buildins, mistah, goin up into de air, where ahll dese bigshots does rule de world like dey in heaven. De hell wit dis, I say. I'm no mahn to give up. I is resistin. I crawl back to Brooklyn. Ahn old auntie take pity on me ahnd give me plane money home. I escape, I escape de dragon."

"Uh-huh!" the other fellow exclaimed, beginning to appreciate the magnitude of Glasford's adventure.

"Daht's a nice piece of story, Glahsford." Fish chewed thoughtfully on an orange, analyzing all that Glasford had said, separating what could be true from what could not. New York City was a hard place—everyone knew that. Somehow Glasford had done okay though. He strutted off the plane in soft, pretty shoes, new Levi's with a crease ironed into them, a shiny brown shirt that Fish knew he hadn't owned before he went north, his hair wilder and longer. Strapped around his wrist he had one of those little cassette units with a good AM/FM radio in it. On the other wrist, pinching his flesh, was a thin gold bracelet that seemed too small for a man the size of Glasford.

Glasford had made out. He had done okay. Something had happened though. Whatever it was, it made Glasford start talking like a warrior.

Glasford's calm, sardonic voice: "So, Fish, you believe I makin a story, eh?"

"Nah," Fish said. "I'm only sayin my ears find an in-trest in de ahccount."

"My bruddah Granville," the other guy mused. "I tinkin now he must be a very lucky fellah to be gettin by so in de States, sendin us money each month."

"Lucky!" Glasford used the word like a whip. "Daht is *bull*shit."

"Come, Fish. Come."

Fish shuffled over to the car and lowered himself in. Glasford slapped him lovingly on the thigh. *Brotherhood.*

Fish suspected the uselessness of it all, but he got in the car anyway, uncomfortable, embarrassed to look at the driver once he saw it was no one he was familiar with. He stared straight ahead, stared directly at the government license pasted to the outside of the glove box without realizing what it was. A car passed. In the light that melted through the interior of the old Ford, Fish suddenly focused on what it was before his eyes. He leaned forward onto the front seat to shout at the driver.

"Stop. Mahn, what de hell you doin pickin us two boys up?"

The driver tapped the brake reflexively but then let off, continuing down the road.

"Mahn, stop. We ain't payin no taxi."

The driver turned to look at them. He seemed quite used to taking his eyes off the road. The three were only dark outlines to each other.

"Look, doan worry wit daht," the driver said. "I just now comin from me suppah."

The fellow sounded friendly enough to Fish so he sat back uneasily. "Okay," he said. "Watch de road. We nuttin special to look at."

Fish could tell the fellow was okay just by the way he nodded and moved and drove—fast, but not out to be fastest. He was an older fellow, probably one of the first drivers around when the hotels were built. His car was clean but coming apart.

"Um hmm," Glasford grumbled. It was a sinister sound. Nobody else said anything.

"Um hmm." Glasford again, only louder. Fish couldn't figure it.

"Um hmm."

Fish wasn't going to pay attention. There was no sense answering a voice that proposed trouble you didn't want. He hoped the driver knew as much. But then the driver was bending around again, his elbow on the top of the seat.

"Here now," he said to Fish. "Why dis guy *um hmm* so? What's on his mind?"

Fish didn't want any sort of conversation. The best policy was to let a man make whatever speech he cared to, and forget about it if it wasn't your concern. Glasford tapped him conspiratorially on the knee.

"Fish, you tink you have de proper ahttitudes and mentalities to be a bourgeois fellah like dis taxi mahn?"

"How you expect me to ahnswer daht?" muttered Fish.

"What you fellahs up to?" the driver turned once more to ask.

"We is de Black Knights," Glasford said. His arms were crossed on his chest and he talked scornfully. Fish looked at him in horror.

"Black nights," the driver said, nodding his head.

"You heard of us?"

"No."

Silence. Fish made himself stone-hard. They were less than a mile from the edge of town.

"You doan hear word of us?" Glasford persisted.

"No."

Silence. They slowed for a stop sign, floated through it into shantytown.

"We is revolutionaries, ya know."

"Oh," the driver said with less interest.

1 1 2

"Revolutionaries," Glasford repeated. He made each syllable march out of his mouth.

"Oh," the driver said. "I first thought you must be some music group."

"No, no," Glasford explained. "We is de words to de music. We is de livin words."

"Oh."

Fish interrupted this nonsense. "Drop us aht de corner, please."

The car stopped. Fish jumped out. Glasford remained in his seat for another minute, continuing his talk.

"We must change our ways ahnd work togeddah."

"Okay," the driver said.

"You is wit us, taxi mahn?"

"Sure, big noise," the driver answered. "I just give you a free ride."

"Ahll right, ahll right," Glasford said as if he had fixed a deal. "Maybe someday we give you a good job, Mistah Taxi Mahn." He slammed the car door behind him and joined Fish, his feet springing lightly off the pavement, a high swagger that Fish couldn't help but admire.

There was not much action on the street. Glasford saluted the few limers and layabouts with a raised fist. They turned their heads to nod tentatively.

"Bruddahs," Glasford declared.

"Yeah," some of them called back. They stepped past a few nice houses, gated and barred, protected from the street by cement walls, and then onto a block alive with hucksters and kids, shops angry with light and noise, trash and stink scattered through the gutters.

Once they entered Billings Road Fish guessed where Glasford was headed. His mood sunk. The Ethiope was a discotheque-bar, too big, too expensive. You had to be a kingpin to feel right there. Or carry a gun—same thing. Fellows bothering you to buy weed at Miami prices or talking a big sell on pills that made you dizzy, or pills that made your thoughts jerk too fast for your brain. The girls stayed tight against the money men, or one of the high-rolling tourists they sometimes talked inside the door. Fish preferred smaller places, safer people, booze that only cost what it was worth.

A bouncer who was all heft checked the entrance. Glasford knew him.

"Steam, my bruddah, out de way. We comin trew." Glasford tried to push by him. The bouncer grabbed his shoulder.

"How you gettin so cocky, boy? Put in my hand a dollah, quick."

Glasford pretended not to hear. "Steam, bruddah," he said with an earnest expression. He placed his own hand on the hump of the doorman's shoulder, so that the two of them formed a box, facing off each other like wrestlers. "Which title sound bettah to you—Black Knights or Black Brigaders? Knights sound too schoolboyish?" Glasford attempted to step inside the entrance but Steam restrained him.

"Doan talk shit," Steam said. Fish didn't like a man who had such a smile, a smile that let you know you were underfoot and easily squashed. He moved back on the sidewalk, from distaste as well as for his own protection.

"Put a dollah in my hand quick." The smile was fading.

"What happened, Steam?" Glasford protested. "I nevah pay a dollah before."

For a second Steam glared at Glasford's hand on his shoulder. "Dis a new policy to keep away a cheap, mouthy niggah such as you," he said. Glasford's eyes shrunk and locked into Steam's, so he couldn't see, as Fish did, the bouncer reach with his free hand behind his back and pull a gun from his belt. He laughed as he slid it up the outside of Glasford's pants, into his groin. Glasford didn't have to look down to know what Steam was pressing into him. The pistol was small, almost nothing, in Steam's massive hand.

"Fish," Glasford said coolly, "bring a dollah."

Without knowing the seriousness of Steam's threat, Fish had no choice but to pass over a bill from his pocket and then

—he had not expected this—another for himself. The gun was lowered and tucked away. Steam's posture flaunted his disregard for danger, his amusement with his own power, as if he were trying to squeeze himself up to beast-size.

"So, Glahsford," he said. "How come it's so long since I see you? How Momma Smallhorne keepin?"

Fish was outraged. "Mahn, what kind of a fool are *you?*" he demanded of Steam. The doorman blinked and grinned benevolently, finished with his big joke and now oblivious to any ill feelings he had created.

"Doan be so touchy," he chided as Fish and Glasford, who was now laughing nervously at the game Steam had played, passed by him through the entrance into the shiny fluorescent oasis of the Ethiope—*E-T-OPE.* The vibrations of the crushing music were like the pressures of rough water against Fish's body, the invisible surging of the bass guitar, the swift tugs of the high notes, then a sucking release as the music stopped and a deejay searched for another record.

"Dey fix dis place up nice since I last come," Glasford observed.

On the plywood and concrete walls, shimmering under the electric voodoo of black lights, were unfinished murals of lions' heads and serpents, naked women and seven-spired marijuana leaves, demons and tribal warriors, and everywhere, even on the floor, the three-bar cake of primary colors—red, yellow, green—of the flag of Ethiopia. Some of the images were crude, some elegant, some elaborate or simple. Apparently, customers were free to add to the art as they wished. Cans of Day-Glo spray paint were abundant along the walls.

"Beautiful inspiration," Glasford said. He penetrated the crowd and Fish rejoined him minutes later at the bar. Once again the music had detonated. Fish stared at the clothes of the dancers that glistened, pale sheets of flashes like phosphorus churning at night in the sea.

"Buy me a beer," Glasford yelled to him.

"Look, slow down wit dis revolution. It costin me dearly."

Glasford seemed to hear only the one sweet word he was operating off of. "Dis beast too big to confront straight on," he said. "Its heart too hard fah weapons to pierce. We must take bite by bite ahnd cripple it so. Zimbabwe take a bite. Cuba take a bite. Nicaragua take one, too. Soon a new world will grow on de ruins of Babylon."

"Um hmm," Fish snorted. "I tell you, daht Steam is de first guy I lock up in dis new world."

Glasford acted surprised. "What! No, he's a good fellah. He knows how to handle heself."

The bartender brought them bottles of stout which Fish, when he heard the price, paid for reluctantly. Glasford slumped forward into the music in a trance. A drunken woman, clutching a can of spray paint in one hand, a drink in the other, bumped into Fish. Without apologizing, she had him hold her glass, and Fish watched suspiciously as the woman bent down, kicked off her sandals and sprayed them a blazing green.

"Girl, you crazy?" Fish said.

"Me?" she answered seductively, looking him up and down. "How you know *what* I am?"

Fish's natural response to women was to be flirtatious. He felt he was drawing her into his charm when Glasford interfered.

"Here now, Fish," he remarked. "Doan distract youself wit dis womahn. Lissen to de music."

As far as Fish was concerned, this was bad advice. He turned back to the woman, but she was brusquely removed from his side by a scowling fellow with eyes like small blue light bulbs in a tarry face. Before the man could drag her back to the dance floor, she thrust her can of spray paint into Fish's hand.

"Discipline you mind to de music." Glasford regarded him fretfully and continued. "Lissen to dese prophets ahnd doan be foolish."

"I hear dis sound ahll de time."

"Yes, but you doan lissen, Fish mahn. You keepin a message from youself."

Because he didn't understand what Glasford wanted from him, and because he was irritated that his friend could talk so big and behave so small, Fish wandered away, surveying the images and slogans on the walls. He looked at the paintings, at the can of spray paint in his hand, and began spraying, first a tentative line, then a curve that sagged from both end points, next a perpendicular line rising from the first, then the sweep of a sail, until he had outlined the catboat built with his own sweat. The way it shone so mightily in the dark pleased him. Since the spray can was only good for broad, bold strokes, he signed the name of the boat, *God's Bread,* in the sky above the mast, so that another fisherman would know it was his. Then, under a squiggle of waves, he sprayed ugly sharks and pretty fishes. When he stood back to appraise his work, Glasford was there.

"Daht's a nice picture. Look, cahn you buy me a next beer?"

"No."

"How you mean *no?* We is bruddahs. We look out for each oddah."

"Dis rich place take ahll me money."

"Ya know, Fish, dis a very sad country if two good men such as we cahnt drink ahnd eat as we need."

"Daht's true."

Glasford took the can of paint from Fish. He shook it violently and began to spray slogans along the wall, disregarding the work of other painters.

Black Power!!!

Babylon Finish!!! He ran out of paint on the hook of the *F* but soon found a fresh can.

More work for people!!!

"Glahsford, if it's work you want, come wit me in de boat."

"Doan talk foolish, mahn. You missin de point."

Fish didn't see the point. Instead, he was bored.

But Glasford had inspired himself. "Okay, let's go," he or-

dered. "I cahnt hold meself back now. I ready to ahk-tivate."
He marched toward the exit, gripping two cans of spray paint
as if they were pistols and he were a desperado. Without much
hurry, Fish trailed after him.

Fish never came to town much at night. Once he came for
medicine for one of his babies, once for a cockfight, several
times to play poker with an old uncle and his cronies. But
generally Fish had no business in Georgetown and no interest
in its activities, designed more for foreigners than for the people of the island.

Glasford armed Fish with the second spray can and led him
up the alleys, through the streets and across the promenades,
commanding *Revolution, Revolution,* in his raw, heroic voice.
The fellows out and about stared, turned away smirking, or
raised their fists in solidarity, observing Glasford painting the
slogan *Black Power* in pink paint on the walls and windows of
Georgetown.

Eventually Fish said, "Here, Glahsford, tell me someting.
How you writin *Black Power* so? You tink Halston ahnd dem
fellahs in Parliment is pink like de words you sprayin?"

"No, no, Fish. You doan catch de music, mahn. *Black* signi-
ficates de Holy Jah, ahnd *Power* symbolize his lovin sword of
vengeance. You see now? I must only write dese expressions
to set dis message trew de blind eyes of de Ministers of Corruption."

Fish wondered if Glasford knew what he was talking about.
He himself had no message to deliver to anybody, so alongside
each incident of Glasford's work he would write the wobbly
name of one of the women he loved: Margareet, Rita, Alvina.

They had infiltrated the city to its core: the hotels, the
casinos, the government houses. As they sprayed their paint
freely on the perimeter wall that enclosed one of the popular
gambling resorts, Glasford explained his forthcoming strategy
to Fish. They would bust into the casino, he said, and grab the
wealthiest white bitch in sight. They would hold her for ran-

som, and they would demand from the slaves at Government House a plane to fly them to Havana. Once they were in Cuba, they would train with Castro's freedom fighters until—

"Doan stop on my account."

Fish looked over his shoulder. There, his legs spread out in a military stance, a nightstick clenched firmly in both hands, was a cop. Fish smiled extravagantly in an attempt to minimize any notion the cop might have that Fish was a threat to anybody.

"I say, gentlemen, doan stop on my account wit dis beautification program."

Glasford was just turning to acknowledge the man's presence when the cop struck them both—*tunk tunk*—so quickly with the nightstick that Fish had to think about what had happened before he could recognize the pain of the blow on his elbow.

"I say *doan stop.*"

"Mahn, what de hell." Fish raised his arms for protection. Glasford was not intimidated. Before he could be stopped, his can of spray paint was level with the policeman's nose.

"You ugly bitch," Glasford snarled. In an instant the cop's round black face blossomed pink. "Dere, you mudhead. Now you a pretty pink-face boy in truth."

Fish was stunned, thrilled. His knees shook. Glasford was finally getting somewhere, behaving such a way to this bigshot, letting him know how people were tired of cops all the time molesting a fellow who wasn't bothering a soul.

"Run, Fish. Fly."

Glasford threw his can at the policeman but missed. The two friends raced halfway down the block before they heard the muffled pops of a handgun behind them. They turned a corner, following the high wall studded with broken glass along its top, turned another corner, then slowed cautiously as they approached the bright entrance to the resort's compound. A guard in a flamboyant colonial costume narrowed his eyes at them.

"We has a message fah dem fellahs in de band," Glasford explained loudly, out of breath. "We comin right back."

"Wait a minute, you."

"Get out of me way," Fish yelled, shoving the guy aside. He was suddenly furious. The man might have the power to prevent his escape. The cop back on the street might beat him and lock him up. How easy it was for a quiet fisherman such as he to so quickly become an outlaw.

They sprinted down the drive and across the lawn to get behind the huge glittering block of the hotel. Then they could cut down toward the bayshore which Fish knew would lead them into the darkness and safety of the harbor. He looked beside him at Glasford, legs and arms pumping frantically. He would never have guessed this lazy guy could run so fast.

Fish was seething with militancy. Dis water rough but I cahn mahnage, he thought. As if he were in a movie, music—the sort of music Glasford was always barking about—began a crescendo that soon enveloped them. They poked through a tall hedge of hibiscus into what surely must be Babylon. The lawn was dazzling with party lights and torches. White folks, hundreds of them, jerked about like land crabs to the din of the reggae being cast at them by five arrogant-looking musicians on a raised platform. Native servants in tuxedos, their hands gloved in white cotton, delivered drinks and food on silver trays throughout the crowd. At the end of the lawn, toward the darkness of the sea, a goat was roasting slowly over an open-pit barbecue.

"Keep runnin. Doan stop." He glanced at Glasford and nodded fiercely. This was not an environment they could lose themselves in.

After his recent persecution, Fish loathed the gay scene he found himself in the midst of and wanted to mar it somehow. He thought he was feeling for the first time the brotherhood of Glasford's emotions, the new community of spirit that the music prophesied, the spirit and its rage. They pushed their way rudely through the dancers, deaf to the protests and shallow threats, but Fish was not blind to the fear their presence sponsored. At the shoreside fringe of the crowd, Fish's passion boiled up into a wicked impulse, and the wickedness made him laugh, at least to himself, and his laughter frightened him but he could not stop. He raised the canister of spray paint gripped tightly in his hand all the time they had been running.

"Look out. Look out. Get away," he shouted. "Is a bomb I have."

There were a few uncertain screams from women. As the news swept through the crowd, the dancing stopped although the music didn't. People struggled to back off from where Fish stood. Fish watched them move away, fascinated by how readily they responded to him. He shook the empty spray can vigorously and pitched it into the barbecue pit. Glasford had halted to hear his proclamation, frozen with his mouth wide open.

"Holy Christ, Fish. What de hell craziness is dis?"

Most people had abandoned the dance patio and were regrouping near the casino's doors, watching Fish to see what would happen next. The lawn around the roasting goat was clear. The aerosol can exploded with a noise like a truck backfire, scattering the coals of the barbecue pit out a few yards as a cloud of embers ballooned into the atmosphere. Fish watched the red sparks swell up, for an instant more radiant than the stars, and felt a small sadness in himself, as if he belonged to another world and had just painted a slogan that nobody could read.

Glasford whooped victoriously. "De Black Knights strike," he said.

They ran along the shore through the shadows of a grove of Australian pines. They kept going to where the lights began again near the harbor, the two of them loping between the few cars on the docks, crouching unnecessarily until they were positive no one followed. Finally they walked out bravely into the open, down along the pier toward the public anchorage where the yachts and sailing ships and some sport fishing boats tied up.

"We need money," Glasford stated. Fish could only sigh. He was weary and wanted the comfort of Althea.

"A hungry mahn must satisfy himself."

"Daht's true."

They proceeded aimlessly down the pier. It was late but the anchorage was filled with boat sounds: rigging slapping against masts, bilge pumps switching on automatically and splattering oily water into the bay, the creaking strain of anchor lines. Not many lighted portholes though. No people around. Fish was ready to reverse direction and start home when Glasford leapt quietly from the wooden pier onto the deck of a sailboat. He snuck along the cabin and disappeared into the cockpit. Fish heard him trying to force the cabin door and felt his loyalties to Glasford begin to split. Fish liked boat people. No matter how well outfitted they were, their good grace was always a question of their courage and their luck. Pirate and prince were often equal, their brotherhood instinctive, on the sea. He wished Glasford had shared a day of fishing with him. An island man shouldn't forsake the sea.

Glasford hopped back to the pier. "Shut up tight," he whispered.

"Glahsford—"

"Come, come." He darted onto another boat but a dog began barking from below deck, and a light flicked on. Fish was off the pier by the time Glasford caught up with him. They walked along the city wharf. There was nothing Fish wanted to say. The triumph at the casino already seemed the secondhand boast of a street hooligan.

They came to the end of the quay. There were no lamp posts here and the air smelled fresher. A piece of moon had appeared over the eastern waters and hung in the sky like a fishscale. Glasford was still acting sneaky.

"*Psssss.* Fish, look." Glasford held a finger to his lips to forewarn silence.

From the cleats on the quay two nylon lines ran over the edge and down toward the blackness of the water. To see what was below, Fish had to step up next to Glasford. At first glance the motorboat was nothing unordinary. Big but not so big, no cabin, nice size engine pulled up and locked. It didn't take so much to buy a boat like this one—lots of fellows had them.

What did surprise Fish was seeing on the exposed flooring of the boat two twisted, humped piles of, what—sheets or light blankets—a tennis-shoed foot connected to a white ankle protruding out from one pile, the round featureless shapes of heads under the bedding, shrouded from mosquitoes and the distant lights of the pier. Toward the stern, placed flat near one of the sleepers, was a large suitcase. If the people on the boat were tourists they were a type Fish had never encountered before. Most visitors to Georgetown were decidedly less adventurous than this.

He didn't have to see Glasford's face to know what was on his mind. Fish felt ambivalent but vaguely curious again, noting how easy it was for Glasford to exploit the vulnerability of the sleepers, as if Glasford were a ghost capable of pranks but not of harm. Sitting himself on the edge of the wharf, extending his legs carefully until they rested on the motorboat's gunnel, Glasford seemed so adept with the stealth of his movements that Fish realized his friend had a talent for the act he was performing.

Glasford put his hand on the back of the pilot's seat to steady himself, stretching until his other fingers found the handle of the suitcase. He tried to ease the suitcase up noiselessly, but his position and the slight rolling of the boat made the task impossible. A scraping noise moved through Fish's blood. Glasford stopped in slow motion as if he were underwater. But then he snatched the suitcase up and braced himself to toss it over to the quay. As Glasford corrected his balance, Fish saw a white man's head pop wildly out from under the blankets, saw the shock pass into the muscles of the man's face, and then grimness and determination engage as the man bolted upright and lunged at Glasford from behind. Glasford's mouth dropped in astonishment. A spontaneous pose of innocence and victimization filled his expression. This not-guilty plea would have made Fish crack up if at that moment the suitcase hadn't slammed into his shins and knocked him backward. He gaped down at its plaid surface, not knowing why it was there.

"Take it up, Fish. Run!"

Glasford's voice was cut off by dread and struggle. The white man wrestled with him. Through the force of his effort, the two men heaved themselves into the water. Fish was about to turn and flee but he paused just long enough to witness the other sleeper appear from undercover. A woman. She was pretty in the sort of bare, hard way white women were. The confusion on her face intrigued him. He wanted to stay and look at her but with the immunity he had felt when she was still sleeping. Her hands desperately patted through her blankets until they discovered a pair of eyeglasses. With her sight came a flush of horror. Fish grabbed the heavy suitcase and started running.

He hadn't taken more than ten quick steps before the woman began to weep and call after him in a wet voice.

"Please come back. Please. Oh, dear God, you've taken everything I own."

Fish kept going but he couldn't run fast enough to get out of range of the despair in her voice.

"Please, please," she wailed. "All that's in that bag is our clothes."

Each of her sobs seemed to add more weight to his feet. What the hell was he doing on this dock, with this suitcase in his hand, running away from a helpless woman who was miserable on his account while Glasford and a white man were thrashing each other in the bay? Fish didn't have much sympathy for the troubles of other people—his own were enough for him—but he was always alert to the needs of a woman. He slowed down and then stopped altogether, unable to work his legs.

Once stopped, he didn't know what he should do. He remained motionless, the suitcase on the street, as if he were waiting for a bus. Glasford finally hoisted himself out of the water, a dark fearsome sea-thing flopping onto the quay. He spotted Fish and staggered forward, gasping and spitting, water squishing around in his leather shoes.

"Daht womahn cryin a big tragedy, Glahsford. How cahn we go on so?"

"He try to kill me!" Glasford shrieked. Fish had never heard Glasford sound this offended. He stood there pounding water from his ears. "She trickin you, boy," he argued angrily. "Ahll dese rich people does cry a storm when dey lose a penny."

Fish wasn't prepared to discuss the matter any further. He spun on his heels, lifting the suitcase, and walked back to the dock. By now the white man had hauled himself back into the boat, looking blood-wild as Fish returned the suitcase to him. Once he had his property back, the mistrust went from his face and he shook his head in wonder. He was younger than Fish and his longish hair stuck to his cheeks and forehead.

"Brother," he said, "you are twice crazy. What if I had a gun? You could've gotten killed, a decent guy like you. You'd be dead right now. I'd damn sure do it, too."

Fish was ashamed by the truth of what the fellow was saying. Robbery without a gun in such circumstances was ignorant. To avoid the judgment of the man, he looked at the woman, her eyes offering gratitude and a forthright curiosity that somehow made him feel proud and countered what the man had said. Maybe there was a better reason for bringing the suitcase back but Fish had no appetite to search for it. The world had become melancholic and too romantic.

Glasford swaggered up, tough and unrepentant, once there was no obvious danger in doing so. The white man stared at him and trembled while he spoke, releasing the last of his anger and fear. "I know how hard it is for you people in the islands." He gritted his teeth, pausing to decide, perhaps, what to say next or how to say it. He shook water from his sodden hair and combed confidence back through it with his hands. "You sons of bitches are going to get killed, though, if you keep doing this." The woman, swaddled in a blanket below the waist, held out a towel to her companion, but when he bent to take it she would not let go until she had persuaded him of something. Fish strained to listen but could not make sense of her whispering.

"Look," the guy continued when she was finished. He dug into his soaked pants. "Here's twenty bucks, you know, for bringing the bag back." He shrugged unhappily. "Maybe it will help you stay smart. Who knows."

Fish had no interest in the money but Glasford snatched the bill from the white man as soon as the fellow's hand came out of his pocket.

"You lucky dis time," Glasford said to the man below him in the boat.

There were no cars on the road. Not even a stray donkey they could hijack into service. Glasford said he wanted to wait for the ride he believed would come but he caught up with Fish when Fish went ahead without him, trekking the long miles back to Momma Smallhorne's. She was already up when they arrived at dawn, a fire sparking in her cookshed, baking soda bread and warming yesterday's coffee.

"I suppose you hear by now," the old woman clucked at them. "I just receive de news meself. Scamps blow up Richmond Park. Is dead white people everywhere. Dey place a bomb in a poor billy goat. Oh, Lahd, when dis wickedness goin stop?"

Momma seemed happy to have a big story to work with. Fish didn't want to spoil it for her so soon by telling her the true account. They settled themselves gratefully into Momma's two shaky chairs and had her bring a pint bottle of rum and biscuits. Glasford poured and drank and appeared revitalized, though his eyes looked slack.

Fish's fatigue left him helpless to prevent the sadness pooling in his outlook for the day. He was sure that the woman in the motorboat would have liked him if only she knew what sort of man he was, that he was a man who had determined truths in his life and tried to live by them. *Don't take from me what I wouldn't take from you.* That's what she had cried to him. It struck a nerve, even if he couldn't be certain that she indeed lived that way herself.

"Fish, drink up, you fallin behind," Glasford said. "What, you sleepy? A guy like you daht blows up white people?" It was a joke but no light came into Glasford's eyes to support it. Fish knew he was being mocked.

Fish's bed was three minutes down the road and he wanted it, but his mind was carrying on against his will and would allow him no peace. Yes, it was true in many ways that he and the people around him were, as Glasford had said, like rocks on the bottom of the sea. What gave a man cause to rise up, Fish didn't know. Glasford on the gallows, Glasford in a limousine, surrounded by flags and personal bodyguards and beautiful women. How much did it matter? A rock had lost its gravity and was lifting toward the surface. Fish could only see the emptiness left by its passage.

Glasford was starting his talk again. Next time, he was saying, we get a gun.

—For Tay and Linda Maltsberger

Hot Day on the Gold Coast

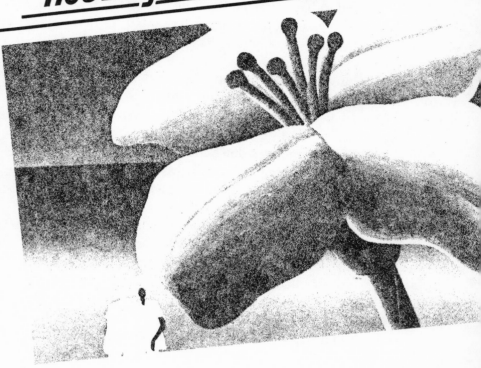

It's steamy hot and the radio's loud. Fifties stuff: *shoop shoop, dee doo, waa-oo, my babee left me.* I once knew the words and sang along in a wine-cooled voice. The blues and the bop dribble my heart between them like a basketball. Here's a ballad of love. Here love is lost and much missed. A saxophone player squirts his high-rising juice out of the box.

The house is blistered white, with gables and gingerbreadish scrollwork milled by some Victorian craftsman gone daftly baroque. It is jungled-up and bug-eaten and can't be seen from the street, a residence that offers no clue to my uptown breeding. We have plenty of privacy here.

The sun has hopped off the ocean and nuzzles through the canopy of ficus leaves to brighten our breakfast on the porch stoop. For me a sweet, stringy mango and a domestic beer suffice, while Tericka picks through a bowl of protein capsules and vitamins. The kid rolls around on a blanket in the grass with a bottle in her mouth.

"Tericka," I say.

"Yes?" she says.

"I feel pretty good."

Tericka was born and raised in Titusville, Florida, the Space Coast. She is nineteen, has a tattoo and a baby. Not my baby. The father's an astronaut but I'm not supposed to know which one. She receives love letters on NASA stationery signed *Ace, Forever.* I lie awake at night counting nose cones like silver sheep. Our man must be one of the newly chosen, still nameless and faceless to the world at large, a fresh Faustian hero in waiting. Tericka won't say; it's been classified. Oh, him, she says dismissively, and smiles wide. When a flame is struck his child displays mothlike tendencies.

The tattoo is of a small rocketship, orbiting her left breast.

We sit side by side on the top step. Elbows on her knees, Tericka's orange bikini top gulps air and my attention is fixed there. On a morning as pleasant as this, I can't take my eyes from it—the rocket, the trace of orbitry, the round atmosphere where perhaps gravity grows, the distant planet, darkish red and volcanic. For the moment all I can think of is that she is very proud of her motherly tits. These are tits like tropical mountains. The Daughters of Oahu. The Pitons of St. Lucia. (I prefer this imagery to the celestial surfaces.) These are breasts that hold no grudge against the natural world.

My own anatomy suggests the need for tuning. The stomach sags, the spine wants to bend, the lungs do penance for various sins. My hips are still very firm and boyish, I think, but there has been much amiss in this temple of flesh for one year too many. The soul has made contingency plans in case of sudden emergency. For my sake and for Tericka's peace of mind I voice a resolution, which as a gentleman I will stick by.

I will jog.

HOT DAY ON THE GOLD COAST

"Oh, Lord," she snorts. "Starting when?"

"Starting now."

Her tone has kicked a small dent in my vanity, but given further reason to honor the commitment to tighten the belly and build the biceps. Flood the brain with baptismal oxygen, add to the expectancy of life.

"You're not going to run in your underwear, are you?"

Already I am doing preliminary exercises to alert unused musculature. I touch the toes, stretch the hams. Perhaps I should fall on my knees and pray for safe passage. "Of course," I answer with the haughtiness of a pro. "Everybody does."

"Oh no, they don't," she says. "You'll flop out the way those boxers are cut. Let me get you your bathing suit."

"No," I say. "These colors just beg for speed." My shorts are sky-blue with a trim of fiery red.

"I'd better get you a safety pin, then."

I do not protest since she has considerable knowledge of the pitch and yaw of various missilery. She fastens my un-stitched fly and gently hefts my thinly protected balls.

"Don't hurt yourself, Weber," she warns.

"I will be a better man for all this," I tell her.

"You'll be a better man if you can think of a less boring way to keep in shape."

"Ah, Tericka," I admonish her. "This sport has swept the nation. Millions of citizens can't be wrong."

"Yes, they can," she says firmly. "You'll find out."

I crouch in starting position. She opens the front gate for me and I fly past her under the arch of yellow allamanda, out of our palmed and fruited shady seclusion and on to the street. I turn down the avenue headed east, toward the coast where I shall take a northward route to the Palm Beaches. The sun is all over me and gee it's hot. The pavement burns through the thin soles of my tennis shoes but I am too much in motion to turn back. Movement and pace are the key now. Cramps threaten the instep but I sprint onward.

The seedy residential blocks of Lake Worth disappear behind me. The voices of many nationalities sweep out of the doorways of pastel bungalows. Finnish. German. French-Canadian. Cuban Spanish. Colombian Spanish. Jamaican. The drawling, spitting, tongue-flopping gobbles of indigenous Floridian humanoids. *Whoim da fuckhell smayshup mah baym-boo bong I'll killem!* Old people everywhere. Dangerous drifters by the dozens. Bohemians and bikers and the lumpenproletariat enjoying themselves in the sun.

Past the all-night shuffleboard courts, lights blink and the barrier tilts down across the railroad tracks. The best I can do is run in place, high-stepping like a halfback, while the engineer spitefully blasts the locomotive's horn. The noise is ferocious. The ground shakes, rumbling under the weight of orange juice being rushed north. I am anxious to be on my way. Beside me, an older woman with sun-wrinkled face and hair white-blond glares at me from behind the wheel of her stupendously long car. The window slides down electrically and she speaks to me words I cannot hear over the roar of the boxcars.

"What?" I shout, beginning to huff just slightly.

She shakes her head impatiently and purses her lips. I learned long ago to ignore the wealthy matrons of the land until introduced by someone trustworthy, because they are righteous, narrow-minded, and sometimes cruel. The caboose thunders by and leaves behind a rare moment of silence, soon violated by the driver.

"Young man, I know you won't mind me telling you this, but you should be in jail." Her voice is refined but conversational. She only wants to assure me that I belong somewhere.

"Thank you," I say, praying for the guard to rise so I can get away from such an awful person.

"You're quite welcome."

There is a note of satisfaction in her voice. I believe I have impressed her with my unexpected gentility. The window returns, the lights cease flashing, the road is clear. The car flows forward with the current of traffic, an unmasted clipper ship, drifting I hope toward some catastrophe with the blessings of my middle finger.

On the flats of my toes, I weave a way through gangs of

consumers in the downtown district. Everyone is sunburned, sundressed, or Bermuda-shorted. Pink faces of *turistas* bob up and down on a sea of fluorescent polyester. I hurdle the occasional poodle that barks into my path, and jump out of the way of roller skaters. Past the butcher, the baker, and the adult bookstore. One entire block smells of spices and fresh coffee. The sidewalk opens up after La Scala Ristorante and my stride becomes less restrained, full of confidence. Bryant Park is empty except for a lone gull feeder and a quiet audience of Royal palms. The bridge across the intracoastal is the first station of my itinerary, and I come on to it feeling that I have miles and miles left in me. Maybe I'm not so bad off after all.

The water below is aquamarine and sparkling. Along the railing all the grandfathers are lined up fishing and I love the tranquil sight of them. Perhaps the best thing my old man ever did for me when I was a kid was take me with him to the jetties and teach me the finer points of cast and reel, the subtle tricks of bait and lure. Until he struck it rich, purchased a yacht, and forgot about me. Months later, my mother refreshed his memory during the course of litigation.

These fellows here are landmarks, as consistent as the warm weather, patient, gentle sportsmen until the big one strikes. I know most of them from my walks to and from the beach with Tericka and child. All of them turn to see what they have never seen before.

"What's the hurry, Weber?"

"Running in this heat? You should be so lucky you don't drop dead."

"Shame. Put some pants on."

Sam, a retired driveway salesman from upstate New York, trots alongside me for a moment. "A school of blues, Weber," he says. "Right underneath me, hitting on anything. Rubin caught one with a candy wrapper on his hook. And me, right there. I didn't getta one, I'm telling you. Maybe I shoulda said a Hail Mary or something. Holy cow, look at that. Watch out!"

Directly ahead of us the aging mass of Guido the Gorilla, a

former soccer player for the national team of Italy, blocks my route. His pole is bent double and he has stepped back almost into the highway to struggle with it. The nylon line slashes left and right. His face sweats with ecstasy.

"Yank him up! Yank him up!" Sam cries. "It's a record-breaker!"

I sidestep behind Guido off the curb just as he gives his pole a tremendous jerk. The rod nearly slices my ear off as it whips by and is snapped in two by an oncoming car, popping out a headlight with a bang. But the force of Guido's effort has saved his catch. A huge, banquet-sized fish sails across the railing of the bridge. It writhes through the air like a gleaming piece of shrapnel, tail twisting and evil-eyed. Over the head of Guido and into traffic, it bounces off the hood of one car which will now need repair. Airborne again, the fish smashes through the window of a delivery van which keeps going after severe swerving. Chased by Guido the Gorilla, caterwauling down the road, retired but not to be cheated. That Guido's in good shape for a man his age.

Over my shoulder, I see that Sam has thrown his arms into the air to exalt his recent vision of the almighty Pisces. "Wow!" he shouts hoarsely. "Weber, wait, where are you going? Come back."

Where I am going I think is obvious, so there's nothing to say. Besides, I feel a bit knackered and at this point it is essential not to disrupt the breathing pattern.

"Weber, come back. It's against the law."

But by now I am on the drawbridge section of the span, the highest point on the bridge. To the left and right the back bay separates the mainland from the barrier island, a skinny piece of real estate known as the Palm Beaches, a place known to the more discriminating European families as the only new world locale with acceptable standards. It is true that certain Americans have declared their aristocracy here.

From my vantage point, the ocean is in view, glittering through the palms and Australian pines. The sight of the sea

HOT DAY ON THE GOLD COAST

invigorates me like no other, my blood jumps from the smell of its primordial salt. Out there beyond the steely horizon is everything else in the world. Although my lungs hurt, there is in me a desire to run forever. I suppose I have encountered that zone in all sports where the metabolic interfaces with the *mysterium tremendum*. A few of my steps fall through time and for an instant I am eternal. Even though the police car slowly tailing me reinforces the uncertainty of my well-being that I think Sam was hinting at.

On the downslope to dry land, the cruiser stalks me like a barracuda. Something is of course wrong but I'll be damned if I know what it is. Out of the corner of my eye I check the immaculate blue uniform of the driver, his humorless mouth, the angry lines of his cheekbones, the eyes entombed in black sunglasses. In a paradise of tanned bodies and bleached hair, his face is unsunned. Trepidation adds a little boost to my stride. As an entrepreneur involved in a very lucrative importation, a business that has in fact kept the Gold Coast golden, neither I nor my banker can afford to talk to this man.

As I leave the bridge my first footfall is acknowledged by the shriek of sirens. There is an amplified rustle, and then a tinny, rasping voice which addresses me publicly. "All right, sport. Hold it right there."

I don't even look at him but keep running obstinately across A1A, the coastal highway, and into Casino Park where the one-way drive loops up around the parking area, then back along the beach, past the pier and the shops, and exits again where I enter. Because the lane is filled with cars headed out, the police car cannot follow me. The cruiser accelerates into the circular drive that will eventually bring him back to me, but even with lights spinning he is slowed by the ubiquitous winter traffic. Not running but racing, I head for the pier to lose myself in the crowd out there. I am panting out of control by the time my feet touch the first brown boards. The wood feels soft and loamy after the gravel in the street. The smell of creosote is as snappy as spirits of ammonia. I am safe among the fishermen but in need of counsel.

I keep moving, trying to regain control of my lungs. Hyper-ventilation helps restore a dreamy sense of proportion to the day. There must be hundreds of anglers out here elbowing each other for a spot along the rail. Down below the ocean is transparent; trash sways back and forth on the bottom.

In a white *guayabera,* linen pants and a Panama hat, my friend Bert stands pensively down at the end of the pier, six lines out into deep water. He has years of seniority in this prime spot. Out here on the pier from seven to ten every morn-ing, Bert has become an expert on the weather, salt-water fish-ing, human behavior, pipe tobacco, and smuggling. He has invested heavily into many local operations. He owns three banks. A courier brings him daily market reports at nine with coffee and croissants. He is my banker and I rely on him. Once again I need his advice.

"Bert," I say.

Bert does not turn around but remains leaning over the pier railing, examining the water.

"Weber, is that you? Why are you gasping? Even if it isn't you, be quiet. There's a cobia down there. I can feel him, I know what he's thinking. He's playing with me, Weber."

I have tried not to hear the siren as it circled the drive, but now the wail is unavoidable. The sound approaches the pier entrance and then stops.

"I think the police are after me," I whisper.

Bert wants to know why.

"I don't know why," I answer, my voice escalating. "Every-thing's airtight, Bert. I have the happiest people in the world working for me. I don't get it. Here I am out jogging and I get a tail on me and then bam, as soon as I set foot on A1A he gooses the siren. Bert?"

Reluctantly, Bert stops watching the water and turns to look at me with his calm, green eyes. He is a little man, thin, and mostly bald. His face is smooth and benign, strangely un-weathered, boyish and intelligent. A real charmer, a sweetheart —all the trademarks of a successful crook. He gives me the once-over and shakes his head compassionately. I am instantly on my guard. Bert's compassion in this sequence is usually a prelude to disaster.

"What is it, Bert? What have I done?"

He sucks professorily on his burl pipe. "Weber," he says. "You remember Jimmy Jamaica, don't you? He got in on the ground floor back in the sixties. Set it up perfectly. Perfectly. Took care of everybody, never stepped on toes. One day he forgot to pay for a pack of Lifesavers in the drugstore. Walked out with them in his hand and they grabbed him. He panicked. One thing led to another and that was that. Remember that fellow named Sundown from Gainesville? He could wheel and deal with the best of them but he lost everything because he shot his neighbor's dog when it wouldn't stop yapping. Alfredo the Ass down in Coconut Grove? Same thing. Same damn thing.

"Carelessness, Weber. People forget that a good business-man is one hundred percent business, no matter what he's doing."

"For God's sake, Bert," I plead. "I was only trying to stay healthy."

"Of course, Weber. Of course. And from the looks of that belly of yours I'd say you have the right idea. Good for you, Weber. Discipline is important."

"Bert, there he is.

"Who? Ah, you mean your officer. There he is, all right."

"Bert?" I am ready to grab Bert and shake the serenity out of him.

"My assumption is, Weber, that this guy wants to arrest you for jogging without a shirt on, jogging on a north-south road, and jogging in what looks to be your underwear. All of these things are illegal in the Palm Beaches. I advise you to get the fuck away from me and jump. Call my secretary on Monday morning and let me know how things turned out. Good-bye, Weber."

I am overwhelmed by my responsibility. Jimmy Jamaica supported everybody in the Keys and kept a Third World econ-omy on its feet. Sundown pumped money into progressive political campaigns all over the country. After they locked up Alfredo the Ass, the sharks took over and people started getting killed. If I go down, Bert might end up with me, and if Bert goes, Statia goes, and golden dominoes are going to fall all over the place.

My knees are weakening. How did the structure wear so thin that the stock market would twitch if somebody got busted for jogging in Palm Beach? Perhaps this is the time to stand in full force and virtue. Give my attorneys something they can sink their teeth into. "Your honor, the bare chest of an athlete, we contend, is not unsightly. There is no more fundamental right than the right to feel good." Oh boy, am I in trouble. The cop is about fifty yards away and I can hear him blasting farts like a galloping horse.

"Jump where, Bert?"

He doesn't want to talk to me but he sees that I am not jumping so he mumbles to me out of the side of his mouth as he casually reels in one of his lines.

"Jump into the water, dummy. Swim out to the black cigarette laying off the reef with those fishing boats. Better hurry, Weber. Your friend is about ten steps behind you."

I am up on the railing poised like a cliff diver. Hands grab me by the waist and squeeze into me, trying to hold on. I try to pry the fingers back but they are gripping me with a maniac's resolve. I push off into space. The hands stay with me for about a second but then slip down and tear away. My impact with the water hurts, it knocks the breath out of me. I plunge deep, waiting for the release of gravity, and when it comes I feel in control again and kick slowly to the surface. Thirty feet above me there's the cop, waving my boxer shorts at me. Man, I wish Bert would get over there and talk him out of shooting me.

I am a man who rarely regrets his actions, but right now I'm a little disappointed with the way the morning has developed. My muscles ache, energy seems in short supply, the policeman may not stand for this sort of resistance, and here, from the surface of the ocean, that black cigarette looks miles away bouncing in the white-capped distance. What the hell, I tell myself. What the hell. I roll in the emerald water and breast-stroke eastward. Tericka, these strokes should be for you.

Like a seal, I duck under crashing waves and pop sleekly up in the calm foam of their passing. The tide is crawling away from land and I am riding its cushion like a victorious athlete raised on the hands of his teammates. It's best to forget about bullets spitting into the water around me, or Bert's big fish nipping off the piece of bait that's waving between my sore thighs. It's best just to stroke, pull, and kick ahead through the dazzling blue and concentrate on this new challenge.

I glide across dark clumps of turtle grass and out over fields of sand bright blue with refraction. At least here a half-mile from shore there is no one to intrude on one's autonomy. Beyond the reef, the fishing boats swing and jerk like white kites against their anchors. Mackerel must be running, dolphin migrating. The coral heads are mottled rose and amber beneath me. The surge is strong and I have about had it but still I frog-kick into deeper, more sinister water where death can flash up from infinity and take a big bite. The ominous black hull of the oceangoing powerboat lures me onward, my dark salvation.

On board the cigarette, two fellows are gauging my progress. One extends a long gaff out to me. I reach for the crook of the pole but it thrusts beyond my hand and twists to hook into the back of my neck. Maybe I am not wanted here. The violence in the motion stops at the surface of my skin. I cannot raise my head but gaze instead into the sheen of the black fiberglass and my reflection sliding by. The desperation of my image startles me absolutely cold. I didn't know, I murmur to myself. There is seaweed in my mustache. There is a familiar Cracker accent calling down from above.

"Webah, is that you?"

In my exhaustion, all I can think of is Chuck Berry. Maybelline? Honey, is that you?

"Webah, is that you?"

"Yes!" I scream it. My voice takes what juice I have left. "You tried to spear me!"

"Now, Webah, don't be like that. I didn't know that was you."

A wave slaps me and my mouth fills with salty water. I sputter and cough and begin to drift away from the boat. A strong hand locks into my hair but I feel no pain. A rope is somehow looped under my arms and I am hauled up over the gunnel and flipped on deck. I land sprawling next to a colossal blue marlin, easily five times my size. Its eye is as big as my fist. Blood has puddled around the torn beak.

"Goddamn, Webah. You're naked, boy."

I can say nothing, only sympathize with the fish. Leo Stubbs, the best diesel mechanic on the Gold Coast and a former employee of mine, crouches down beside me and helps me to sit up.

"Webah," he says. "I know there ain't no sense in askin' what the hell you doin' bare-assed a mile offshore. Things happen to workin' men. But Webah, my man here and me's on a business trip, ya know, and this is my man's boat, and he wants you to catch your breath and leave."

"Leave to go where, Leo?"

Leo suffers the telling of his message. Loyalty and friendship are not in excess in Leo's life, but here they have crossed tracks. His weather-eaten eyes appeal to me for understanding and he lowers his voice.

"Come on, Webah. My man the captain here is a fuckin' renegade, a regular shitball Ernest Hemingway. You won't believe what he done. Webah, I'm sorry I don't have time to be more hospitable, but you gonna have to go over the side and swim to that drift boat passin' by. Let's get together tomorrow and have us a clambake or somethin', drink some ten dollah bourbon."

I look at Leo's man to try to get a feeling for the situation. He is up in the bow lackadaisically casting a silver spoon over the reef. He's dressed in a white cotton T-shirt and seersucker pants, unstained by salt or sweat. His face is bright red but clamped shut by wraparound shades and a stiff blue captain's hat. In his back hip pocket is a conspicuous bulge and anybody would know this is intentional, for there's more heat per capita in Miami and the Gold Coast than anywhere north of Bogota.

"Been fishing, eh?" I ask Leo.

"Oh, brother, have we ever. You said it," Leo says, narrowing his eyes.

"Square grouper, is it?" I ask. Square grouper is a very popular catch these days in south Florida. It stacks up neatly in the cargo hold and is the only fish I know of that stinks sweet.

"No, Webah. Wrong."

Leo has seen too much sunlight. He is a perpetual squinter. His hands, the hands of a marine mechanic, lead a rough and reckless life. They are everywhere scarred, the fingers crooked, the nails smashed off. They tell me Leo is the one man I would want with me on a boat, but he's a loner and won't stay put.

"Shit, Leo," I tell him. "We worked together, we survived a hurricane together. You even fell in love with my wife, didn't you, and now you're telling me—"

"I'm not lying, Webah."

I look at his hands, the course of the palms black with grease, and shake my head sadly.

"And Statia ain't your wife no more."

"Nobody takes a boat like this out fishing. You picked up the marlin at dockside in the Bahamas. Come on, Leo. This is me, Weber."

"No, Webah, you ain't gonna believe this. It's black gold we got. My man Captain Shitball here has himself forty-six Haitians down below sittin' on each other's feet. We picked them up in Freeport last night and each of them handed over six hundred bucks to the captain. I don't know where people like that get that kind of money."

Something is wrong here. A big boat like this one crosses the Gulf Stream in an hour, one thousand horsepower boiling the sea astern. Live cargo is off-loaded on the golden beaches in the dark morning hours. Leo and his man should have been at the night deposit window of their bank hours ago.

"Webah," Leo says, "my man here is insane. As soon as we're out of the harbor last night he rigs up a trawl line and sets it and we take it real slow 'cause we got time to kill. Then about twelve miles out the clothespin snaps off and the line rings through the reel. My man goes berserk. I tell him cut the fuckin' line and let's go. He pulls this runty piss-ant little pistol on me and says, 'No, I want the fish.' Well, hell, that big marlin swam us up to Abaco and then back down toward Eleuthera and this way and that way. At five this morning I could still see the lights on Bimini.

"Finally he lands the son of a bitch and struts around like a commandante. I turned the boat west and let her fly but by the time we got here the sun's up twenty degrees and we're down to the last sip of gas. Damn the man! Webah, this is the truth. We're just waitin' for nightfall."

This is not where I want to be. Nothing looks more suspicious to the Coast Guard than a cigarette, especially one this size, lying offshore all day long.

"Leo," I say, "give me a pair of pants or a bathing suit and I'll be on my way."

"Can't do that, Webah. Only got what I have on."

"Hell, give me your underpants then."

"Ain't wearin' any."

"What about the captain?"

"I'll ask."

My strength is returning. I am prepared for the swim to a nearby boat but I am, when possible, a man of standards myself, and would prefer not to impose my nakedness any further. I try a shaky push-up on the hot deck. Leo's conversation with his man is very short.

"Captain Shitball says go below and take what you need from off the cargo and then beat it. Come on, I'll show you the way."

I follow Leo's taut little body into the cockpit and down a ladder into a spotless, ultramodern galley. Beyond this there's only a bulkhead, teak from beam to beam, and Leo unlatches a door into the forward hold and opens it to the escaping darkness and the smell of poverty. I step through the passageway and can hear teeth chattering nervously, stomachs gurgling, one or two babies crying.

"Leo," I say, "this isn't the business for you."

Leo ignores me. My eyes adjust and I can make out the round, black faces framing the neon glow of eyes and teeth. The air is low on oxygen but satiated with hope. Several women giggle and I instinctively cover my genitals with folded hands.

"Welcome to America," I say.

"Izt Meeami?" a girl's voice sings.

"Oui oui," Leo answers, although it sounds like *whey whey.* "My mammy soon foof come-go yeah yeah, y'all dig that?"

The people nod their heads understandingly, joyously.

"Leo," I say, "you're a pig, telling these people you'd take them to Miami. Give me some money, man."

"What for?"

"I'm going to buy myself a pair of pants."

"Webah," he says impatiently, but I won't let him go on.

"Just lend me the money," I tell him, "and leave it at that."

"All I got is hundreds," he says, digging into his cutoffs. I pluck a bill from the tangled bundle he reveals.

"That'll do." I tuck the money into the shirt pocket of a man in front of me and motion for him to take off his pants. He gives me a nice smile and obliges. Most probably the captain prohibited his cargo from carrying luggage, so I am not surprised to see that the man has a second pair of short pants underneath his outer ones. I have enough foresight to ask him also for the Salvation Army suit jacket that matches the pants. I shake the man's hand and the deal is complete.

"Webah, you're crazy to give a hundred bucks to a nigrah that don't even speak English."

1 4 2

I don't want to argue with Leo. It was a discussion much like this one that lost me the best mechanic I know of on the water. (Webah, you're crazy to walk away from a woman like Statia.) I shrug and begin to step into my recently purchased trousers, blue serge circa Korean War era. Two things happen.

As if it had a nervous system for chills to run through, the boat gives a silent shake, a sequence of twitches, and then a roar crescendoes behind us. Like a horse rearing suddenly up, the bow of the boat rises, the stern punches into the water. My ankles are tied by the trousers I am struggling with and I pitch backward through the passageway and crash into the galley. Leo tumbles after me, banging his elbow into my mouth with such force that I want to cry. We are two grains of salt instantly buried by a rain of pepper. By the time I am able to breathe freely and move again, Leo has somehow clambered up on deck and now is back down in the galley, pushing Haitians out of the way and furiously searching the cupboards, throwing things around. He looks like a man who has just been electrocuted and enjoyed the volts.

"Leo!" I shout.

Leo has found a jar of instant coffee and from the way he's gulping the dry brown granules you'd think he had a cold beer in his hand.

"Lord, Lord, Lord," he says. "Marine patrol comin' outta Boynton inlet. Lights, siren, a big show. Shitball's borrowin' time."

Leo is grinning, he's having a good experience. My mouth, I realize, is bloody. My ribs feel cracked. Leo throws more condiments out off the shelves, finds a baby food jar with about a half-inch of powder in the bottom. He dumps its contents on a countertop and begins frantically chopping at the crystals with his buck knife.

"Wanna line, boy?" he asks, talking fast. "Fortify yourself for the ride. Come on now, blow summa this snow and grab a handful of vitamins there in that jar." He looks away from his project to nod toward a mason jar filled with a tropical flora of pills. In his haste he chops into the hump of his thumb. He jerks his hand away to keep the blood from spilling into the cocaine. He holds the deep gash up for me to inspect. His eyes are all squinty.

"How's that for a pain threshold, Webah? I don't feel a damn thing."

I take a pinch of the coke and rub it across my busted lips. Hoisting myself up the ladder, I reel through the hatchway into the cockpit, gripping desperately for any handhold that will keep me from catapulting out of the boat as we hop and skip over the ocean at tremendous speed. Captain S is at the wheel, as indifferent as any midweek commuter. I'll bet catching that marlin made the worms in his heart glow. The lights of law and order are shrinking far astern.

"How many horsepower you got in this thing?" I yell idioti-cally. I cannot hear my own voice, but a hand cups my ear. Leo has joined us, his wound bandaged with gray duct tape.

"Damn impolite!" he screams. His mouth is cold on my sunburned ear.

"WHAT?"

"Damn impolite question. After a thousand, it ain't no-body's business!"

I turn to grimace at the bouncing, jolted face but his eyes cut me away. Here's a man whose sureness and certainty are proportionate to the degree of chaos he is able to sniff out. Tericka says the same of me but she's wrong. I am satisfied enough keeping capitalism and myself healthy. I am satisfied by the girl, the tits, the baby, the house, the mango and grape-fruit trees, the weather, the music, and the money. I am a gentle man, for God's sake.

The gash of our wake is as tempestuous as a squall line on the surface of the water. The Moorish towers of the Breakers Hotel rise ten degrees off our portside. We are no more than a quarter-mile out. Amid the flying spray, the crashing and pounding, the extreme noise, something within this fiberglass behemoth slips, and the kinetic clutch of our motion relaxes for a second. The air stutters but then the roar continues.

"All right, goddammit," Leo is shouting. "That's it. That's all she wrote. Son of a bitch, put her on the beach, man."

Leo's man, the captain, one gets the feeling, is dozing behind his sunglasses. The air cracks and stammers. *Vaa vaa vaa va va.* The passengers that have come up on deck crouch like Muslims at prayer. Leo shoves the captain aside and spins the wheel to port. The cigarette arcs and slams broadside through the water. The force of the maneuver sends several Haitians crashing through the lifeline, which they grab and dangle from like eels. Just as we regain our forward momentum, an unnatural silence implodes down into us. We are out of gas.

Captain Shitball *has* pulled his pistol and he waves it at Leo. This sort of behavior depresses the hell out of me. I try to make myself small, but the captain says in a high Latin accent, "Keep those folks there away from my feesh."

We have enough glide left in us to coast within fifty yards of the shore where up above the concrete breakwater, in the glassed bays of the Breakers' dining room, I can see the faces of the aristocracy turn with concern from their fois gras and Châteauneuf-du-Pape.

To the north and south red lights are flashing out beyond the reef and you know the sirens are blasting even if you can't hear them yet. I tell Leo good-bye, and Leo's man thanks for the ride.

"Miami!" Leo announces. "Miami! End of the line." He begins to throw the Haitians overboard. They are shrieking and wailing hysterically. For some of these immigrants in the past, this point has truly been the end of the line, but the water here seems shallow enough to stand in. I dive over the side and freestyle as fast as I can toward the beach. Leo follows close behind. The captain has chosen to stay with his marlin, a man intent on legend.

We must seem a very peculiar aquacade to the ladies and gentlemen lining the oceanfront windows of the hotel. Surely money is changing hands over the prospect of our individual arrivals. Small fortunes suddenly made or lost. America, I am back ashore again and ready to run.

The wet worsted of my suit chafes against me like sand-paper and I would like nothing more than to sit down in the hot sun and let everything dry up and calm down, but in a few minutes the Marine Patrol, the Coast Guard, the State Police, the local guardia, and all my friends at the DEA will be here to welcome everybody, so I must be on my way. I hurdle over Haitians and puff up the slippery steps of the breakwater, across the perfect zoysia lawn toward the circus colors of the poolside cabanas. I am thinking that this is all a rather shame-ful matter and that I've been made to feel embarrassingly law-less.

I think my form is pretty good as I approach the pool; the old spirit shines through. My legs still feel a bit jellylike from the vibrations of the boat but my knees are rising respectably and I keep my elbows tucked into my side, my hands pumping out in front of me. Bikinied women on chaise longues lean forward to check me out. A well-tanned attendant in lime-colored sportswear is striding toward me, waving his arms for me to stop. I collar him around the neck with my forearm and together we rush somewhat awkwardly into the nearest ca-bana. I must say this part of town brings out the worst in me. We stumble to the Astroturf floor. I am holding his head down by the ears. I try to talk to him.

"I'll kill you, I'll rip these things right off your head. I'll bite your fucking nose off."

"Mister, please—!" the fellow says. There is terror in his preparatory blue eyes. I am not behaving properly, I see.

"Excuse me, I'm overwrought," I say apologetically and roll off, still holding on to one ear so I don't lose him. "I was out jogging and ran into some trouble. Understand?"

He nods his head very quickly. After all, he is a young man who has been trained to be of service to people who have everything and still want more.

"Mrs. Gerald Silverhartz," I say. "Statia Silverhartz." His eyes widen appropriately. "Do you know who she is?" He nods his fair head vigorously after I let go of his ear.

"This is a private, personal matter. Understand?"

Again, a satisfying nod.

"Ms. Silverhartz and I are business associates and I need to talk to her. Find her, please. Tell her Weber needs her. She'll come. And, of course, if you'll see to it that I am not disturbed while I wait, Ms. Silverhartz and I will express our gratitude in generous ways. Okay?"

"Okay." More than a nod now. Genuine enthusiasm. I am pleased by his resilience and help the lad to his feet.

"And look," I say cheerfully, "could you send in a sandwich and a beer for me? I've worked up an appetite this morning."

I stand behind the door while he opens it to leave, but still I can see through the crack at the hinges that the Haitians are discovering Palm Beach's most exclusive hotel. Welcome to America, I say to myself. Good luck. The first of many uniformed men bounds out of the bushes and draws his gun on a black woman with a scarf wrapped around her head.

I slam the door quickly and sit back in a rattan chair to await dear Statia, the woman who once made my heart sweat: my former beauty, lean and restless, hard-mouthed and cat-faced. The first time I ever saw her, almost twenty years ago, was on the cover of the Shiny Sheet stacked inside the pink vending machines along Royal Poinciana Way. She was a debutante, she was coming out, she was bending over a table signing the *Social Register.* A presidential candidate had his hand on her hip. She was lovely. Three weeks later I was in bed with her learning the game I've Got A Secret Place. I never knew for sure if we were right for each other, or if our relationship was simply a prerequisite for growing up.

What I do know is we were married once and pissed away a fortune. Which under her guidance we promptly recovered. By age twenty-six she was sneezing blood into the finest Chinese silk. By twenty-seven her septum was reinforced with stainless steel plating. By age twenty-eight we acknowledged our hatred for each other; at thirty she wed Gerald Silverhartz, well-known bauxite tycoon and international power broker.

Now, six years later, we are still in business together and the hatred's gone, replaced by a quiet, honest affection. That's best, because I don't want her out of my life. She is someone to look at and say, we're alike, you and I. Hell bent, the both of us, and yet heaven does its best to stay on our side.

From Statia I inherited Tericka. On the surface, the acquisition was another convoluted, hushed, little-said-much-implied business deal. Statia sent a messenger across the bay one day ten months ago with a monogrammed note: *Weber— Please house mother and child for a day or two until we can put them on one of our boats to the islands. Stash.* Tericka stepped out of the limousine, looking very girlish, very fragile, in a flowered dress and straw espadrilles. The baby was asleep in her arms. Stash had managed to put one of the new astronauts on the payroll to deliver from Florida to Houston a special something for a special someone. Tericka was a clause in this unwritten contract. Which said, I imagine, get her and the kid out of my life. I let them in reluctantly. After three days, I couldn't let go, and nobody came to retrieve them.

I begin to worry that perhaps the attendant fellow is right this moment turning me in to a roomful of arguing Pinkertons. A knock on the door makes my adrenaline zing, my heart fly about like a loose bird inside me. Nothing matters more here than tone of voice. Statia was the first to teach me this.

"What is it, damn it?" I shout curtly.

"Room service, sir. Roast beef and Guinness."

"Is the roast beef bloody rare?"

"Yes, sir."

"Horseradish?"

"Uh, yes, sir."

I pull the door open so that I'm hidden behind it. "Push in the service," I say, "and that will be all." I grab the silver cart and wheel it in, taking a quick bite of the sandwich, which I must instantly spit out because my mouth hurts so much. What I see outside stops me from closing the door fully. The Haitians are all queued up, cowering before a force of lawmen. One old man is weeping, pulling a few dirty dollars out of his ragged pants and throwing the money on the ground. In front of my cabana, several of the local citizenry review the situation. Perhaps they hope for a good price on a gardener or yardman. Goddammit, where is Statia? I haven't seen her for weeks. For all I know she's still in New York, or God knows where, allowing the clergy of commerce to worship her. Leo, I see, has been nabbed and handcuffed. He is set down in a lawnchair and doesn't hesitate to call the bartender for a cocktail.

I withdraw back into my cabana, resigned to my skewed fate. Statia could be anywhere, could be receiving the dry old tongue of a Trade Commissioner at this very moment. My attendant taps on the door and enters carrying a telephone which he plugs into a wall jack. "Sir," he says respectfully, "I haven't had much luck locating your party. Would you care to use the telephone." I must tell him I am too distressed to push the buttons properly and he must do it for me. For a half-hour I call out numbers, the boy dials and makes the necessary inquiries without success. My resolve for good health dissipates with each click of the receiver and I experience a terrific urge for vice. Nothing to do but send the attendant for cigars and vodka, and when he leaves I rise from the rattan chair where I've been sulking and stab out the numbers to Gerald's private beeper. In but a few minutes he rings me back.

"Silverhartz here, what is it?"

"Gerald, this is Weber and—"

"Good-bye, Weber."

"Gerald, don't hang up, I have the stink of scandal and grievous harm on my breath today."

"One of your many stinks. How did you get this number?"

"I must see Statia. She must come rescue me at the Breakers."

"Heh-heh, that's a good one."

"Gerald, you are a flaccid debilitated kraut and of limited interest to me. I hope you have enough socked away to survive the economic ruin that shall now descend upon your house.

You won't have a penny left to pay the young boys you bugger on your jaunts to Martinique. Good-bye, butt rash."

I pitch the receiver back to its cradle and congratulate myself on gaining Mr. Silverhartz's avaricious attention. He is a bully, a pigoid, a charge-ahead pomposity but not so much a fool to keep Statia away from me if he suspects his ass is in any manner endangered by my indiscretions. I am furnished with cigars and clear liquor and send the attendant out to the drive to escort Statia to my little cage when she arrives.

The room is well fouled with tarry smoke, my blood rushes through my heart vents and valves like the Volga by the time I hear the familiar gravel of her voice pelt the ears of the crowd outside my louvered window.

"Get out of my way, please. I said *move.*" Ah, the charm of authority on the lips of a self-possessed and desirable woman.

Skillfully elbowing a bewildered cop from her path, she points at Leo in his lounge chair, the mechanic double-fistedly gulping a tall yellow drink, and says to a man in a gray business suit, "Rubin, you're making a mistake arresting that citizen. My lawyers will be glad to explain." The man sneers back at her but everyone knows Leo is home free. Nobody suffers the lockup in Palm Beach until deserted by the moneylenders.

She breezes past this scenario, nodding her head appropriately as the poolside attendant points out my cabana to her. Even at this distance she projects invulnerability, even to me, and I know better. I tuck my hands glumly into the pockets of my damp trousers. She enters the room looking eternally young and ready for sport, dressed as she is in a snappy short white tennis skirt and sleeveless jersey. She is full of energy, terrifyingly confident, though her mouth has found the reproach she so commonly employs on me these days.

"I was over at the Fays' when Gerald rang, *livid,* let me tell you," she says as she closes the door behind her, and then, "Oh my, what happened to you?"

I smile sheepishly, shrug my shoulders, feel the unwanted scratchy beginnings of the affection I have for the lady. She looks good, though perhaps a bit overwintered from the recent business trip to the cold offices of New York. Her thick dark hair is drawn back from her bony face and held with a peach-colored ribbon. Her lower lip is naturally swollen, a fat slice of fruit. Her eyes are aggressively green. I have remained loyal to all this yet others have remarked that her features suffer from too many fast stops and starts.

"Statia, sorry to bother you but I'm in a jam."

She stands off from me, taking account of my condition. "Ee-yuck," she says, "that suit looks horrible on you." She clucks out mild disappointment. "And who hit you in the mouth? It's all bloody, let me see." From somewhere in her skirt she has extracted a crumpy wad of Kleenex and dabs at my lips. She sticks a finger in my mouth and tenderly probes. I try to explain.

"I waa yawging," I say.

"Weber," she says sympathetically, "your front tooth here is broken. Jesus, doesn't it hurt?" She removes her finger quickly from my mouth.

"It just throbs," I say, unwilling to examine the damage myself or to think much about it.

"What in the world were you doing?"

"I was jogging."

Her geometric eyebrows furrow and she looks at me suspiciously. "You were jogging? My goodness, how did you end up with Leo and those poor Haitians and enough cops for a baseball game? No, don't tell me, Weber," she says, exasperated with me, testing her forehead with the back of her hand as if I had just sent a fever into her. "I'd rather not know."

"Well, I think you should know," I say. "I want you to know I was not behaving frivolously."

"No," she says, growling. "I definitely do not want to hear about it. Let's just clean you up and get you out of here."

"Statia, dear," I say, since I must match her hauteur, "don't dare patronize a fellow careerist. We are spiritual comforts to one another. A matching set of bookends on the literature of indulgence and immoderation."

She blinks deliberately slow and says, "Where's that boy

with my mineral water? I asked him to bring me mineral water. Idoona Fay and I were playing doubles against John and Yoko and I'm thirsty. Idoona's selling them the McLean estate. You'd never believe it, but she's really quite good with a racket."

This chatter, I know from experience, is a way of punishing me and my trivial concerns. She keeps on until she gets her water, and with her throat freshly doused she turns on me.

"What has gotten into you lately, Weber? Where's the class and the dash gone? That tumbledown shack you live in with that child and her baby. It's just too perverse, even for me. And now this escapade with Leo. And oh what a fool you were to phone Gerald and threaten him."

"I panicked," I admit.

"I'll say. He's furious, he wants you disappeared."

"I worry about you, Statia," I say, trying to make a joke out of it yet unable to prevent a certain amount of righteousness from my voice. "Is there life after Gerald Silverhartz and unrestrained decadence?"

"How dare you?" she hisses back. "I'm a happy woman, Weber, and you know it. I am hardworking and loved. I am not idle or world-weary like you. Go back to where you belong with your teenybopper. I should tell you that we've closed the Space Shuttle deal with Tericka's bum from outer space, so if you were ever motivated by certain business-wise obligations, you are free of them now."

"For your information," I say, "I love Tericka, I like the baby. You always checked into the headache clinic whenever I tried to talk to you about kids." I surprise myself because I've never said this aloud before. It sounds good to me.

"Oh, Weber," Statia says, "you make me feel old and tired. But I'm happy for you, really. In fact, I'm relieved, although it all sounds painfully mature for a fellow like you."

I suppose I could bite down on that but I don't. Her voice has been icy, but she steps away from me with just a brush of melancholy across her mouth. We were most ourselves when we were in bed or bickering, and we both ran like hell from each other when we figured this out.

Statia picks up the receiver and dials, doing what she does best—business in extravagant fashion. I watch her, thinking, I'm glad I stopped *needing* you, I'm glad we're still friends. Statia, you're a woman, you're good-looking, you're awfully rich, your life is sinfully exciting. I try to add all these facts up, try to attach some great meaning to the gilded patterns, the exaggerated blessings, of your life. I can't do it, for you or for me. We have strong hearts and a certain arrogant commitment to excellence of one sort or another, whether we are outlaws or saints of the new world. And we never gave up anything without a fight, including our marriage. When we were so much younger, down on our luck, very scruffy but destined to rise again, a salesman in a used-car lot condescended to our few dollars that we hoped would buy an old VW bug. I want to smack him, I said to Statia then. Oh shit, Weber, forget it, she said. He's not tall enough to look down his nose at us. You know what I mean? Why do you have this need to apologize or attack?

Within minutes Statia has orchestrated a dignified ending to my day. She phones her tailor, her prosthodontist, her chauffeur. She puts her cool hands on my neck and kisses my cheek. I hug her tightly, this woman who is now a goddamn institution. "Good-bye, Weber," she says. "I've got to get back. Let's get together Monday or Tuesday with Bert. Wear something nice." She smiles warmly, showing a neat line of teeth, and is gone.

I feel better. By tearing the roast beef sandwich into little bites I am able to chew it on one side of my mouth. I suck vodka gingerly from its chilled bottle, light a second cigar to keep me company now that I'm alone again. The tailor comes first and leaves me wearing satin racing shorts with a chamois crotch, expensive running shoes, a cotton pullover, and sunglasses capable of concealing the most public of identities. The prosthodontist arrives shortly thereafter and fits me with a gold cap he selects from a small leather boxful of them. "It's only temporary," he says. "Of course, many gentlemen today are finding that a golden smile is also a sound investment." He

HOT DAY ON THE GOLD COAST

has amused himself and he cackles. "Think it over," he says, handing me a script for codeine.

Like clockwork, Statia's chauffeur Raans enters the cabana and waits quietly at parade rest until the doctor leaves. When we are alone, he whips off his cap and bows. "Boy oh boy, Weber," he says, "you're looking slick."

Indeed I am in awe of myself, that simple exercise can provide such change. "Don't you find it a little queer, Raans," I say, "that Statia and I share this phoenix quality, that the second we start to smell like shit you can bet roses will be delivered?"

"Ah yes, you bet. You bet," Raans says, amiable Raans, so happy to be a handsome Scandinavian in cockstruck Palm Beach. "Where can I take you? The beach? Your broker's? Down to Hialeah to watch the ponies?"

"Just home."

We walk out side by side, assured and unapproachable. The Haitians are being whisked away in paddy wagons. Leo is gone but I doubt he will be forgotten because too many of the gentry depend on him to keep their intrigues running smoothly. Stash's Silver Cloud is parked close by. Raans holds the door for me as I slip onto the expansive leather seat. Raans gets behind the wheel and soon we are southbound on Ocean Boulevard, across the Causeway and not far from my neighborhood.

"Raans, stop," I say. "I want to get out."

"Okay, Weber."

I spring out of the car and onto the sidewalk, marveling at how comfortable the new shoes are on my feet. Every muscle is sore but the pain fades as I pick up speed, press ahead to find the limit.

The Pelican

In the quiet kitchen the old woman slowly prepared a breakfast of mashed sardines and cocoa tea for the white man and set it before him on the rough, oil-stained table, mumbling at the easy thanks he returned her. She stood back then, watching him begin to eat, sucking her teeth at his hesitation, the reluctance with which he tasted his food. He waited for her to walk to the back of the house, her heels squashing down the backs of her undersized slippers, before he dumped what was on his plate out the window for the cat and left.

It was Saturday, no need to work, but Bowen rose early in his room at the guest house and decided to hike up the mountainside to the museum. No one bothered him in the streets. Walking Victoria Drive to the upper reaches of the city he looked down on the waterfront to the crowds gathered in the open market but could not hear their noise. The peace of the early morning was strengthened by the sea beyond, crystalline and windless. Two fishing boats were out with sagging sails, frigate birds circling and circling high up off the harbor point, a wheel of black dots that gave Bowen the impression of magnification, seeing beyond the visible, microbes swimming soundlessly on a laboratory slide. To the west off the point, a line of four big-winged birds, probably pelicans, swooped in formation down toward the barrier reef.

The air was clear and sweetened, unpenetrated by weekday noise, until he crossed the block that separated the government houses from the shanties of the ghetto and then the city smelled like rotting fruit and kerosene, urine and garlic, and the sun burned with a cruel intensity. It was a reggae bass he heard first, syncopated and booming, unmistakably provocative, a strong narcotic presence in the empty street. The music fizzed at high volume from the cracked speakers of the Black Cat bar—the Black Cat open all night, a chapel where men came to release the duty of hard living. A beam of sunlight edged past the entrance to a man asleep on a board bench, a beer bottle sparkling on the dirt floor. Ahead a group of fellows leaned against a parked taxi. As Bowen walked by they stopped talking to take a cold look at him. Bowen nodded politely but instantly regretted it. He had called attention to himself as an easy mark; the gesture was an unwitting invitation to sell him dope, beg his money, to let the antipathy surface. They watched him as if he were an event they did not yet understand.

But nobody said anything and he passed by unmolested.

He was from the States, too new to the island to be relaxed but beginning at least to be annoyed by the endless rituals of the street. This world stunned him, produced its own measure of guilt and yet excited him. The fieldwork was his first, free of graduate school and swept up by Smithsonian omnipotence and a rebirth of interest in the Pre-Columbian Conference of the Antilles. Stepping from the Liat Avro onto this land, he felt like something unjustly sheltered, brought up from underground and deposited in the sun.

Behind Bowen a car honked and it startled him fully awake. He jumped off the pavement into the dry, scattered saw grass that pricked his sandaled feet. A chip of red pottery lodged in the black dirt drew his attention and he stooped to pick it out. The piece was embedded in the baked soil and he was forced to dig around it with his pocketknife. Wherever Bowen walked he searched the ground, eyes downcast like a penitent, for clues to a new site: shards and chalky shells, a rock worn smooth by human friction, a discolored patch of earth; or colonial rubbish—old bottles, oxygenated crumbs of iron, the verdigris of a copper nail, anything that spoke honestly of the past, a mindprint or a voice that he must hear first before the distortion, the objectification, of exposure. The cataloging, the collected data thereafter would always be in accessible public domain; the pleasures of the first touch would remain private and real. Bowen flipped the shard in his hand and rubbed the dirt away. The surface had been pebble-polished, diagonals scratched through a white slip glaze with a fish bone or thorn. He slipped the fragment into the pocket of his khaki shorts. The horn, he realized with vague irritation, was still bleating impatiently.

An old Morris Minor, once bright red, scarred from front to back by bad roads and haphazard driving, had pulled over. Bowen couldn't see down inside so he came over and bent to the window for a look. Inside he saw a dark, blunt face, eyes that appeared abnormally convex, a nose that seemed like the first blow of an irregular bubble. The man's kinky hair was longish, combed up and back to where it curdled into short locks. The man grinned charitably, his pale palm beckoning Bowen into the car.

"You goin up?"

Bowen crammed his large body, as pale and sharply pink as the man's hand, into the passenger seat. "Marcus," he said, acknowledging the driver. The car leapt forward. "It's getting hot, isn't it."

"Every day, mahn."

"I forget what I'm doing."

"I see you stop to make a study ahnd I tell myself you goin up de hill."

"Yes. That's right."

Marcus was the deputy agricultural officer, a prize for the ministry, young and talented, willing to forsake the lure of the north for his homeland. He was responsible for the care of the Botanic Gardens, the hemisphere's oldest. His predecessors to a man were British and white: loyal adventurers, disciples of Kew and the Royal Society. Bowen saw Marcus frequently, for the fledgling museum was housed inside the gardens in the cottage of the old overseer. The colonial residence was ramshackle when Bowen was first shown it, the only blemish in the extraordinarily ordered world of the gardens' property.

They made their turn off the main road and started up the greater incline of the hill. Where the land leveled to a small plateau the jungle had been stripped and the gardens laid out two centuries ago. From here the countryside pleated and rose symphonically, soaring to the vertical peaks that flanked the modest industry of Kingstown. Marcus accelerated to the right to bypass a taxi that had slowed in front of them. A white woman, one of the many gray-haired dowagers out inspecting worlds their husbands had never thought to show them, had twisted herself halfway out the window to photograph the view of the harbor below, the Grenadines like haloed gems falling into the horizon. She yelped girlishly as the Morris Minor passed close to her extended shoulder on the narrow road and popped back into the cab, losing her sun hat in the process. Bowen smiled sourly, disapproving of the woman's ostentation, that type of blatant tourism that marched over the precious subtleties of a culture as if nations were only artifice, extravagant Disneylands. And yet what was so wrong with an old woman snapping a picture.

Another few minutes of vigorous steering and downshifting up the grade and they were at the main entrance to the gardens, the tall wrought-iron gates chained across the road. Marcus left the engine running as he unlocked the gates and swung them back on their stops. The taxi they had overtaken pulled alongside Bowen. Marcus stood proudly in the center of the road underneath the arched iron letters. *St. Vincent Botanic Gardens.*

He walked back to the taxi and chatted with its occupants, welcoming them with the benign smile of ownership. "Lady, I hope you okay. You okay, eh? I doan want you comin ahll de way to find de gate close up." But the woman and her two companions were delighted by the incident. Her sun hat had been crushed by another car before she could retrieve it. They worked themselves out of the taxi, the woman with the camera displaying her ruined hat with satisfaction. It would transform into a story of adventure; she was having one of the best times of her life, she said. She leaned over and framed her face in the window by Bowen's seat, oil that had run from her skin beaded into her makeup, the enthusiasm of her bright red mouth almost grotesque.

"Hello, who are you?" she said with gay familiarity.

"Good morning." He felt as if his mother had somehow found him out here in the backwater.

"Come have your picture taken. Come on," she coaxed.

"No thanks."

She made Marcus stand straight and still by the entrance as she photographed him. While Bowen remained in the car, the black man accommodated his passenger's fellow countrymen with easy graciousness, even warning them not to pay more than two dollars to the shantytown boys he had trained as guides. The questions and answers between them seemed formed by complicity.

Marcus returned to the car and drove slowly ahead into the gardens through a channel of purple bougainvillea cresting overhead. Bowen expected the man's mood to reverse itself now that they had escaped the women, but it did not. He asked,

"Does it bother you to have them running all over the place like that?"

"What? Dem people?" Marcus answered, swinging his head back. "No, mahn. Dis place made fah outside folk to come see, see someting done right in dis shitty-ahss country." He said it without irony, without an inflection of regret. Bowen did not believe that Marcus was telling the truth. He was surprised, at least, that he resented the offense of tourists more than the black man did.

They turned and stopped behind a walled hedge of crimson ixora that hid from public view a double row of long ramadas canopied with black nylon screening. This was the propagation center for the gardens. In the coolness of wet stones, a half-light filtered down upon line after line of seedlings, their rich black scoops of earth girdled in plastic sleeves. The air was moist and thickly powdered with fragrant pollens. Marcus pushed his seat forward and began to unload trayfuls of young plants, mintlike but fat and deep green, from the rear seat and floor. Bowen had not noticed them before; now he was aware of their peculiar scent.

"Can I give you a hand?"

"Ahll right," Marcus replied, but it didn't sound like it mattered to him one way or the other.

"What are these?"

"Here, mahn," said Marcus, breaking off one of the sticky leaves and crushing it below Bowen's nose. "You tell me."

The pure, hot aroma of the sap expanded in Bowen's nostrils, triggering a line of emotions, images into his memory. It was the smell of women he had slept with, of people crowded against him in bars, of hitchhikers, of a certain type of music —the smell of an era in his life.

"Patchouli. I never even knew it was a plant. I don't know what I thought it was."

"Dis a good cahsh crop," Marcus said seriously. "We has a guy in Chateaubelair tell me he want to try it, so I bring some down fah him from de Windwahd Station. When de bush young like dis, it doan carry much stink. But a mahn in Queenslahnd keep ten acres. In de rainy seàson, when de plahnt juicy ahnd de fellah staht to cuttin it, you smell de oil on de whole mountahn."

"I'd like to see that," Bowen said. "If you go up when the harvest begins, will you take me with you? Would you mind?"

Instead of answering, Marcus continued removing plants from the car as if he hadn't heard. Bowen stood waiting for some response but when it was not forthcoming he shrugged his shoulders and put himself back to the job, a little hurt at being ignored. When they had finished, Marcus showed him a spigot where he could wash the dirt from his hands. They were very close together sharing the stream of chilled water, squatting on their heels. Marcus looked carefully at Bowen without regard to how improper the act might appear, his eyes impenetrable, monochromatic like the highland rain forests, as dark as the soil they washed from their hands. Bowen saw something in them he recognized but could not name. A magnetic resonance that did not seem clearly placed in time.

"So you in-trested in plahnts, eh?"

"Sure." Bowen was uncertain whether he should say more. He did not want to commit himself too eagerly or somehow be pretentious. Or be rebuked.

The agriculturalist dried his hands on his pants and started talking, the love of his words a fact Bowen appreciated more than the knowledge they spoke for. Bowen followed him through the hedge that separated them from the formal realm of the gardens.

"See dis," he said, pulling out a branch from a wall of rampant vegetation shifting in the breeze trickling down the mountainside, a bank of organic flags collected from many nations. "*Amherstia nobilis.* We cahll it Flame Amherstia. Dis tree very rare, mahn. She comes from India or somewheres like daht. A British fellah bring it here in 1906. Lot of guys bringin stuff here den.

"Ahnd see dis white greeny stuff wit stickah? We cahll dis

Wait-a-Bit. It grow too fahst ahnd everywheres daht I must send a mahn to chop it every week."

They went over to a towering tree shedding its large compound leaves for the magnificence of a downpour of yellow blooms. "*Cassia fistula.* You like de sound of daht? Golden Showah. Muddahs like dese fruit pod very much fah a sick child. *Monstera deliciosa.* Some cahll it Cerimahn, some cahll it Delicious Monstah. You cahn eat dis spike comin out de bloom, ya know.

"Milk-ahnd-Wine Lily. Lobstah Claw. Firebrush. Womahn's Tongue. Jerus-lem Thorn. Look here. Pelicahn Flowah. Feel how nice de leaves lay. Nobody bring dis plahnt from somewheres else."

The unopened flowers of the vine were pelican-shaped, a pointed beaked crest arching into two wide wings folded down in rest. Bowen plucked one of the larger flowers and cradled it in his hands. The flower seemed like a womb, an egg, something ready to give birth to a small life. It was too awkwardly shaped to be stuck into a vase in the museum so he passed it over to Marcus. Marcus examined the blossom for a moment as if he might find a flaw and then tossed it on the ground.

The tour continued. Ornamental and blandly functional, toxic or medicinal, aquatic and xerophytic, Marcus revealed them all, often naming family, genera, or land of origin for Bowen. *Dis one good fah shade, come from Africa, mahn. Dis one here kill you. Dis one de best fah keepin dirt on hillsides. Some crazy guys eat ahnd smoke dese seeds to feel nice.* He pulled the milky green buds from the ilang-ilang and squeezed them between his red fingertips so Bowen could smell this, the flower of flowers, the world's most exotic essence.

Marcus's involvement as a master of his silent, perfect domain made Bowen anxious to get on with his own work, to immerse himself in the chaos of the inanimate morsels of the past, to puzzle the fallen world back together again by matching cracks, designs, colors. The agricultural officer offered to walk over to the museum with him to check on the progress of the Amerindian plants he and Doc Kirby had cultivated there —Doc's idea for using the native flora as a device for the past to enter the future. Savages knew the pleasure of lemon grass tea and the comfort of tobacco. Visitors to the museum identified with that.

They passed through a grove of ginger, the arrow-shafted stalks drooping with clusters of pearly buds, and stepped into a grassy glade surrounding the long shell of a tree toppled by its own fatigue years ago. A sign nearby on a post explained the historical importance of this, the gardens' most acclaimed attraction. The park had filled with tourists by now. They cluttered around the naked husk of wood, its inside soft as cake, and photographed it from different angles. Bowen had known the tree was in the gardens someplace but he had not seen it until now. The sight was anticlimactic, a contrived presence, a false relic.

"Bligh's gift to niggahs," Marcus said with a contemptuous grin. Bowen was grateful for this bluntness and hoped now a deeper alliance would form between them in opposition to the needless romance of the tree. He heard cynicism in the black man's voice, what he had anticipated hearing much sooner. "Dem wicked slaves doan eat cotton, cahnt stew sugah cane. Mahn, what you goin do?" Captain Bligh's breadfruit tree lay on the neat turf, an idol rotting back into the earth though its tendrils had spread throughout the islands to nourish the bodies of souls abandoned in purgatory, to keep their feet and hands and backs on earth.

The lady from the taxicab emerged from the group of admirers and approached them. "Just think of it," she said breathlessly. "That old tree was right there with Captain Bligh on *The Bounty*. It survived so much!"

"No, no," Marcus corrected her. "Daht voyage de specimahns ahnd de cahptain did not fare well. But dis mahn Bligh was stubborn. He try it ahgain. Now everybody eatin breadfruit, even de hogs.

"Den he bring some teak. Soon teak tree everywheres you

look, ahnd a fellah cahn make a dollah choppin it. Now people prayin strong to de cahptain, prayin *Ol mahn Bligh, come bahck. Bring me womahn, bring me husbahnd, bring me pot to cook in, bring me piece ah meat to eat wit dis breadfruit.*"

"I am fascinated by it all," the woman said earnestly, her forehead shining, her fingers stroking the camera mounted on her belly. She drifted back to her companions and Bowen could hear her repeating the information to the group as if she had been asked to interpret what the black man had said.

Marcus seemed self-conscious after he had spoken to her. "I know what it sound like, mahn," he explained to Bowen, "but I was only jokin wit she. She take it too straight."

"Not at all," Bowen said, dismissing what he took for an apology. "Most people like that like their history under glass. Otherwise they don't know what it means."

The approach up to the museum had once been terraced, perhaps to make the premises more English and impressive, to assert the dominion of the residence over the lush grounds. Marcus had recently restored the house's rose garden, returning it to the precision that had once comforted the lonely wives of the men sent here from Devon or Lancaster, transferred from Bombay, Kabul, Singapore. On the other side of the walkway, antithetical to the roses, Marcus had planted the Amerindian flora for Dr. Kirby, the retired veterinarian who had devoted himself to preserving the island's heritage. Bowen left Marcus to tend to these, climbed the wooden steps of the museum's veranda, tested the front door but found it locked, knocked loudly but Doc was not inside although he had said he would be here.

Bowen dug in his pockets for his own key but he did not have it. He turned back to Marcus, who had forsaken the freshly rooted Amerindian plants and was on his knees in the rose garden inspecting the browning leaves of a flowerless bush.

Bowen called down to him. "Do you have an extra key?"

"What?" Marcus said absently, barely audible across the short distance. Bowen was going to repeat himself but Marcus pushed himself up off the ground, brushing his pants with his hands, his attention returning from the problem that had attracted him to the roses. He was coming up.

"Well, I remind myself to stop by you anyways fah a look. Doc tell me dis place gettin full of rocks ahnd bone ahnd broken pot."

He tried several keys until he found the proper one. Past the door the air was noticeably drier. The front rooms were empty, the ancient wood floors coarse and noisy, gray with a layer of dust. Doc had still not settled on the design for the display cases, although a cabinetmaker had been commissioned and set to work on storage shelves. Marcus followed Bowen down a center hallway to the rear of the building. The work area resembled a garage and had once served as both carriage house and kitchen. The floor was rough cement, artifacts everywhere upon it—in loose piles, in burlap bags, in boxes, in coffee tins. Rock carvings, some weighing hundreds of pounds, were stacked against two walls. The men stepped cautiously through the jumble to a table alongside a set of windows which Bowen shoved open to allow the air to circulate. Marcus examined the room with severity.

"Stone ahnd bone ahnd broken pot," he said. "Indiahns doan leave much."

Bowen wanted to return to the intimacy that he had experienced between them when they were walking the gardens. There was a level in each man's work that bonded to the other —a sublime level—and Bowen felt he was on the verge of identifying it. The feeling needed expression but he felt doomed to the visible, the prosaic, for only this was left in each piece after the wonderful burn of the first touch.

"All the pottery fragments you see on the table are called *adornos,*" he said. "They are images of an animal, a fish, a bird, or sometimes humanoid, that were formed onto vessels. Like cooking pots or bowls. Water jugs."

Marcus picked through them. "Why is daht?" he asked.

Pick them up and feel them and listen, Bowen wanted to

answer, but couldn't. Doc can tell you better than me. He has seen them, graced with a vision in the Yambou Valley; he swears he was among them for a morning. Before our history there was this, this silent world of men and birds and fish. Am I saying it right? Bats swarmed the air at night and were gods or devils or something not men, not man, with knowledge and power. In the silence that covered the planet, manatees somersaulted in the lagoons, sea turtles rasped lungfuls of air on the empty beaches, squeezing their eggs into the land. Man was no different and when he killed he was satisfied with that act. Women spoke a spirit language of clay and fire. Here the clay suffers, here the clay honors man and here it pities him. The potter, a girl, a young woman, marked these lines with her fingernail. In these indentations, put your own flesh; she has found you then across time and the pot knows your touch, the pot is whole again, has waited and waited for it and recalls the day of its creation. The blood moves again into the head of the lizard thing that lives dormant in this pot, that watches through this image. Do you understand? She was just a child and forbidden to speak the same words as men. She took dolphins from the waves and twisted them into clay. I do not know if there was happiness in this act, but there was knowledge. Power.

Bowen finally answered, his sense of futility lessened by the interest evident in the stern set of the black man's jaw. "We are classifying them in terms of period, character, function— whatever helps us identify them. Usually they were formed as handles or spouts. Occasionally they were merely ornamental, although ornament is most often expressed through geometrical patterns and color." He stopped. The words were not what he wanted, only what he couldn't prevent. But Marcus was listening so he continued. "Some, like this frog, have the nostrils hollowed out. A powder, primarily jimson weed, would be placed in these small bowls and sniffed during ceremonies."

Marcus flipped an *adorno* over and over in his hands, put it down, looked for another. "Very simple work, mahn. Like a cahtoon, no?" He took another piece made of darker clay. It had been burnished to make it shine like vinaceous enamel. "What is dis?" he said, frowning.

The face itself was flat, the features plain but inscrutable. Triangular mandibles erupted from it into a peaked snout, thick, fanged, forceful. "A bat," Bowen said. "Bats were special to them."

"How you mean 'speciahl'?" Marcus persisted. "It too fuckin ugly."

"I don't know," Bowen said, recoiling from the sudden disgust in Marcus's expression. He had looked at Bowen as if the white man were responsible for encouraging a bad habit. "The Indians were primitives. The Caribs associated magic with the bats and wanted their power."

Marcus grunted disapproval and quickly replaced the *adorno* with one of the rare shards that showed the man-image. Rarer still was the emotion of the face, grief-stricken, eyebrows collapsing down over deep concave eyes, the mouth an imperfect hole, utterly helpless. Both men were mesmerized by the clay's countenance. Nowhere in the room was there another piece to balance it, to match or offset the pathos. The rest of the work, a millennium's worth—demigod, man, animal, reptile, bird, fish—was all expressionless, detached and accepting.

Bowen told himself that the artifacts were not inconsequential to Marcus; perhaps he had found a friend and fellow seeker. There was something there in the inanimate fragments, a weak memory or emanation of humanity, but he suspected that here, as they stood together, the past bothered them both more than they could casually admit, it suffered mutely in the pale orange face of the man-image, a tiny death mask denied mortality. If they could find a way to speak about this there was no telling what might come of it.

Outside the windows a pickup truck had stopped at the maintenance shed across the drive from the museum. Two men rode in the cab, a third rode back in the rusty bed, clinging to the sides to keep from bouncing out. Marcus observed their arrival and returned the *adorno* to its position on the long table.

"Daht's Henry Wilkes. He come to collect dem patchouli."

Through the windows, Bowen watched Marcus exit the building and walk toward the truck. The black man had left without saying anything more; Bowen was both disappointed and petulant, a part of him reacting like a missionary who had lost his first convert.

Driver and passenger climbed out. The third rider reached into the bed and raised aloft a large broken mass of brown feathers. Marcus spoke to the man but Bowen could not understand what was said, the words more quickly fired and less carefully enunciated. He knew he should get on with his work, most of the morning was gone, but he wanted to see what the man had held up from the truck so he went out to it.

Overspiced air was steaming out of the jungle above them. Back toward Kingstown, above the treetops, the slate of ocean was canescent with glare. The carnival colors of the gardens were drained and shadeless. A single-barrel shotgun and several red-papered cartridges were placed precariously on the truck's sloping dashboard. Marcus was laughing appreciatively at the driver's story of the hunt. The man's two companions held the bird between them to measure its wingspan. It was a pelican. The long canelike bill was missing, and without it the lolling head, only eyes and skull, looked mammalian, monkey-like, its mouth a bloody circle. Bowen's revulsion was immediate.

The men began plucking the bird, tearing out the soft chocolate feathers in patches that separated from the skin with dull, sucking pops. Bowen watched aghast as the pelican was reduced to a purplish bloated lizard-thing. In the air the bird was so stylized, such a bold silhouette, a pterodactyl soaring effortlessly through history, adjusting its tremendous wings with the most delicate trimming, intelligent and masterful—an aviatic dolphin. Now it was an obscenity. Bowen turned to walk back

to the museum, commanding himself to forget about this business, there was nothing he could do, but as he passed the rear
of the truck and looked in he saw two more pelicans there.
One was limp, its chest split by buckshot. The other was alive;
one wing raised at his approach, the other wing hung loose
and glistened with a coat of blood. The bird clacked its bill
defiantly.

One of the men came beside Bowen to get the second bird,
the dead one, for cleaning. "Dis bird meat very sweet," he said.
"Bettah dahn chicken." Because Bowen could only stare grimly
he explained further, "Pelicahn is fish-fed, mahn. Daht make it
tendah. Fowl is pebble-fed. It just peck de dirt ahnd grow
tough."

For the first time on the island, Bowen spoke in anger. "Why
don't you kill the damn thing?" he demanded, pointing at the
remaining bird.

The man opened his dark eyes in mock surprise and smiled.
"Yes, mahn. Doan worry bout daht, suh. Cahnt eat him wit de
flahp still dere, ya know." He winked, already pulling feathers
from the bird he held.

When the man refused to respond to his sense of outrage,
Bowen felt abandoned and betrayed by his own emotion. He
was not a man of action but now an obligation seemed to echo
from his words. Several of Marcus's boy-guides had gathered
around to see what was happening; tourists wandering by
came over as if attracted by blood. "Poor thing," Bowen heard
an American voice saying. Bowen glared at the anonymous
white faces lingering on the perimeter, expecting to see the old
woman from the taxi. She would blame him for something like
this, wouldn't she.

Bowen climbed into the truck, taking his pocketknife from
his shorts, and pinched open the single blade. He paused before grabbing the pelican to register the sadness within it, and
its final dignity, but the bird's eyes were remote. Marcus and
the hunters had stopped what they were doing to watch him,
and their eyes, too, when he glanced over at them, were indif-

ferent. As he reached out the pelican snapped his hand with its ridiculous hooked beak; it felt like bamboo, hard but almost weightless. He took the bird up. Its body seemed pathetically small in his hands, awkward in design, all elbows and knees and no substance. In his fingers the neck rolled under the feathers like a long silk cord. He laid the edge of the knife against it and started to cut. The bird struggled against him but he held on. The pelican's supple neck, covered in short dense feathers like fur or velvet, would not cut. He crouched above it, sawing and sawing, waiting for the flesh to break and the gush of blood but the blade had been dulled by digging shards out of the dry volcanic soil of the island. It would not open the bird's throat. He was determined to kill the bird and when the knife wouldn't cut, he could not see through his frustration to an alternative. He felt increasingly imbecilic, slicing at the slippery wires of the bird's neck. Someone laughed, and someone called out, "What de hell, mahn, bite de head! Step on de belly."

The three men from the truck were no longer paying attention; they joked loudly with each other and began to gut the first two birds with a machete. He saw Marcus shake his head and signal over one of the young boys that worked for him in the gardens. The boy listened to his instructions and then searched the ground, found what he wanted and leapt into the truck with Bowen. Bowen still gripped the pelican at the top of its neck, unaware of what the boy was up to. He had decided to puncture the bird with the point of the knife, but by then the rock had smashed the bird's head, delivering a flutter of death into Bowen's palm. He dropped the pelican and saw the boy standing there, smiling confidently, undaunted by Bowen's hatred. He took the pocketknife from Bowen's hand and pressed a finger down along the cutting edge.

"Dis knife no good, mistah. You need a stone to rub it."

From the crushed eyes of the pelican, the blood flowered in little round blooms, ixoralike pinwheels. Bowen's legs had been splashed by blood and he tried to wipe away the stains with his bare hands. Marcus was there, offering him a work rag to clean himself. Bowen would not dare look at him for fear he had shamed himself. Marcus took the rag back when Bowen had finished, said he would stop by the museum again soon to see how everything was progressing. Then he ordered the boy to take the white man's knife and sharpen it.

Hunger

Here in the cays away from Providence and the villages, there was a fellowship among the fishermen in their isolation. They did not mind that they were utterly alone and apart from the world—this was their life. The darkness completed itself around them, throwing the horizon across the water until it lay beneath them and they could walk it like a tightrope, toeing the distance underfoot. The great distance, the cusp of nowhere from which they worked a living.

Among them only Bowen, a white man and an outsider, did not share their history and so the solitude was more powerful for him. The sea had fuzzed out into invisibility, joined to the sky in a solid cliff of darkness. From where he stood on the cay that was like a shallow china bowl turned upside down on the water, the sea was still in his hair, in his eyes, everywhere, a wetness that wouldn't wipe away. There was nothing he could do about it. It pushed in when he opened his mouth to speak, and swept out again when he exhaled, stinging his tongue. It blew against him in the night breeze and added weight to his salt-encrusted clothes. Air and water and small scab of land wrapped into each other and floated the men in the middle of darkness. Not even his grave held such magnitude for Bowen, not even that seemed so empty as this darkness. This was Bowen's feeling. It didn't worry him; it made him hungry.

On the mother ship *Orion,* anchored in the lagoon, a light in the galley flickered on. The light weakened and broke into particles only a short distance from the ship, a globe of blurry color suspended in the dense moisture. The silhouette of a man in a straw Panama passed across the yellow moon of the galley's porthole. The moon blinked. On the cay, matches were struck and placed to wood. A line of cooking fires wavered on the sand but the light revealed nothing more than the shapes of men crouched close to the auras of slow, lambent flames.

Bowen brought up more firewood from the beached cat-boat. He could see each arm of flame playing with hundreds of grape-sized hermit crabs that clicked and tumbled and rolled over onto their shells, escaping the heat and illumination.

The crabs provoked Gabriel. He grabbed any he could between his thumb and index finger and snapped them into the fire. He didn't want them crawling on his face at night, he said, he didn't want to awake to one of them picking its way across his cheeks or down his neck. In the flames, the tiny animals shrank in their red-white shells, burst and bubbled. It was a game Gabriel liked, but he was not a malicious man, not like Sterling, the murderer, who shot his mother's lover in the head with a speargun and raped the boys who were his cellmates in prison. Or Ezekiel, who was drunk all the time and let his wife and children go hungry. Everybody found it easier to forgive Sterling than to forgive Ezekiel. No one cared that Gabriel burned little crabs.

The night ran up the long shadows of the boatmen, merging with their black outlines as they tended the fires. Heavy iron caldrons and sooty Dutch ovens were shoved down into the coals as the flames waned. Into each pot was placed something different to cook. Men moved in and out of the shadows joyously, with clear purpose, racing back and forth to the boats from light to darkness to light again, carrying calabash shells brimming with portions of the first day's catch. The work they had done after setting up camp at the banks that afternoon was for themselves alone. No unseen white man could put a short price on the fish, not even on the tiniest mullet; no sprat had to be ferried aboard the *Orion* tonight and packed into the ice holds. The real work would come tomorrow when the Dutchman brought his scales ashore, and his tally book. But tonight was jubilation. Tonight every man was free to eat as much as he wanted. It was a spree, an eating fete, and everybody was happy. *We feedin weselves, mahn. Nobody else!* Bowen listened out of curiosity for a moment and then went about his business. *No dahmn bean big wife makin babies in she belly, five, six, sevahn kids cryin "poppa"; no grahnmuddah, uncle, ahntie or cousin John Robinson ten times removed and livin in de mountain so a boy must go up wit a dish fah de guy. No coolie mahn stockin de freezah in he shop, no tourist place on de mainland, no big goddahmn Texahn cowboy. We eatin everyting we got.*

Sterling's boys fixed the birds' eggs. They had pilfered them from the nests on Southwest Cay when the *Orion* stopped there earlier in the day to report to the four lonely soldiers sent to guard the fishing grounds from Jamaican poachers. With perverse authority the mainland government dropped off young recruits here for their first duty, left them with a sack of rice, fishing line and hooks, no boat and no shortwave radio, hundreds of miles from the shores of their homes, for six, eight, sometimes nine or ten months to enjoy the skeleton of a freighter, their only skyline, locked onto Pearl Henry's Reef.

It was this freighter, the *Betty B,* that the men on the *Orion* first sighted after their long passage from Providence. The massive wreck perched on the bleak, sun-scarred horizon like something ripped away from a city and dropped out of the sky to crumble and rust secretly, away from mankind. Captain Sangre anchored the *Orion* in water as transparent as coconut oil, over a sandy bottom dotted with thousands of conchs five fathoms below. One of the fishermen's catboats was unlashed from the deck and lowered over the side. The captain was rowed ashore to deliver the government permit, a preposterous formality, since the soldiers were helpless to enforce anything out here. Sterling and his boys went along to collect the eggs from the stick and pebble nests of the boobies, the frigate birds, the gulls and terns. The soldiers insisted that the eggs were under their protection and the fishermen couldn't touch them unless they paid a tax. After stone-faced negotiation, a bottle of rum, an old coverless *Playboy* magazine, and twenty pounds of cassava were handed over to the military.

From the rookery Sterling had gathered perhaps two hundred of the eggs speckled pink and blue and brown. After leveling the bed of embers, the boys boiled a ten-gallon can of seawater and threw in the eggs. The Bottom Town men stewed fish heads: triangular jaws gaping as the cartilage that held them melted, poking through the steaming surface of the liquid among an archipelago of eyeballs and flat discs of severed brain and bone. At another fire one man tossed the backs of spiny lobsters and their thick antennae into the vapor of his pot. The tails earned the best money and were saved for the Dutchman. All of the fishermen agreed the meat of the lobster, except for the fatty parts, was too rich-tasting anyway.

White gleaming wings of mashed-up conch simmered in another stew. Hot lard splattered and sizzled, foaming over dark orange sacks of roe. Turtle eggs that looked exactly like Ping-Pong balls boiled in the pot at the center of several men who poked a wire leader through the shells of uncooked ones and sucked out the raw yolk. Bowen was called over and given one as he passed cautiously by in the darkness on his way from scrubbing the fish slime from his hands in the wet sand at the water. He sucked the shell hollow but the egg felt syrupy and inedible in his mouth and tasted like something that shouldn't be swallowed. He spit it out in his hand to examine what was there, squatting down near the light of the fire. It was all bright viscid yolk threaded with a design of red capillaries. He slung the mess out into the night for the crabs.

"Dis stuff make yah seed grow straight, mahn."

Bowen returned to his own fire. Gabriel was watching intently as Mundo pitched a row of oval fish steaks into their pot: yellowtail and red snapper, hogfish, amberjack, gray vertical sections of barracuda. Bowen was surprised at the amount of fish being cooked, but he did not doubt the three of them would eat all of it. Mundo pulled plantains, brown and soft, and a giant yam from a burlap bag, cleaned and sliced these vegetables, added them to the stew with lime juice, salt, cornmeal dumplings, a handful of garlic cloves, and small green cooking peppers. Bowen took a mouthful of stale water from a jerrican to wash the globs of egg gel from his teeth.

"It's beginning to smell too good, Mundo. I'm dying from the smell."

"Oh yes? If you staht to die, Mistah Bone, you must finish, too. Nobody to help you here, mahn. Who goin help? Tell me daht."

The overpowering aroma of the cooking, as distinct and potent and wonderful as the smell of water in the desert, rose from the pots and encircled Bowen, a warm, copious, life-giving atmosphere. As quickly as that, the sea that had racked him all day and all of last night, the presence that seemed to be a second skin he must learn to move in, abated. Freed from one sensation, he was enslaved to another. The sea was now part of his viscera, part of his strength, and Bowen knelt down to limit the pressure of hunger in his stomach, cloistering the force of it with crossed forearms. It was, he thought, the perfect gesture.

Mundo leaned behind himself into the darkness and re-emerged with a young hawksbill turtle, its eyes already shining with martyrdom, the flippers lashed together like hands in prayer with palm fronds weaved through cuts in the leathery skin. He held it by the tail over the pot and cut its pale extended neck with an easy pull of his machete. Black blood squirted into the stew. The act disgusted Bowen but he couldn't prevent the hunger from swelling up inside him, so foreign and portentous, unlike anything he had ever felt about food. It stunned Bowen to realize he had not learned that hunger was the pure voice of the body, of being alive. He did not know what had insulated him against this knowledge. He would rather have seen Mundo kill a worthless man like Ezekiel, the drunkard and child-beater, than butcher the magnificent sea creature that was so close to extinction, but he imagined the blood hot and salty as the brine that nourished it, the blood spilling from the opened neck of the turtle into his own mouth, seeping under his tongue, filling his mouth completely, gulping it down too fast to breathe until whatever was there that demanded so much was appeased.

Gabriel turned on the balls of his feet, calling out, "Who de hell burnin mahnchineel tree?" Mundo clamped a lid down on the cooking pot and the three of them moved away to investigate the source of the smoke from the poisonous manchineel wood. Bowen's face and arms had begun to itch and his eyes felt as if soap had gotten into them. The search brought the men to Sterling's fire. His younger boy, Jambo, was responsible for the wood and had mistakenly put a piece of manchineel on the coals. He should have known better but nobody expected very much from Jambo. The can of eggs was pulled off and the water poured on the fire until the eggs drained. A fat column of smoke, spreading out around them, drove everyone upwind, rubbing their eyes, cursing and scratching.

"You a dahmn monkey, Jahmbo."

"How daht boy chop dis wood ahnd cahrry it to de ship witout blisterin he hands?"

"How you get a boy like dis, Sterlin?"

"Take ahn egg, mahn."

"Dey finish up cookin?"

"Dey feelin too hot."

"No, look. Dis one too juicy."

"Look here. Dis one nice."

"Dem eggs no good anyway. Dey too old, mahn."

"Dis one makin a bird."

"Teach it to fly, boy."

The man studied his egg for a moment and then flipped it onto the ground. Bowen bent over to look at it and saw the well-developed embryo of a man-of-war cooked white, almost plastic. Some men were tearing the shells off and popping the eggs down their throats without looking if the meat was bad or not. The close, wet air began to smell faintly rancid.

"Lord, dis guy nevah eat egg before. Sylvestah eatin de shell too."

"He mahd."

"How many eggs daht make, Sylvie boy?"

"Twenty-two." Crumbs and drips of brown-gold yolk stuck to his chin and fingers. "I ready fah someting new." But Ulysses said he had eaten twenty-three, so Sylvester ate one more out of pride.

Most of them had no desire to eat the eggs since there was an abundance of food at hand to reward patient stomachs after the long sail aboard the *Orion*. If the eggs were nice, they agreed, that was one thing, but they weren't: they were rotten. Watching Sylvester and Ulysses gobble the malodorous, runny eggs was good entertainment, but their own suppers were waiting. The groups wandered back to their own fires, stirred their pots and began to eat. Sterling was the only one who hadn't fished that afternoon. He thought everybody would appreciate the eggs and eat some and then share their own food with him. Mundo called him over to take a piece of fish. His two boys, Ulysses and Jambo, went with the Bottom Town men because they wanted to smoke ganja while they ate.

Sterling, a tall, lean mulatto with stark eyes, sat down in the sand cross-legged, enamel dish in one hand, spoon in the other, stoically waiting to be served. With an empty oatmeal can, Mundo scooped into the pot and overfilled Sterling's dish until gray sauce oozed across the rim. Sterling's thanks were harshly whispered; the man seemed obligated to quiet gratitude. To Bowen, the relationship between Mundo and Sterling was a mystery. He had watched them closely ever since Gabriel told him it was Mundo's first fishing partner, Gabriel's predecessor, whom Sterling had killed. *Dis guy was real dahk ahnd Sterlin crazy from his momma sleepin wit such a blahck blahck mahn so he shoot him in de face ahnd den take a stone ahnd bahng him. Sterlin young ahnd foolish den, mahn.* At the time of the murder, Mundo himself turned deadly and swore he would avenge his mate, but for once the police reacted swiftly and got to Sterling before Mundo could. Now Mundo treated Sterling like an older brother would. Frequently they competed against each other in the water to see who was the best sailor, the best diver, the better shot underwater. But never on land. On land Sterling was most often deferential, even helpful. He knew that Mundo's white friend collected seashells and so the mulatto gathered them when he was working on the reefs, offering them shyly in his cupped hands to Bowen. Bowen was thankful Sterling would rarely look straight at him. There was an exclusive intensity in the fisherman's eyes, a dangerous fascination. When their eyes met for the first time, it made Bowen apprehensive, and now that he knew what Sterling had done, he could easily tell in his resinous, never-blinking eyes that Sterling had killed a man, that Sterling had watched a man die by his own hand and for a moment had believed completely in his own power and will. It was like a brand.

With his spoon Sterling poked through the food on his dish, ostensibly waiting for it to cool, but he would not eat until Mundo had served himself. For everyone, the first taste was an immense relief, a reassurance that life was good and not only toil uninterrupted day after day. They ate from old cans or held tin bowls between their splayed knees, gouging the sand with their heels to make a trough for the bones and fat, rubbery skin. Mundo was the most serious eater. He had a big family— Gullie, his wife, and her seven children, his wife's parents and his own half-Chinese grandfather to support under his roof, plus a scattering of outside children, and though he fed them well, he always needed more to eat than he could get at home. He passionately sucked the grouper head he held catlike between both hands—it was bigger than his bowl—licking the delicate flesh of the cheeks and digging out the brain cavity with his fingers. The marble eyes were relished, the bones cleaned diligently: not a speck of meat eluded him. Gabriel would take a handful of snow-white steak and squeeze it into his mouth, chewing until it was all mashed up and half swallowed, and spit out as best he could the needlelike bones. He didn't bother that he lost large chunks of meat in the sand by doing this. Bowen was more methodical. Somewhat self-consciously, he picked the flesh free of bones before he took a bite. When invariably he missed one of them, he rearranged his mouthful with his tongue so that the bone was pushed to the forefront and then extracted, or failing this, he dropped whatever was in his mouth into the palm of his hand and pinched around until he found the damn thing. Judged by the pile of offal in front of him, knobs of vertebrae, long rows of dorsal spines like serrated knives, flaps of mottled skin, Bowen was eating the most, but the opposite was true.

Sterling talked a lot to himself while he ate, sometimes only moving his lips silently with the food, spit seldomly, and hacked without concern when a bone stuck in his throat until it blasted out. Sterling behaved like this occasionally, chattered away like an old woman, and then slipped back abruptly into his diffidence, embarrassed when he realized what he was doing. Like everyone else, he took second and third helpings and curled over his dish to slurp up the spicy gravy. Even Bowen, as careful as he was, had stains all over the front of his shirt, and his fingers and lips were sticky with the paste of boiled cartilage.

The men ate on and on. The darkness no longer seemed bleak but was comfortable and intimate, its vastness a barrier against any force that could possibly disturb the eaters. The fires dwindled to passive ruby clusters of coals, mystical and beguiling, as though something other than wood and flame created them. Stars began to drop through the black canopy of haze. The men did not so much decide to stop eating as they did fall thoughtlessly away from the pots exhausted, collapsing as athletes do after their greatest effort and concentration. They were stupefied by their extended stomachs and patted themselves delicately, croaking with gratification. For a moment Bowen experienced a release, an awakening of something sublime, but he told himself that was nonsense, he had misinterpreted insight or oneness for the dull contentment of a full belly. He let gravity take over and set him back into the broken coral that the sea had outcast to form the cairn of land where they camped. His dirty hands became gloved with flakes of cool sand. All around the cay the prone lengths of the fishermen groaned peacefully; with the increasing quiet, the hiss of the ocean surge on the reefs became audible, absolute energy leaching through the night from the interface of living earth and crashing, merciless water, ghost-white, somewhere in the distance.

One shadow still danced among the cooking pots, a faceless ebony shape that seemed intent on searching everywhere. It jumped from group to group like an obeah man, grunting and devilizing, its rasping steps circling closer to where Mundo and the other three sprawled around the remains of their dinner, not talking much, staring without expression or need for meaning into the sky. The spirit rose out of the darkness before them but nobody paid much attention. It was Ulysses, Sterling's oldest boy, a burly young man.

"Ahll right dere."

Sterling shifted, nodding to his son.

"Okay, Mundo."

"Ahll right."

"Mundo," Ulysses asked with quick, deep words that were almost unintelligible, "you got more to eat here?" The features of his round face were knotted together by a big ganja smile.

"Go look in de kettle," Mundo said with some annoyance. "Sterlin, what's wrong wit dis boy? How's daht he doan get enough to eat?"

Sterling shrugged. Somebody was always asking him what was wrong with his boys. Ulysses eagerly removed the lid from the pot and peered in. From under his white cotton T-shirt, his black gut humped downward like the hull of a boat. He dredged the bottom of the pot but found only a few bones there and sucked them dry.

"I still hungry," he announced.

"Go beg a piece ah fish from Mistah Dawkin."

"Him finish up."

"Go ahsk Henry."

"Dey ahll finish."

Sterling said to his boy, "Go eat dem eggs. Lots ah dem left."

"Dem eggs bahd."

"What de hell, mahn," Mundo said sternly to put an end to it, "eggs still eggs, even if dey bahd."

This logic appealed to Ulysses's sense of gluttony. He retreated back into the darkness headed for the eggs, driven to clear the hunger out of his mind. From where they lay, the four of them half listened to Ulysses bumping into the gear, clanking over pots like a bear in his blind hunt for the eggs.

With his head back facing the stars, Gabriel sighed. "I like it like dis," he said. After a pause he continued. "But dis a lonely place. Dis place doan even smell like lahnd."

"I nevah been lonely. Not once," Mundo said, as though the matter was unimportant.

"Give me a cigahrette, Mistah Bone," said Sterling quietly. There was no need for politeness here away from everything, away from the world. Among the fishermen, all requests were straightforward and a man either helped another or he didn't.

Anchored by satiation and fatigue, Bowen did not want to move. He invited Sterling to reach over and take the pack of Pielrojas from his pants pocket. Earlier he had been afraid that the men would not accept him in close quarters, but now he didn't care. Mundo and Gabriel were no problem because he worked with them, but back on Providence the others watched him cautiously, suspicious of his whiteness, never speaking to him. Mundo's own mother-in-law looked at Bowen as if he had come to steal the toes from her feet.

Sterling never took the cigarette from his mouth when he smoked. He rested back on his elbows and the ashes sprinkled down his bare chest. "Mistah Bone," he said tonelessly, "why a white mahn like you come to de cays?"

The question amused Mundo. He answered, "Mistah Bone come fah experiahnce. He want to study how hahd de blahck mahn work." He winked at Bowen and Gabriel as he said this and tugged his red baseball cap down clownishly over his eyes to indicate the absurdity and also the sufficiency of this reply. They did not pretend to understand why the world was the way it was, but among themselves they assumed that a man had good reasons, however offensive, for his actions. That was enough. Sterling's public showing of curiosity was easily dismissed, for Sterling was a strange man, a man who sometimes couldn't control himself. The fact was Bowen was there: He and Mundo had befriended each other. That was enough. The others were disconcerted by the enigma of a white man working with them; always and always black men had worked for clear-skinned people. That the pattern was disrupted was easy to see, but only Mundo accepted it nonchalantly as a natural course.

"I watch Mistah Bone takin notes," Gabriel spoofed, referring to Bowen's letter writing. "He come to write history of de cay in a big big book. He writin 'Dese bunch ah blahck men sail up to Serrana, go ashore ahnd eat like hogs!'"

Bowen laughed halfheartedly, satisfied that he didn't have to say anything. He was convinced there was nothing to look back to—not here anyway, not in the middle of the ocean with men so different from him. Secretly, he trembled from a new sense of freedom, not prepared for the truth of it, faithless but full of modest expectation like a baptized sinner, carried to the river by force.

A shot of light, vanishing and then reappearing more brilliantly, drew their lazy attention to the camp of the Bottom Town men where a rag had been twisted into the neck of a soda bottle filled with kerosene and ignited, creating a phantasmagoria of gleaming skin, light sparking from eyes and angles of metal, the choppy flash of a single thick flame, orange and greasy. The men could not relax for long. They had found their second wind, were standing and stretching and beginning to talk loudly.

"Sterlin, come play *pedro,* mahn. You got money to lose? Mundo, come play wit Sterlin."

Sterling yelled over, "I smokin dis cigahrette. You wait." The cigarette was only a nub of ash stuck to the roll of his lower lip. More kerosene torches flared from the camps of the other fishermen.

Ulysses came back clutching his stomach. He went to the white man first.

"Mistah Bone," he pleaded, "you got some medicines?"

"What sort of medicine?"

"Stomach powdah."

"No, I don't have anything like that," Bowen answered. He was concerned though because Ulysses's stomach was squealing and making duck sounds.

"Where'd you find the duck?"

The boy began to wail. "Oh, Christ. Oh, me ahss, me ahss."

He turned to the other men for help but they wagged their heads without sympathy. Mundo said mockingly, "Dem eggs real good, eh?" and Gabriel turned to Bowen and asked, "You evah see a mahn eat like dis?" Bowen had no answer because he was fascinated by the clamoring coming from inside Ulysses.

1 8 4

Now Ulysses's indulgence was a big joke. He stumbled toward the slick black ocean, stomach quacking hysterically, and Mundo hailed the others to come witness the boy's trouble. The digestive storm at his center doubled Ulysses over and he crawled the final yard to the water, set his face into the glinting surface of the lagoon and drank like a horse, sucking the water into his mouth. The fishermen banded around him; their hooting chorus of laughter escaped out across the expanse of the sea, breaking against the austerity of the fishing grounds. Ulysses jerked his head out of the salt water and roared. The men catcalled above his noise.

"Look, look, him got enough food in he belly to feed ahll Cuba."

"Hey, Ulysses boy, you doan has to feed dem fish. Dey get plenty."

"Maybe he gonna be like dog ahnd eat daht mess right bahck up."

When Ulysses had finished purging himself, he rolled over and smiled up at the men, not like a fool, and not with shame, but like a man whose relief is genuine, a man reconciled past a moment of bad judgment. His father knelt down beside him and gently lifted his son.

"You bettah?" Sterling asked. "You ahlright now?"

"I eat too much of dose dahmn eggs," Ulysses explained without much remorse. "Mundo say eggs still eggs even when dey snotty ahnd stink, but I eat too much. De first one taste good ahnd I must keep eatin dem."

Bowen stared at the boy and felt himself gagging reflexively. He felt his eyes squeeze tight with convulsion, his jaw thrusting away from his skull, his insides closing in upon him as though he, too, had stumbled to his hands and knees to gulp seawater the way a dog will chew grass to make itself heave. The sensation passed into a weightlessness, a rough freshness, and he turned away from the water and walked back to camp.

The men scattered to play *pedro,* to wash the cooking pots, to listen to Gabriel tell a story about a Providence boat that disappeared in Serrana with his father aboard. The wind fell off completely. A small flake of moon rose and gelled the sea. Out in the darkness the coral reefs relented and let the tide pass over them unbroken. Bowen lay on his blanket in the sand, waiting for sleep. The cards ticked loudly against the *pedro* players' soft conversation. The words spread entropically out into the night and somewhere, far out to the black sea, slipped underwater and were lost, flying like souls through an exquisite silence.

Mundo's Sign

In the fading darkness, the small boats, twelve in all, were dragged into the water from the camp on Southwest Cay. Masts were stepped quickly and the sails unfurled in the placid security of the coral lagoon. Wind-filled and ghost-white, they rounded the leeward edge of the cay and scattered in all directions across the fishing banks.

Bowen was in the bow of Mundo's catboat, huddled against the cool dawn breeze. He and Gabriel faced each other, their knees bumping together, but Gabriel lay back relaxing, his arms spread out along the gunnels as if he sat in a bathtub. Mundo was in the stern, his brown flesh sallow without true light, eyes and cheeks puffy, evidence that he had not slept well. Bowen hugged himself, his head down, shivering as the veiled pastel sun lifted from the sea behind him. A bird landed on his shoulder.

"Doan move, mahn," said Gabriel. "Daht is good luck."

The white man turned his head slowly to look at the bird. It was a green finch, little enough to fit in his hand. Through his T-shirt, Bowen felt the light pricking pressure of the bird's claws as it balanced to the rock of the boat.

"A bird never landed on me before," he said.

"Daht is good luck," Gabriel insisted. "Good fah de boat."

The bird fluttered from Bowen's shoulder to the gunnel and then hopped down between his feet, pecking at flecks of dried fish. It ran rodentlike under Gabriel's seat, in and out of sight in the shadows.

"Keep you head down low, Mistah Bone," Mundo said. The word *Mistah* was a joke, a taunt that Bowen had finally to accept. A friendship with Mundo had not been easily established. Bowen had come to Providence because he had heard that sea turtles were still numerous in the waters of the archipelago. They were something he wanted to know about, creatures whose habits informed his own pursuits, the omnibus sciences that made his life what it was, a quest for worlds lost or hidden, for knowledge unavailable to ordinary lives. His interviews with the fishermen led him to Raimundo Bell, the man most respected on Providence Island for his abilities in the water. Mundo had no interest in him at first beyond a natural suspicion, but Bowen offered to trade a share of the everyday work for a seat in Mundo's boat. If it was a question of proving oneself, Bowen did so, he hoped, through his sweat and dirtiness and exhaustion. The difference in the lives of the two men gradually diminished until they took each other for granted. Still, Bowen could not talk Mundo out of calling him *Mistah,* or pronouncing it in a tone that underscored the conspicuous nature of their relationship.

Mundo balanced upright in the back of the boat, the two rudder lines gathered from behind him, held in his big hands like the reins of a horse. "Gabriel?" he warned. Mundo was rarely more than laconic and yet Gabriel always responded precisely. Mundo stooped down, dark and solid, steering for extra wind.

"Yes," Gabriel answered, rising up. "Goin speedify directly, mahn." He began to coil in the mainsheet. The boat heeled and pressed into the tinted water, going faster, bracing the men against the windward hull. Mundo jibed the boat. Once the sail had luffed Gabriel allowed the boom to swing over, combing the back of Bowen's hair. The canvas inhaled again and held the breath. Bowen sat up straight and repositioned his weight in the boat. He could see the sunrise now, chalked with lavender towers of clouds lining up away from it. The light was like a warm hand on his face.

Behind them they heard the slapping of another sail as it dumped wind. "Look dere," said Gabriel. "Ezekiel turnin ah-cross, too,"

"Daht bitch," Mundo grumbled, and twisting his neck he shouted back, "Ezekiel, you old piece ah fuck, you tink you cahn race me, mahn?"

Ezekiel would not answer, nor would he look toward them. Within minutes he had let his boat fall far in their wake. Months ago, Bowen had approached Ezekiel because he heard the doddering fisherman had once caught a malatta hawksbill, a crossbreed between a hawksbill and a green turtle that the experts Bowen had read insisted was only mythical, a tall tale. He wanted to know if they were wrong. Mundo said he himself had shot a malatta, two years ago on the fishing banks in Serrana, and that he had seen the one Ezekiel had netted before it was butchered and sold to the Japanese. When Bowen went to Ezekiel for verification, the old man was incoherent, a pathetic figure who could not focus his memory. Bowen pitied him out loud to Mundo. Mundo said *Daht mahn steal from de mouth of he children. He beat de wife fah rum money. Mahn, when de devil need feelin sorry fah?*

"Mundo, where you goin, mahn?" Gabriel finally asked. Bowen had watched him fidgeting, building up to the question until he was certain of their course. Gabriel was a handsome man and knew it well, shaving his sideburns into broad flairs and wearing a gold cross on a thin strand of wire around his neck. He had once told Bowen he was too good-looking to be a fisherman, that he would like to work in a shop or as a waiter. But on Providence there was no other work but fishing for a man who did not own land. Mundo didn't seem to care though. Mundo loved the sea and never questioned what it brought him or what it took away.

"Mundo, you sleepin?"

"Jewfish Hole," Mundo said, spitting into the water and watching it twirl out of sight. "Headed up daht way."

"True? Not Five Shillin Cay?"

"No."

Gabriel licked his teeth and asked why not. Last night after supper they had discussed where they might fish today. Mundo had argued that if the wind stayed the direction it was, they must sail for Five Shilling Cay or Aguadilla Reef instead of closer waters. That was fine with Bowen because he wanted to go ashore on the cay and see what there was in a place where man never came. *Light bulb, whiskey bottle, piece ah plahstic baby, dead fumey stuff ahnd birds,* Mundo told him. Maybe a malatta hawksbill, too, Bowen added, and Mundo had said *De malatta can be anywheres, mahn. Daht's only luck.*

"Mundo, wake up now. Dis a bahd wind fah Jewfish Hole."

Mundo peered at them both through hooded eyes. "I get a sign," he said. Bowen wondered what he was talking about. Mundo stared past him, out of the boat, measuring the waters of Serrana as if these eighty square miles of unmarked banks were city streets he had grown up on. He veered several degrees off the wind; Gabriel automatically trimmed the sail.

"So you get a sign, Mundo?" Gabriel probed.

"Yeah."

"What's that supposed to be?" Bowen wanted to know. Perhaps the two men were humoring each other to pass the slothful time of the sail. Mundo was too serious and impassive this morning. He should have been singing. He liked to sing when they were sailing: Jim Reeves, Bing-Bing, salsa, anything.

"I get a dream lahst night daht was a sign."

Bowen sniffed at this revelation, fretting. Back on Providence, Mundo didn't play the lottery so he never talked about his dreams like those who did. The town would stir in the morning and somebody would be claiming they had a dream, a good one, and then the dreambook would be consulted, a finger-worn copy published in Harlem in 1928, and the dreams figured out. *No, I tellin you, a white horse is six, de white cow is two six, ahnd a white lady is six one one. In dis dream you see a white lady milkin a white cow? Oh ho! De lady come first, so daht six one one two six. No, I tellin you, is de lady come first, mahn, not de cow. If blahck on de cow, daht six two.* A boy would be sent running to Alvaro's shop to buy the number. But Mundo always said the lottery was foolish.

Bowen dipped his hand over the side to feel the water. He liked the unworried, surging speed of the catboat, the white and rose and amber colors of the bottom refracted and blurry, just colors streaming by through the window of the surface. "Is that so?" Bowen asked. "You had a dream?" Mundo said yeah.

"I didn't know you dreamed, Mundo," Bowen said. "Did you dream you saw a white lady wearing a white dress riding a white jackass?"

"Mistah Bone think you makin joke, Mundo," said Gabriel. "He believe you jokifyin."

Mundo's eyes sparked, showing Bowen the hubris he saw in many black men. "Dis a sign fah dis place only," he replied harshly. He was moodier than Bowen had ever seen him. This place, Bowen thought. This place wasn't a place at all. It was wide open. It was openness, sunlight shattered blue and unstopped in all directions. There was another world beneath, a mint-cool wilderness, treacherous and lush, but here on the surface the boat pushed into an empty seascape.

"No kidding?" Bowen asked.

"No."

"What's the sign?"

"Fuck a mahn."

"Oh yeah?" Bowen said incredulously.

"Fuck a mahn."

"Daht a funny sign, Mundo," said Gabriel.

"What's he talking about?" Bowen asked Gabriel almost incidentally, squinting beyond him to study Mundo. His skin was slicker now in the sun and the light stuck across Mundo's narrow face in sharp pieces, leaving him cheekbones but no cheeks and emphasizing his stolid mouth, lips parted but no teeth visible. Bowen expected Mundo to grin at him but he didn't. His distance seemed acted out, like part of a magician's masquerade. He's playing with me, Bowen thought. No, he decided, looking at him again, he's serious.

"So Mundo, you fuck a mahn, eh?" Gabriel said.

"Yeah, boy," Mundo answered. He began to uncurl his arms and legs from the tight ball he sat in and warmed up to his story. "I dream I fuck a mahn. I stayin in Costa Rica, in Puerto Limon, when I play basebahll in de leagues, ahnd I stayin in dis residencia. Dis girlie mahn come to visit wit a bottle of aguardiente. We drink de bottle, den I fuck him."

"Oh ho," said Gabriel, as if he were saying, Yes, I see.

Mundo navigated the boat through a porcelain blue channel that furrowed between two ridges of coral. Outside the reef, the water deepened abruptly, a darkening translucence. The waves rose to one-third the height of the mast. They were on the open sea now, outside the coral walls. The faraway sail of Ezekiel's boat had disappeared. Mundo followed the reef northward. Already the sun was strong and Bowen was acutely aware of its power to stupefy. Before the words dried up in his mouth and his mind muddled, he wanted to know what it was about the dream that meant something to Mundo.

"You dreamed you fucked a man," he said cautiously. "What does that mean? What kind of a sign is that?"

"A good one," replied Mundo.

The bird reappeared on Mundo's knee. He made a quick

grab for it, but the finch was in the air, scooting low over the waves.

"Come again next day," Gabriel called after it. The bird hooked east toward whatever land might lie that way.

The mystery had become too much for Bowen. He mimicked Alvaro the bookie and his high rapid voice, like a little dog's: "Costa Rica, dat's two oh one; mon's arsehole, dat's nought; drinkin aguardiente, dat's oh oh oh. Boy, you get a nice numbah dere, Mundo. Put a fiver on it, mon."

Mundo's weak smile made Bowen feel patronized. The black man blinked ostentatiously, widening his hidden eyes as if only now he had reason to come awake, to come away from the dream.

"No, let me tell you, Mistah Bone. Dis sign mean I must shoot a big he hawksbill," Mundo said emphatically. He raised his thick right forearm. His fist clenched, the dark muscles flexed from elbow to wrist. "Big!" he said.

"Mistah Bone doan believe," said Gabriel in a sad, false voice. He nodded at Bowen. "He is a sci-ahnce mahn. He only see sci-*ahnce.*" Then Gabriel laughed, pushing Bowen's knee good-naturedly.

Hearing Mundo and Gabriel talk about the sign made Bowen feel for a moment that he had lost all contact with them. He leaned forward earnestly, resting his forearms along his bare thighs. He could not resist speaking and yet he hesitated, sure that he was being drawn into trouble.

"Tell me, you can shoot a hawksbill turtle because you dreamed you assholed somebody?" An image of the dream flicked through his mind: Mundo bent over slim, tar-black buttocks, mounting like a beast, the *girlie mahn* in a stupor, slurring a languid, corrupt Castilian. "How is that?"

"How you mean, mahn?" Mundo looked keenly at Bowen, a challenging eyebrow cocked, teasing him with a crooked smile, ready to invite Bowen into his house and then beat him at dominoes all night long. "You evah fuck a mahn, Mistah Bone?"

"No," Bowen said immediately. He was surprised that the

question had embarrassed him so easily, as if it exposed a level of manhood he had not achieved.

"Mistah Bone want to investigate everyting, but he doan fuck a mahn yet?" Gabriel said, his voice scaling to a parody of a question.

"Some men just be like womahn. Gabriel—right?"

"Daht's true. It's de same, mahn."

"Oh, Christ," Bowen said, shaking his head ruefully. He tried to play along. "Let's let it all out."

"So Mistah Bone," Mundo continued, "you evah take a womahn like daht?"

"My God."

"You doan like it?"

Bowen folded his arms across his chest and refused to answer. There were pieces of himself he did not wish to share, even in a game. To be forced to this realization, to admit that something in him would instinctively retreat into rock like a sea anemone, made him angry.

"Mistah Bone," Mundo said, "when we reach bahck to Providence we find you a mahn to fuck." Gabriel winked at Bowen.

"No thanks," Bowen answered coolly. "You two black queers."

Separating himself from the conversation, Mundo came up off his seat to look around. Bowen wondered how he could know where they were when there was absolutely nothing out there to sight on. Mundo sat back down, rocking rhythmically from side to side, letting the waves loosen his shoulders and neck, danced by the sea.

"Fuck fucka fucka mahn," he chanted.

"Sail the boat."

"Sailin like a real bitch right now."

"Black man bullshit. Jungle stuff."

"Uh-oh, Mundo. Mistah Bone vexed now wit dis dream bodderation."

"All right. All right. Enough," Bowen declared. "Do that trick, shoot the turtle, then I'll start fucking men. Maybe you first, Gabriel."

"Oh me God, Mundo." Gabriel laughed. "Look what you talk Mistah Bone into."

"He gettin de picture now, boy," Mundo said. "You doan worry, Gabriel. Mistah Bone lookin hahd to fuck dis bunch ah guys bahck in de States who say malatta hawksbill a make-believe. You not hear him say so?"

"I got the picture now, so let's drop all this somethingness out of nothingness."

"Pretty talk," said Gabriel.

Bowen resented his ambition described through such a coarse metaphor, but now that the point had been made, he felt comfortable again with the two black men. Mundo said nothing more but sat quietly like a schoolboy with an expression of overbearing innocence.

They sailed for another twenty minutes, cutting progressively nearer to the reef until they were only yards away from the foam left behind by the waves that broke across the shallow coral. Then the reef bowled inward, pinched by a channel which they rode through into calmer water. After a short distance, Mundo tacked back toward the inside of the main reef, and when they were a couple of miles down-current from the channel, he steered into the wind.

"Come, you workin today, mahn?" Mundo called. Bowen looked at him stupidly. He had let himself fall into a daze, the light, like thick crystals growing on the water, overcoming him. His deeply tanned skin felt scratchy and sore and gluey.

"Get de sail, mahn. Quick."

Bowen jerked himself out of his lethargy and stood up, holding the gunnels for balance. He concentrated on his equilibrium, judging how the water moved the boat until he was sure of himself, straightened up, and then leapt from the bottom of the boat to his seat. He grabbed the mast with one hand and extended the other one out toward Gabriel. Gabriel stood behind him, rolling the sailcloth onto the boom as far as he could, passing it to Bowen until the flour-sack sail was furled around the wood and the boom was parallel with the mast.

"Gabriel, watch out," Bowen said.

"You okay, Mistah Bone. You become ahn expert."

But Bowen wanted to know that Gabriel was ready if he should lose his footing in the pitch of the boat. He lashed the boom and mast tight together with the sheet line, grunting as it took all his strength to lift the long heavy mast from its step. He rested the butt on the seat, spread his arms on the poles like a weight lifter and lowered the mast slowly to Gabriel and then Mundo, who had their arms up ready to receive it.

When the mast was down, they passed it back to Mundo far enough so he could get it under the seats to stow. Bowen pulled the two handmade oars from the gear in the bottom of the boat. Slipping them through the rope oarlocks midway on each gunnel, he jammed them back into the boat and left them ready while the boat drifted. It was still early in the morning.

"Sun hot," Gabriel said. He always said this before he set to work.

"Daht's right."

"Watah too cool," he said, cupping his hand into the sea and splashing his face. Bowen stood up to negotiate a piss with the churning of the boat but remained there for some minutes prick in hand, unable to relax.

"Mahn, jump in de sea if you want a piss."

He removed his shirt and sat down with his legs over the gunnel. Mundo and Gabriel leaned to the opposite hull to counterbalance the canoelike boat and then quickly leaned back after Bowen hefted himself over the side. He let himself sink a few feet below the keel, felt the temperature subtly change, cooler and cooler until it was all the same, the blue pressure bearing against him completely. He opened his eyes briefly, welcoming the rough bite of the salt that took away his drowsiness. He kicked back to the surface, spinning in slow circles for the pleasure of it, relieved himself and struggled back into the boat. Without a diving mask to clearly see what else was there with him, he did not like to stay in the water long. No matter how casual Mundo and Gabriel could be around sharks, Bowen couldn't muster the same aloofness. They chided him about this, but still, Mundo wore a cummerbund of old sheet around his waist for bandaging in case of trouble. And Gabriel's left arm was arced with purple scars across his bicep. *Ahn eel do daht. Shark doan molest mahn. It's true.*

Bowen dried his face and hands on his shirt and put it back on as protection against the sun. Underneath the bow seat he kept an oatmeal tin. He stretched and found it, unscrewing the lid. Inside, wrapped in a plastic bag to keep out moisture, were a pack of Pielrojas, a box of matches, the precious spear points, and a sack of hard candy labeled simply *Dulces* which he had bought at Alvaro's right before the fishermen had set sail on the *Orion* from Providence eight days ago. The candy had turned gummy in the sea air. He took a red piece and bit into its waxy surface, chewing vigorously and swallowing the whole lump without determining its flavor. The sweetness took the salty, sour heat out of his mouth. Mundo asked for a Pielroja and Bowen lit one for him, smoking it down a bit before he passed it along with the point for Mundo's spear. Bowen switched places with Gabriel and began to row, bringing the boat around into the current, pulling against the tide just enough to stay where they were.

The black men silently outfitted themselves and to Bowen they already had the grim look of hunters on them. The cigarette jutted straight out like a weapon in Mundo's tight lips. He propped his long metal gun between his legs and unclasped its spear, screwing on the point, securing the catch line, and then set the gun aside while he pulled black flippers snug on his white-soled feet. Bowen watched him; each piece of equipment he added on seemed to alter his humanness, and now, more so than with the dream business, Mundo was becoming inaccessible, the friendship between them a triviality. From under his seat the fisherman took his diving mask and spit on the inside of the glass, spreading the tobacco-flecked phlegm with his fingers to prevent the glass from fogging. He washed the mask out in the sea and adjusted it to rest on his forehead, pressing into the short curls of his hair, not kinky hair like Gabriel's but

more Latin, straighter and oily. He sucked the ash of the cigarette down next to his lips, knocking the butt off into the water
with his tongue before it burned him. He exhaled deeply, and
then inhaled, and then exhaled normally. Turtles made that
same noise when they sounded for air, thought Bowen, that
sudden, single gasp of inhalation bobbing out of the sea from
nowhere. Mundo's eyes were featureless, without pupils, the
irises dark, without color. Go fuck your big turtle, Bowen said
to himself. He began to see that the prophecy was an easy one
—like a handsome man boasting he would seduce an available
woman—because there were plenty of turtles in the water.
This was their mating season, the end of the hurricanes. They
had come from all over the ocean to return here to breed.

"Ahll right," Mundo said softly, and pulled his mask down
over his eyes and nose. He was out of the boat promptly, disappearing below the surface.

Gabriel procrastinated, sharpening the point of his spear
on the block of limestone they carried in the boat. Bowen
heard Mundo purge his snorkel. Looking over his shoulder to
check the diver's position, he began to row.

"Wait a minute, Mistah Bone," Gabriel said. He slung his
legs over the side and crossed himself vaguely, lifting the cru-
cifix from his chest to kiss. He fitted the mouthpiece of the
snorkel behind his lips and they bulged apishly. Splashing into
the water, face down, the gun ready, he turned a spiral to
examine what was there below him.

Bowen pulled ahead six times and then paused, unable to
locate Mundo. Gabriel was to Bowen's left, kicking mechani-
cally into the two-knot current, his gun cradled from elbow to
elbow. Mundo surfaced ten yards ahead, going down again like
a porpoise. Bowen went after him, quickly over the glossy boil
that marked Mundo's dive.

He leaned out of the boat and looked down. Below him in
about eight fathoms of water he could see Mundo in pieces,
distorted fragments of motion rising and coalescing into
human shape, the curve of his dark back floating up to him, the
red faded trunks looking like raw skin under the water.

His back broke the surface first, a long brown bubble, smooth and headless. The snorkel poked up, gargled and wheezed. There was a moment's calm before the water in front of the diver was flying apart, twisting and scattering and white. Blood swelled olive-green from the center of it all. Mundo fought for control over something Bowen had not yet fully seen. Again there was quiet. And then this: Mundo's torso suddenly out of the water, pendulous beside the boat, his arm dipping the spear down inside and letting a slab of great, furious life slide off it at Bowen's feet. The fish was as long as the arm that had released it, violently thrashing, the fan of its dorsal spines sharp enough to cut through leather. Bowen fell back off his seat, drawing his legs out of the way.

"Jesus."

He found the ironwood mallet and bent over, striking at the fish, unable to hit it effectively. Blood and bits of rubbery tissue sprayed on his chest. Finally its movements slowed and he was able to direct a clean blow to the broad, bull-like slope of its head.

"Goddammit."

The shot had not been clean. The spear had struck behind the head but too low to hit the spinal cord. It had entered through the huge gills—thus the excess of blood now in the boat—and come out on the other side below the pectoral fin. The blood all over Bowen made him feel filthy. He was stone-eyed now, full of his job. Mundo's head popped over the gunnel. He was amused.

"You like daht one, mahn?"

"Shoot better," Bowen said.

Mundo laughed wickedly and sank out of sight. Bowen could hear the click of the spear sliding into the latch of the trigger as Mundo reloaded the spring-action gun against the hull of the boat. Gabriel was calling. He held his spear in the air, a lobster skewered on the end of it. Bowen was there in a minute, screwing off the flanged spear point to take the catch into the boat.

He set the oars and stood up to rearrange the gear under

his seat. Mundo's fish was a grouper, by Bowen's estimate twenty-five to thirty pounds. To shield it from the sun he tugged it into the cleared space below the seat. The lobster was thrown into the stern behind a coil of rope. He used to put the lobsters with the fish, but if they weren't dead they kept crawling out from beneath him and he would stab his feet on the thorns of their shells. Before he could sit down again Gabriel was beside the boat with another lobster.

"Four more in de hole, boy. I tellin you, de bird was good luck."

Bowen hovered over Gabriel until the diver had brought up the remaining lot. It took some time and only then did Bowen search for Mundo. He spotted him far off, impatiently waving the boat forward. The muscles in Bowen's arms cramped from the fast rowing. By the time he reached him, Mundo had his face back down in the water, staying afloat with his fins. Bowen had to shout to get his attention. Mundo raised his head, a glare in his eyes exaggerated by the mask. He lifted a fish up and hurled it into the boat.

"What's the matter?" Bowen asked defensively. "Sharks?"

"Keep up, mahn. Keep up."

"Yeah, yeah." Bowen shrugged off Mundo's admonishment. It was impossible to stay with both divers unless both divers stayed together. He took his own mask and held it on top of the water, providing a small round view of the scene below. There were no dark, darting shadows, nothing ominous at all.

Mundo swam crosscurrent into deeper water, his flippers continuously paddling the surface. In pursuit of something beneath him he doubled back and sped past the boat headed in the opposite direction. He vanished as Bowen put all his effort into turning the boat around, determined to keep on top of the action. He heard the rasp then, a sound like a vacuum filling with air. Off the starboard he saw the green, pale-throated head of the turtle bouncing in the swell and he understood Mundo's urgency, because two or three turtles would double the value of a day's work. He couldn't see Mundo, but he knew the man was carefully ascending beneath the creature, taking slow aim. The turtle lurched forward and tried to submerge as the spear shot through one of its hind flippers. Mundo surfaced, hauling the spear line in until the turtle was beside him, hopelessly struggling to shake the iron rod from its leg. Bowen was right there.

"Nice work," Bowen said. "You did it."

Mundo handed the gun to Bowen. While Bowen held the turtle by the rim of its shell, Mundo wrestled to extract the spear. Once he had succeeded in unscrewing the point, it slid out easily from the thin flesh of the flipper.

"He's a big one."

"Not so big."

"He's a male and pretty big. That was your sign."

"Nah," Mundo grunted.

"Close enough."

"Dis no hawksbill. Lift him up now."

The green turtle weighed close to a hundred pounds. Bowen almost fell out of the boat pulling him in. The turtle banged down the curve of the hull, its flippers clawing for water that wasn't there, a dull calloused scrape across the wood, its mouth gasping, the lower mandible unlocked like an old man's jaw. I'll be damned, thought Bowen, this was the biggest turtle their boat had brought in here on the banks. Only two logger-heads netted by the boat with the old men were bigger.

He turned the heavy green on its back. The yellow plates of its belly glowed like pinewood. He set his feet on them, feeling the turtle's cold-bloodedness. Its sea-smell was clean, without mucus or secretion. From inside a wooden toolbox Bowen took the small bundle of palm fronds that every Providence fishing boat carried. He pulled two short strands from it. Grabbing one of the turtle's anterior flippers, he placed it against the hull and with the tip of his diving knife punched a small hole through the glazed flesh that formed the shape of a man's hand with the fingers fused together. He did the same to the flipper behind it and then threaded the cuts with a frond, tying the ends off in a square knot. With its fore and hind legs thus bound, the turtle was immobile.

Prayin from both ends, the fishermen called this.

"Why don't you use fishing line?" Bowen had asked when he first saw Gabriel bind a turtle.

"Palm leaf nice," Gabriel told him. "Turtle ahpreciate daht."

Bowen rowed on, occasionally pausing to fill the calabash bailer with seawater and cool the turtle that now suffered the sun. The first time he did this the turtle curled its head and appeared to look at him. Bowen turned away. It made him feel foolish but he did not like to see a sea turtle's eyes. The eyes were too mammalian and expressive, a more vivid brown than the eyes of a human being, lugubrious. They teared out of water, salty silk tears beading down the reptilian scales, and he did not like to see it. In the ocean there was no movement with more grace, no ballet more perfect, than the turtle's.

The men worked for several more hours before switching. Mundo shot another turtle, an average-size hawksbill which Bowen tied and was able to fit under the seat. There was a long period with no luck. Then, like a magic returning, the divers found fish again. The boat began to fill up.

Bowen tended to the divers, the citric tang of sweat in his nostrils, his eyes closed now and then to soothe them from the glare. His blue trunks and white T-shirt were smeared with blood and the gray slime that came off the fish. Trailing the swimmers, his back to them as he rowed forward, he counted the strokes of the oars, an empty meditation broken by the need to cool the turtles or take another fish into the boat. Alone again he would look up, his thoughts not yet refocused on his labor, and be startled by the uncut geography of the sea, the desolate beauty, the isolation.

The sun was straight up and fierce. Patches of wind blew off the glassy veneer of the surface. The waves lumped high enough to conceal the divers if they weren't close to the boat. Mundo and Gabriel trod water together, talking in bursts, their snorkels jutting out from under their chins. Bowen came over to them. Hours in the sea had made Mundo look younger, Gabriel older. They clung to the side of the boat.

"Mistah Bone, dis Jewfish Hole a pretty spot. Come give Gabriel a rest."

Bowen stowed the oars and went to the bow for his diving gear, anxious to leave the confinement of the boat, the blind sense of being denied something others took for granted. They would not always let him fish. They had spent their lives on the water; for all his effort, Bowen could not begin to match their skill. On a good day, though, he would take over for Gabriel. Mundo had an appetite for the reef and knew that Bowen, more than Gabriel ever would, felt the same way. There were times when he would come and hurry Bowen out of the boat if there was something extraordinary he wanted the white man to see. They swam together like two farm boys at a carnival, exploring everywhere, the joy of it all and the mystery running between them like an electric ribbon.

Bowen lowered himself into the water after Gabriel was settled in the boat. His ears filled with the steady fizzing static of the ocean moving against its cup of earth. The reef seemed scooped out here, forming a wide horseshoe-shaped arena, ten fathoms deep in the middle where they were, the bottom tiering up in shaggy clusters of coral until the perimeter shallowed in a dense thicket of staghorn branches. A school of fry, a long cloud of flashing arrows, passed with the current toward them herded by watchful barracuda. It parted and reclosed around the divers, obscuring them from each other's sight for several moments.

The sandy paths of the surge channels wove through the swaying flora on the bottom, continuing up like white banners from the open end of the pool where the water gathered more dimension and the channels disappeared into a fog of infinite blue. Here the current pushed in from outside the reef.

They started to swim. Bowen followed Mundo's lead. Gabriel stopped them with a shout.

"Mundo, me see a boat."

Mundo swam like a dog with his head up and coughed out his snorkel: "Who?"

"Cahn't see. He way up, mahn."

Mundo stuck his head back in the water, uninterested in this news. He led them closer to the coral walls, turning again into the current when the water reached about forty feet, the depth at which Bowen managed best. They swam toward the wide mouth of the canyon which kept expanding as they kicked onward. Beyond, the visibility closed and faded, a chiaroscuro lanced by drifting shafts of sunlight. The blank distance shadowed and materialized into shapes, accumulating more and more detail as they moved ahead.

Bowen swam with his gun out in front of him like a soldier on patrol. Surveying an isolated button of brain coral, Mundo pointed to the antennae of a spiny lobster. Bowen jackknifed and dove, missed the first shot. On the second shot he took aim more carefully. There was a screeching sound of old armor when he yanked the lobster from its den. He ascended quickly, fighting for the sterling surface as he ran out of air. Gabriel came alongside.

"I see two guys," he reported, taking the spear from Bowen and removing the point. "Maybe daht's Ezekiel." Bowen didn't respond. It wasn't so unusual to see another of the boats off in the distance during the course of the day. The fact that the boat was close enough for Gabriel to see the men in it didn't mean anything to Bowen. He reloaded his gun and swam away to catch up with Mundo.

Together they continued ahead, frequently descending to inspect a cave or niche in the polychromatic reef. Fish were everywhere but they sought only those that appealed to the restaurants of the mainland. Cutting in and out of a gray forest of gorgonian coral, a mako shark rose toward them curiously but then stopped halfway and returned to its prowling. The shark was too small and too preoccupied to worry Bowen; still, he had tensed upon first seeing it, and adrenaline drove into his heart. Mundo plummeted down, found the shark interested in a red snapper nosing in the silt for food, and shot the fish. The shark skirted away when Mundo jabbed at it with his empty gun. The boat was there when he surfaced.

"It's Ezekiel," Gabriel told the two of them. He slipped a hand into the gills of the fish and took it from Mundo. "Ahnd Henry Billings. Dey driftin on de current from down de outside."

"Turtlin," Mundo said. He handed his spear to Bowen while he defogged his mask.

Ezekiel and Henry were too old to dive anymore—*divin squeeze up a mahn's insides*—but they came along on expeditions to the banks to line fish, net turtles, and collect conchs from the shallows. They did not mingle much with the other fishermen who were mostly young and scorned the insipidness of fishing with a hand line and hook. Gaunt and unhealthy, Ezekiel looked like a wrinkled black puppet, simian with lackluster eyes. He suffered the bitter condescension of the islanders because he was too much a drunkard. Most people treated Henry Billings, round and smooth-faced, as though he were a moron. Bowen had never heard him speak a word, and neither had anybody else for more than twenty years.

"Dey lookin excited, boy," Gabriel said, standing up to get a better view. Bowen and Mundo could not see the other boat from the water. "Ezekiel buryin he head in de glahss, ahnd Henry rowin hahd hahd like he racin home fah pussy."

Mundo pushed away from the boat, followed by Bowen, who had trouble catching his breath. They were now approaching the same windward channel in the barrier reef that they had sailed through earlier in the morning. The water doubled in depth, the bottom became more sand than coral. Bowen kicked harder to keep up with Mundo as the current increased. It tugged against him relentlessly and he began to tire. He halted and pressed himself out of the water as far as possible but could not see Mundo over the swell of the waves. He tried to move ahead again, grew discouraged and let the tide sweep him back to the boat.

Gabriel helped him aboard. Bowen saw that they were going out through the channel while Ezekiel's boat was steering in a hundred and fifty feet or so in front of them off the port. Mundo was almost halfway between the two boats, still headed straight upcurrent.

"Dey on de trail," Gabriel said. They watched Ezekiel take one hand off the waterglass and reach behind himself to grasp an iron-hooped net used to catch turtles. Ezekiel called back to Henry, urging him forward. He held the net over the bow, waiting for position. Mundo spun in the water. He looked quickly around and then back at his own boat. Bowen saw him, imagined he saw the calculating look in his enlarged eyes. He stood on the aft seat and waved his arms at the diver. Mundo put his head back down and charged across the channel, angling toward Ezekiel's boat.

"Mundo!"

Bowen was not certain if Mundo realized Ezekiel's boat was so close. He yelled again.

"Mundo!"

Ezekiel positioned the net and dropped it. Mundo was past the center of the channel and nearing the other boat. In an instant he was out of sight under the water. Perched in front of the boat, his face hidden by the wooden sides of the waterglass, Ezekiel became more and more animated until he had come to his feet, his head still stuck ostrichlike in the box. He took one hand off the glass to shake his fist.

"Mundo," he shouted in a garbled voice, difficult to understand. "Mundo. Wha de fuck!"

"Oh, shit," Gabriel said. "Look Ezekiel dere bein so voicetrous. Mahn, he cryin a lot of nonsense, you know."

Mundo had been down for about two minutes and his limit was four. Bowen pulled on his mask and rolled over the side of the boat, biting down on the mouthpiece of his snorkel just as he hit the water. Son of a bitch, he said to himself, seeing what was happening below.

Suspended in deep water six or seven fathoms down,

Mundo labored to free the turtle from Ezekiel's net. One hind flipper was loose, pierced by the spear and sea-anchored by the gun which Mundo had let drop. The diver held the turtle by the stub of its penis-tail and used his free hand to untangle the netting from the other back flipper. Bent around the turtle so his feet were in front of him, he kicked himself backward to resist Ezekiel's effort to raise the net. The turtle's flipper finally pulled clear and flailed wildly about.

With one set of flippers extended, the turtle was easily Mundo's length, the caramel and yellow carapace twice the man's width. Its great size magnified by the thick lens of water, the turtle seemed unreal, like a comic-book monster, to Bowen. Mundo moved spiritedly, hovering now on the back of the turtle. He reached for a front flipper but the turtle fought him. Each time he worked the limb out of the net the turtle jerked and recaught itself. The diver sprung off the turtle as if he were a rider being dismounted into the sky. He exhaled as he ascended, silver spheres of air boiling from his mouth, forming a column which he appeared to climb hand over hand to the surface. Bowen heard the agonized suck of his inhalation— "Mundo!" this from Ezekiel—and then he was down again.

By the time Mundo was back to the turtle, Ezekiel had hauled the net up nearer to the surface. Bowen dived to help his partner but he had entered the water without his fins and could not make the depth. At the bottom of his descent, he saw Mundo bend the turtle's left flipper back through the net and wrench it over the shell. As Bowen turned upward, he heard the crack of the turtle's elbow joint dislocating.

Gabriel threw Bowen his fins. By the time he had them on, the turtle was out of the net, its two foreflippers dangling awkwardly, the third flipper weighted by the spear, the fourth performing its sad ballet. Mundo dipped below the turtle, retrieving the gun that hung from the spear by its line. He swam sluggishly toward the air with the turtle in tow by its impaled flipper. Bowen watched them rise. The sight of the black man and the turtle was like a dream-borne image floating in cool ether. The bright surface gleamed like the edge of sleep, the head of the leviathan turned from it toward the indigo mouth of the channel that sloped down and down and away.

They came up between the two boats. Ezekiel began his protest.

"Daht my hawksbill, Mundo. Wha hahppen, mahn? Wha hahppen?"

"Here now, Ezekiel," Gabriel shouted back. "You makin a mess ah noise, boy. Stop dis ugliness."

Mundo kept his back to Ezekiel's boat and would not answer the charge. He dragged the spear line in, bringing the turtle between him and Bowen. Both men caught hold of opposite sides of the shell and waited for Gabriel to position himself. The turtle wagged its huge head back and forth out of the water.

"Wha hahppen, mahn?"

"Ezekiel," Gabriel said across the negligible distance between the boats. "You shut up."

"Wha hahppen, mahn?"

"Shut up now or come here ahnd take some licks."

Mundo and Bowen faced each other over the mound of the carapace. Blood clotted on the side of Mundo's face.

"Doan move up too high, Mistah Bone," Mundo warned. "Keep in de middle or he snahp you."

"You're bleeding some."

Mundo grinned. To Bowen his grin seemed to celebrate only mischievousness.

"Did you shoot him," Bowen asked quietly, "before they netted him?"

"You have to guess, mahn?" The tone of Mundo's voice didn't answer Bowen but simply posed the question. Bowen suspected that the net had reached the turtle before Mundo had but there was no way to prove it. Only Mundo and Ezekiel knew for sure.

"This is a fucking big turtle," he said.

It took them awhile to get the hawksbill into the boat. Ezekiel and Henry raised their mast and set sail for the camp on Southwest Cay. Gabriel restepped their own mast to give them more room in the bottom of the boat, but even so they had to remove the middle seat to fit the turtle in. Bowen straddled the shell. He subdued the flippers and tied them off with palm fronds. He was shivering unconsciously, a condition Gabriel called *dog-leg*. When Mundo joined them the boat sank low in the water. He took his seat in the stern and stared thoughtfully at the turtle as if he were preparing to interrogate it.

"Dis beast must weigh tree hundred pounds, Mundo," Gabriel proclaimed.

"Daht's good luck."

All at once Bowen was throbbing, tired, hungry and thirsty. The oatmeal can and water bottle were buried in the chaos of fish and rope; he had no energy to look for them.

Gabriel unfurled the sail and changed places with Bowen on the turtle to work the sheet line. They began the long sail back. Because there were only a few inches of freeboard left to the boat Mundo would not let Gabriel trim the sail too tightly. The boat plugged languidly through the head seas. When they were on a direct course, Gabriel put the sheet line between his horny toes and stepped on it to keep it in place. He and Bowen scaled the fish and cleaned them, dropping the guts overboard into the water that was still clear but now colorless again, the blue gone out of it with the beginning of twilight. *Come, shark, come,* Gabriel said each time. *Here's a nice piece ah food. I treat you good, you know.* Mundo sang country and western songs, throwing all the melodrama he could into them. The air became steely and dense with haze.

They entered the lagoon shortly after dark. For some time they had been seeing a flickering bright light coming from the camp; even from a mile off at sea it cast a wobbly, liquid thread of illumination that ran out from the cay to their boat. It was obvious now that someone had built a large bonfire on the shore, and as Mundo steered into the shallows and they prepared to beach, a man moved out of the darkness into the firelight, the flames curling above his head. To Bowen the silhouette was crippled—the shadow of a beggar.

"Mundo," Gabriel said. "Ezekiel want to make a cry, mahn."

Mundo thieved the hawksbill from him, Ezekiel shouted crazily. The other fishermen gathered around him now. *Mundo teef de hawksbill. Wha hahppen, Mundo? Henry, come tell dem, mahn.* But Henry would not come out of the darkness and speak. As they dragged the boat ashore, the fishermen moved down next to the water to help them and to have a look at the big turtle. Amid the crowd, the talking all at once, the three of them were solemn and efficient, anxious for an end to the work. Ezekiel pushed forward, keeping the boat between himself and Mundo.

"Wha hahppen, Mundo?" he said witlessly. "Wha hahppen, mahn? You fuck me."

Mundo would not acknowledge him but spoke instead to the other men assembled around the boat. He looked predatory in the changing light of the fire, dangerous.

"I shoot de hawksbill," Mundo said. "You see it dere in my boat. De hell wit daht bitch Ezekiel." He wouldn't say anything more. Together he and Bowen lifted the two big turtles out of the boat and placed them gently in the sand. The old man yelled a lot but Bowen could not understand what he was saying. Colbert, a fisherman from the same village as Ezekiel, called out boldly from the group.

"Gabriel, speak up, mahn."

Gabriel talked softly as though to counterbalance Mundo's bitter disdain for Ezekiel. Although he would not speculate about what happened in the water, he explained how on their way out in the morning Mundo had revealed his dream, and how the bird had flown into the boat. Immediately the excitement returned. The dream and the bird inflated the drama and the importance of the dispute, and this pleased the onlookers. Someone called for Bowen to tell what he knew. Most of the men stopped arguing to hear him. Bowen was reluctant to speak, aware of his difference and how it would distort what he said to them, how it would become a story that began, *Ahnd den de white mahn say . . .*

"It was like Gabriel said. Mundo told us he had a dream about fucking a man. He said this was a sign that meant he was to shoot a big male hawksbill. There's the turtle right there."

"Sci-*ahnce* mahn doan carry faith in dreams," someone yelled at him. "Dreams is fah peoples like we."

"That's so, but this one came true, didn't it," Bowen said calmly.

Ezekiel shoved forward toward him. "No," he shouted. "Dis dream a lie. Mundo teef de hawksbill. Wha hahppen, Mundo?"

"The dream is no lie," Bowen said, unable to avoid his irritation. He hated the way the focus had been transformed entirely onto him. It seemed that everyone except Mundo was ready to grant him the full authority of his judgment because he was white and educated.

"Yes," a voice agreed. "But you see Mundo shoot de hawksbill before de net reach?"

Gabriel spoke before anyone else could. "Mahn, what de fuck it mattah? De dream come true. Daht's daht. Quit dis fuss."

Bowen bent over into the boat to collect the spear guns, wary that Ezekiel would see only him, blame only him, and that if there was uncertainty on his face he must hide it from them, because he knew now what he had to say. On the sail back Mundo and the turtle wouldn't leave his mind. There was the dream, as undeniable as it was incomprehensible, a coincidence announcing itself, a magic somehow conspired between man and beast.

Out of the corner of his eye he saw Mundo watching him. Bowen wished he could know what the black man was thinking, but he had no intuition for what was at stake between them. His only clear impulse was to protect the mystery of the dream.

"Mundo shot the turtle. The net wasn't there yet."

"You see it, mahn?"

"That's how it happened."

"You see it hahppen daht way?"

MUNDO'S SIGN

"I'm telling you what I know."

Bowen's proclamation put an end to it. Everyone agreed then that the hawksbill was Mundo's. Ezekiel wouldn't be quiet, but he walked away from them anyway, still shouting passionately, and others shouted back at him to shut up. The men went back to their cooking fires to have their suppers. The three of them were alone again. As they finished unloading the boat, Mundo whispered to Gabriel, "Mistah Bone find a mahn to fuck."

"Oh ho," said Gabriel, turning around to see if Bowen had heard. "Maybe next he get a sign, too. Mistah Bone—right?"

No guilt burned into him, or sympathy for Ezekiel. The dream was more important than what he had or had not seen. Mundo had come to the turtle first, through the dream, and that could not be changed, not by Bowen, not by Ezekiel's net. It frightened him that something so intangible could become so absolute in his mind. He confronted Mundo.

"Was I wrong?"

"You must decide, mahn. But you doan has to lie fah me."

"I did it because of the dream."

"Maybe daht's so," Mundo said, watching Bowen carefully. "Maybe you find out someting."

"I should have stayed out of it," he said.

"No, mahn, you was right, so you must fuck Ezekiel so. De hawksbill was mine no mattah what you say to dem."

They picked up their gear and hauled it to camp. While Gabriel prepared to cook their supper, Bowen found his tape measure, notebook and pencil and went with Mundo back to the boat. Together they carried the turtles down the beach and set them under the narrow thatched ramada built by the fishermen to shelter them from the sun. Bowen tallied the ones brought in today by all the boats, measured the length and width of their shells, counted the dorsal plates, recording the sex and species. As always, he checked for the milk-white markings of a malatta hawksbill. Mundo scratched his initials into the chests of his turtles with a diving knife.

"Damn," Bowen said, finished with his notes. "No malatta."

"Daht's only luck, mahn. Have faith."

The firelight rubbed weakly on the carapaces and spun small gold drops orbiting in the eyes of the turtles. Their flippers crooked front to back underneath the rows of shells, the palm fronds pinning them firmly together in a frozen clap, an endless prayer.

"I goin bahck."

"All right. I'll be there in a while."

Bowen did not know why he wanted to stay with the turtles but he lay down in the broken coral, too tired to help with supper, and listened to the sea creatures take their air, the gasping litany that committed them to the surface and to men. He saw them in the sea again, male and female clasped together, hawksbill and green turtle, the plates of their shells flush. They would join each other in this embrace and mate, drifting in the shallows, pushing up together to breathe, the female encircled by the flippers of the male for a day and a night until the mythical pas de deux ended and a new form conceived from different bloods. Then they would unlock to spend a year alone in the sea. The images stopped there and he felt himself falling asleep. He did not want to sleep here in the ramada with the turtles so he rose and walked back to camp, to the men and to the pleasure of food. The sea pulled back off the reef, its tidal sucking audible, the air brought down through coral bones and exhaled again and again.